I0634787

Francis Jeffrey, Lewis E. Gates

Selections from the Essays of Francis Jeffrey

Francis Jeffrey, Lewis E. Gates

Selections from the Essays of Francis Jeffrey

ISBN/EAN: 9783337277123

Printed in Europe, USA, Canada, Australia, Japan

Cover: Foto ©Andreas Hilbeck / pixelio.de

More available books at **www.hansebooks.com**

SELECTIONS

FROM THE

ESSAYS OF FRANCIS JEFFREY

EDITED

WITH INTRODUCTION AND NOTES

BY

LEWIS E. GATES

INSTRUCTOR IN ENGLISH IN HARVARD UNIVERSITY

———••———

BOSTON, U.S.A.

GINN & COMPANY, PUBLISHERS

1894

PREFACE.

THE following Selections from Jeffrey's Essays have a three-fold purpose : first, to illustrate Jeffrey's style and methods as a critic and his most characteristic opinions ; secondly, to give examples of what was in its day deemed the best literary criticism, with a view to suggesting the changes in methods and aims that have since been wrought ; thirdly, to bring together elementary discussions of a few terms and topics in literature which students are always supposed to be familiar with, but which they can hardly find treated in ordinary manuals or reference-books. With these aims in mind it has seemed best to limit the Selections to essays on literature. This limitation ensures unity, and the resulting volume may well be used by classes that are beginning the independent study of literary topics and of methods of criticism.

On the other hand, this limitation prevents the Selections from doing justice to Jeffrey's versatility, and from illustrating satisfactorily certain points on which much stress is laid in the *Introduction*, — the range of the *Edinburgh* essays, and their courage and vigor in the treatment of religious, social, and political questions. The reader who wishes illustrations of these points, must consult Jeffrey's four volumes of *Contributions to the Edinburgh Review*, or turn to the files of the periodical.

The text of the Selections is entire as far as it goes, except in five essays, where omissions are marked by stars; but every Selection ends, when Jeffrey turns from his discussion of general questions, and begins to deal specifically with the book before him by means of summaries and extracts. It has not been thought worth while to mark this form of incompleteness with stars.

The best short sketch of Jeffrey's life is that of Mr. Leslie Stephen in the *Dictionary of National Biography;* the standard biography is Lord Cockburn's *Life and Correspondence of Lord Jeffrey*, in two volumes.

The text of the Selections, including punctuation and spelling, is precisely that of the London edition of 1844, save for the correction of a few obvious and trifling misprints.

HARVARD UNIVERSITY.
December 26, 1893.

CONTENTS.

————◆◇◆————

INTRODUCTION.

I.

DURING the thirty years after his death Francis Jeffrey was remembered in literature with very little honor. Those of his essays that were most often recalled were his attacks on the Lake poets ; and as Wordsworth and Coleridge had ultimately persuaded the public, or the larger part of it, to take their poetry at their own valuation, Jeffrey's reputation as a critic suffered proportionally.

Of late years, however, two sets of causes have been tending to gain for Jeffrey a second hearing and to secure for him a fair recognition. In the first place, the mystical view of life, which he found so offensive in Wordsworth and attacked so relentlessly, has been more and more falling into disfavor, and giving place to a positive and scientific habit of thought. The positivism of to-day is not Jeffrey's positivism, and our insensibility to Wordsworth is not Jeffrey's insensibility ; and yet the temper of our time is perhaps nearer like Jeffrey's than like Wordsworth's ; and Jeffrey's frank, comprehensible blunders are nearer tolerable to a latter-day, prose-loving public than are the extravagances and cloudy mysticism of much of the poetry he assails.

Then, in the second place, the mere passage of time has been in Jeffrey's favor ; the historical point of view has largely replaced the partisan point of view in discussions of the early literature of the century, and a

scientific recognition of Jeffrey's former prestige has
replaced an impatient dislike of his critical opinions.
Questions of cause and effect, of action and reaction, of
movements and tendencies, have more and more come
to the front ; and for a student of problems of this kind
Jeffrey is not a quantity that can be neglected.

It is hardly possible to glance through the life of any
literary man of the early part of the century without
chancing on evidence of Jeffrey's popularity and prestige.
Macaulay, for example, was a·devoted admirer of Jeffrey.
One of his letters of 1828 deals wholly with his impressions
of Jeffrey, at whose home he had just been staying ; the
tone of the letter is that of unmixed hero-worship ; no
details of the Scotch critic's appearance or habits or
opinions are too slight to be sent to the Macaulay
household in London. "He has twenty faces almost as
unlike each other as my father's to Mr. Wilberforce's."
. . . "The mere outline of his face is insignificant.
The expression is everything ; and such power and
variety of expression I never saw in any human countenance." . . . "The flow of his kindness is quite
inexhaustible." . . . "His conversation is very much
like his countenance and his voice, of immense variety."
. . . "He is a shrewd observer ; and so fastidious
that I am not surprised at the awe in which many
people seem to stand when in his company."[1] These
are only a few of Macaulay's details and admiring
comments. Nor did Macaulay outgrow this intense
admiration. In April, 1843, he writes Macvey Napier
that he has read and reread Jeffrey's old articles till he
knows them by heart ;[2] and in December, 1843, on the
appearance of Jeffrey's collected essays, he expresses

[1] *Life and Letters of Lord Macaulay,* chap. 3.
[2] *Ibid.,* chap. 9.

himself in almost unmeasured terms : " The variety and versatility of Jeffrey's mind seems to me more extraordinary than ever. . . . I do not think that any one man except Jeffrey, nay that any three men, could have produced such diversified excellence. . . . Take him all in all, I think him more nearly an universal genius than any man of our time." [1]

Macaulay's opinion, however, may not be wholly beyond suspicion. He himself had much of Jeffrey's dryness and positiveness of nature, and was temperamentally limited in much the same ways ; he was, moreover, like Jeffrey an ardent Whig of the Constitutional type ; and for all these reasons he may be thought to have been prejudiced. But in Carlyle we have a witness who was never for a moment in sympathy with Jeffrey's neat little formulas in art and in politics, and who has never been accused of registering unduly charitable opinions of even his best friends. Yet of Jeffrey he says, " It is certain there has no Critic appeared among us since who was worth naming beside him ; — and his influence, for good and for evil, in Literature and otherwise, has been very great." . . . "His *Edinburgh Review* [was] a kind of Delphic Oracle, and Voice of the Inspired, for great majorities of what is called the 'Intelligent Public'; and himself regarded universally as a man of consummate penetration, and the *facile princeps* in the department he had chosen to cultivate and practise." [2]

These quotations may stand in place of countless minor ones that might be marshalled ; they will serve to make real to readers of to-day the magnitude of Jeffrey's power in literary matters during the first quarter of the century.

---

[1] *Life and Letters*, chap. 9.
[2] Carlyle's *Reminiscences*, ed. Norton, II, 271.

Horner's nickname for Jeffrey, "King Jamfray,"[1] was not a misnomer.

What, then, were the causes of Jeffrey's prestige and popularity? To find a satisfactory explanation, it will be necessary to look beyond Jeffrey's personality, beyond even the band of brilliant workers with whom he was associated, and of whose cleverness and knowledge he made such well-advised use. It will be necessary to take into account the nature of the new venture in literature by means of which Jeffrey won his reputation, the *Edinburgh Review*, and to consider carefully its organization, its relation to earlier Reviews, its principles in politics and on social questions, its grounds of appeal to the public, and even such prosaic matters as its business arrangements. But before taking up these broader questions it will be well to examine briefly Jeffrey's individual characteristics as a literary critic.

II.

The point on which Macaulay laid greatest stress in his praise of Jeffrey's work was its versatility; and to-day as in 1843 this versatility is noteworthy, even after standards of acquirement and performance have had a half century in which to develop. Jeffrey ranges with the same unfaltering step over the most diverse fields of knowledge. He seems equally sure of himself in dealing with politics, history, fiction, poetry, and philosophy. That his air of bravado and of unquestionable mastery was something of a trick, we now know very well. But even with our latter-day knowledge of the tricks of the reviewer's trade, we cannot help admiring and being impressed with the masterful air with which

[1] *Memoirs and Correspondence of Horner*, II, 140.

Jeffrey at one moment sketches the history of English poetry, at another analyzes the questions at issue between materialists and idealists in philosophy, now argues against the doctrine of perfectibility, and now discusses points of constitutional law and of government. A little careful study of Jeffrey's work will usually show that he has had nothing startlingly novel to say on any of these questions. And yet our admiration for the critic's cleverness of manipulation survives even a series of such disenchanting analyses. If these analyses fail to show much reserve power or originality, they make perfectly clear the skill of treatment, the thorough command of essential facts, the readiness of illustration, the keenness of vision within a certain range, and the ease of presentation, which are characteristic of Jeffrey's best work. Admirers of his versatility, then, will not claim for him great originality or vast˙ erudition, or that kind of transforming insight that gives familiar facts an unsuspected significance by bringing them into relation with a new set of first principles. But they will insist on their right to delight in his readiness of adaptation, in his quick-eyed perception, in his tact in simplifying complex problems, and in his unfailing certainty of aim and sureness of motion. He always bears himself gracefully and confidently and threads his way with the perfection of sure-footing to the goal he has from the first foreseen ; and he does all this with equal precision and clairvoyance whether he is dealing with Scott's *Marmion*, or the *Memoirs of Dr. Priestley*, or Dugald Stewart's *Philo-sophical Essays*, or the French translation of Jeremy Bentham's *Works*. Jeffrey's mastery of his subject is like the successful barrister's knowledge of his brief ; he is sure to know whatever he needs to know in order to carry the matter in hand triumphantly through.

Indeed his readiness and his plausibility are not the
only points in which Jeffrey the critic suggests Jeffrey the
advocate. He has the defects as well as the merits of
the lawyer in literature. He is always making points;
he is always demonstrating. The intellectual interest
preponderates in his critical work, and his discussions
often seem, particularly to a reader of modern impressionistic criticism, hard, unsympathetic, searchingly analytical,
repellingly abstract and systematic. He is always on the
watch; he never lends himself confidingly to his author
and takes passively and gratefully the mood and the
images his author suggests. He never loiters or dreams.
He is full of business and bustle and perpetually distracts
one with his sense of what is coming next. He might
well have been in Wordsworth's mind when the poet
wrote of those who think that

> " Nothing of itself must come
> But we must still be seeking."

Of course, however, it must be borne in mind that this
tone and manner, so objectionable to some, and nowa-
days perhaps not wholly winning in the eyes of any, are
common to Jeffrey with all dogmatic critics; and unquestionably it is as a dogmatic critic that Jeffrey must be
classed. By the theory of criticism that had been in
vogue during the eighteenth century, there were certain
laws of composition and principles of taste which must
needs be observed, if the literary artist were to attain
any degree of excellence. These laws and principles
had been partially set down in various treatises, and in
this form were within the ken of the critic and ready for
his use as he might need to appeal to them in praising or
blaming the productions of would-be authors. But even
where these laws had not been codified, they existed, so

ran the ingenious and comforting theory, implicitly in the mind of the critic. In short, the dogmatic critic regarded himself and was generally regarded as able to apply absolute tests of merit to all literary work, and as the final authority on all doubtful matters of taste.

Now, Jeffrey was the inheritor of this tradition in criticism, and naturally adopted at times its prophetic tone and its pontifical manner toward public and authors. Yet, following his temperamental fondness for compromises, for middle parties and mediating measures, Jeffrey never tried formally to defend this old doctrine or represented himself as an absolute law-giver in literature. Nowhere does he lay down a complete set of principles, like the rules of Bossu for epic poetry, or those of Rapin for the drama, by which excellence in any form of literature may be absolutely tested. Such a high-and-dry Tory theory of criticism does not suggest itself to Jeffrey as tenable. He is a Whig in taste as in politics, and desires in both spheres the supremacy of a chosen aristocracy. In his essay on Scott's *Lady of the Lake* he declares the standard of literary excellence to reside in "the taste of a few . . . persons, eminently qualified, by natural sensibility, and long experience and reflection, to perceive all beauties that really exist, as well as to settle the relative value and importance of all the different sorts of beauty."[1] Jeffrey regards himself as one of the choicest spirits of this chosen aristocracy, and it is as the exponent of the best current opinion that he speaks on all questions of taste. His business, then, is to dogmatize, to pronounce this right and that wrong, to praise this author and blame that one; but his dogmatism is not the dogmatism of reason, but the dogmatism of taste; he justifies his decisions, not by

[1] *Selections*, p. 39.

referring to a code of written laws from which there is no appeal, but by a more or less direct suggestion that he has all the best instructed opinion behind him.

For the most part, therefore, in his condemnation of an author, he makes no use of scientific terms of disapproval and he appeals to no abstract principles; he simply expresses his personal discontent with the author in commonplace terms of dissatisfaction. Goethe's *Wilhelm Meister*, for example, is "sheer nonsense," "ludicrously unnatural," full of "pure childishness or mere folly," "vulgar and obscure," full of "absurdities and affectations." These terms are, for the most part, mere circumlocutions for Jeffrey's dislike, mere roundabout ways of saying that the book is not to his taste. As for any attempt to come to an understanding with author or reader about the ends of prose fiction or the best methods of reaching those ends, Jeffrey never thinks of such a thing. He simply takes up various passages and declares he does not comprehend them, or does not fancy the subjects they treat of, or does not like the author's ideas or methods. He gives no reasons for his likes or dislikes, but is content to express them emphatically and picturesquely. This is, of course, dogmatism pure and simple, and a dogmatism, too, more irritating than the dogmatism that argues, for it seems more arbitrary and more challenging. It is of this tone and method that Coleridge complains in the twenty-first chapter of his *Biographia Literaria*, when, in commenting on current critical literature, he protests against "the substitution of assertion for argument" and against "the frequency of arbitrary and sometimes petulant verdicts."

But irritating as is this pragmatic, unreasoning dogmatism, it is nevertheless plainly a step forward from the view that makes the critic absolute law-giver in art. As the Whig position in politics is midway between absolute Monarchy and Democracy, so what we may term the Whig compromise in criticism stands midway between the tyranny of earlier critics and our modern freedom. The mere recognition of the fact that the critic speaks with authority only as representing a *coterie*, only as interpreting public opinion, is plainly a change for the better. The critic no longer regards himself as by divine right lord alike of public and authors; he no longer measures literary success solely by his own little cut and dried formulas of excellence ; he admits more or less explicitly that the taste of living readers, not rules drawn from the works of dead writers, must decide what in literature is good or bad. He still, to be sure, limits arbitrarily the circle whose taste he regards as a valid test; but it is plain that a new principle has implicitly been accepted, and that the way is opened for the development and recognition of all kinds of beauty and power the public may require.

Jeffrey himself, however, seems never to have suspected the conclusions that might legitimately be drawn from the ideas that he was helping to make current. He seems never to have had a qualm of doubt touching his right to dogmatize on the merits and defects of art as violently as a critic of the older school. In theory, he held that all artistic excellence is relative ; but in practice, he never let this doctrine mitigate the severity of his judgments. He asserts in his review of *Alison on Taste* that "what a man feels distinctly to be beautiful, *is beautiful* to him ";[1] and that so far as the individual is concerned all pleasure in art is equally real and justifiable. Yet this doctrine seems never to have paralyzed in the

[1] *Selections*, p. 154.

least his faith in the superior worth of his own kind
of pleasure; and he rates Wordsworth and Coleridge
just as indignantly for not ministering to that pleasure,
as if he had some abstract standard of poetic excellence,
which he could prove they fell short of.

When we try to define Jeffrey's taste and to determine just what he liked and disliked in literature, we
find an odd combination of sympathies and antipathies.
Mr. Leslie Stephen has spoken of him as in politics an
eighteenth-century survival;[1] and this seems at first a
tempting formula to apply to his taste in literature.
But a little consideration will show the impropriety of
any such use of terms. The typical eighteenth-century
man of letters is a pseudo-classicist; and beyond the
pseudo-classical point of view Jeffrey had passed, just as
certainly as he had never reached the Romantic point of
view. Of Pope, for example, he says : he is "much the
best, we think, of the classical Continental school; but
he is not to be compared with the masters — nor with
the pupils — of that Old English one from which there
had been so lamentable an apostasy."[2] Addison he condemns for his "extreme caution, timidity, and flatness,"[2]
and he declares that "the narrowness of his range in
poetical sentiment and diction, and the utter want either
of passion or of brilliancy, render it difficult to believe
that he was born under the same sun with Shakespeare."[2]
These opinions are proof patent of Jeffrey's contempt for
pseudo-classicism. Then, too, Jeffrey is, as he himself
boasts, almost superstitious in his reverence for Shakspere.[3] More significant still is his admiration for other
Elizabethan dramatists, like Beaumont, Fletcher, Ford,
and Webster. "Of the old English dramatists," he

[1] *Hours in a Library*, III, 176.   [2] *Selections*, p. 10.
[3] *Selections*, p. 21.

assures us in his essay on *Ford*, "it may be said, in general, that they are more poetical, and more original in their diction, than the dramatists of any other age or country. Their scenes abound more in varied images, and gratuitous excursions of fancy. Their illustrations, and figures of speech, are more borrowed from rural life, and from the simple occupations or universal feelings of mankind. They are not confined to a certain range of dignified expressions, nor restricted to a particular assortment of imagery, beyond which it is not lawful to look for embellishments." [1]   Finally, he even commends Coleridge's great favorite, Jeremy Taylor, as enthusiastically as Coleridge himself could do : "There is in any one of the prose folios of Jeremy Taylor," he asserts, "more fine fancy and original imagery — more brilliant conceptions and glowing expressions — more new figures, and new applications of old figures — more, in short, of the body and the soul of poetry, than in all the odes and the epics that have since been produced in Europe." [2]

All these judgments tally exactly with the faith of Lamb, Coleridge and Wordsworth ; and as one after another they fall under his eye, the reader is led to fancy that he has to do with a devotee of Romanticism, with a critic who is thoroughly in sympathy with the new spirit in literature.   But soon, judgments of an altogether different nature force themselves on his notice.   The long series of essays is encountered that discusses Crabbe's poetry ; and the reader sees at once hôw far Jeffrey is from welcoming heartily the new age in poetry ✦ or even from allowing its prophets to prophesy in peace and obscurity.   Throughout his praise of Crabbe Jeffrey is by implication condemning Wordsworth ; nor does he confine himself to this indirect method of attacking Roman-

---

[1] *Selections*, p. 16.   [2] *Selections*, p. 5.

ticism. In the very first essay on Crabbe he turns aside from his subject to ridicule, "the Wordsworths, and the Southeys, and Coleridges and all that ambitious fraternity," and contrasts at great length Crabbe's sanity with Wordsworth's mysticism. "Mr. Crabbe exhibits the common people of England pretty much as they are;"[1] whereas "Mr. Wordsworth and his associates . . . introduce us to beings whose existence was not previously suspected by the acutest observers of nature; and excite an interest for them — where they do excite any interest — more by an eloquent and refined analysis of their own capricious feelings, than by any obvious or intelligible ground of sympathy in their situation."[2] With Crabbe, Jeffrey feels he is on solid ground, dealing with a man who sees life clearly and sensibly, as he himself sees it; and in his enthusiastic praise of the minute fidelity of Crabbe, of his uncompromising truth and realism, and of his freedom from all meretricious effects, from affectation and from absurd mysticism, we have at once the measure of Jeffrey's poetic sensibility and the sure evidence of his inability to sympathize genuinely with "the Lakers."

Of course, for the classic passages expressing his impatience of the new movement, we must go to the essays on Wordsworth's *Excursion* and *White Doe.* Jeffrey's objections to the Lakers fall under four heads: First, the new poets are nonsensically mystical; secondly, they falsify life by showing it through a distorting medium of
♦ personal emotion, i.e. they are misleadingly subjective; thirdly, they are guilty of grotesque bad taste in their realism; fourthly, they are pedantically earnest and serious in their treatment of art, and inexcusably pretentious in their proclamation of a new gospel of life.

[1] *Selections*, p. 57.   [2] *Selections*, p. 58.

To consider these points in detail would lead to a discussion of Wordsworth and Coleridge rather than to a
discussion of Jeffrey. Still, Jeffrey's position toward the
Lakers is very characteristic of the man, and illustrates
admirably both his limitations and his positive qualities ;
moreover, his treatment of the Lakers has become · a
tradition in the history of criticism and deserves for that
reason some discussion. A little closer examination,
then, of the grounds of Jeffrey's objection to the new
movement in literature will not be out of place.

When Jeffrey praises, as he often does, the poetry of
the Elizabethan age, delights in its passion, celebrates its
imaginative beauty, its figurative richness, its fervor and
wayward splendor, the reader seems to be listening to a
genuine disciple of the new school of poetry ; and he
cannot but expect Jeffrey to show the same hearty
appreciation for Coleridge and Wordsworth as for the
writings of their chosen models. Jeffrey's rejection,
however, of the new school begins at the very point
where for their admirers their superiority to the older
school begins to show itself, — viz., the moment they
commence to interpret life in terms of the infinite.
The intenser spiritual consciousness of Wordsworth, his
constant and unchanging recognition of the relation
of every-day life to ·the unseen world, are for Wordsworth's admirers characteristic sources of power which
place him above the Elizabethan dramatists as an imaginative interpreter of life. For Jeffrey they are the
precise qualities which lead to Wordsworth's worst absurdities and most appallingly nonsensical rhapsodies.
After quoting some typical passages where Wordsworth
gives free utterance to his idealism, Jeffrey exclaims : —
" This is a fair sample of that rapturous mysticism which
eludes all comprehension, and fills the despairing reader

with painful giddiness and terror."[1] This is a perfectly sincere expression of genuine suffering on Jeffrey's part. We cannot doubt that his whole mental life was perturbed by such poems of Wordsworth as the great *Ode*, and that it was an act of self-preservation on his part to burst into indignant ridicule and violent protest. To find a man of Wordsworth's age and literary experience deliberately penning such bewildering stanzas and expressing such unintelligible emotions, shook for the moment Jeffrey's faith in his own little, well-ordered universe, and then, as he recovered from his earthquake, escaped from its vapors, and felt secure once more in the clear every-day light of common sense, led him into fierce invective against the cause of his momentary panic.

Hardly less impatient is Jeffrey of Wordsworth's subjectivity than of his mysticism. Why cannot Wordsworth feel about life as other people feel about it, as any well-bred, cultivated man of the world feels about it? When such a man sees a poor old peasant gathering leeches in a pool, he pulls out his purse, gives him a shilling, and walks on, speculating about the state of the poor law ; Wordsworth, on the contrary, bursts into a strange fit of raving about Chatterton and Burns, and " mighty poets in their misery dead," and then in some mysterious fashion converts the peasant's stolidity into a defence against these gloomy thoughts. This way of treating the peasant seems to Jeffrey utterly unjustifiable, in the first place because of its grotesque mysticism, and in the second place because it thrusts a personal *motif* discourteously into the face of the public and falsifies ludicrously the peasant's character and life. Wordsworth has no right, Jeffrey insists, to treat the peasant merely as the symbol of his own peculiar mood. Here, as in

[1] *Selections*, p. 115.

his protest against Wordsworth's mysticism, Jeffrey pleads
for common sense and the commonplace ; he is the type
of what Lamb calls "the Caledonian intellect," which
rejects scornfully ideas that cannot be adequately expressed in good plain terms, and grasped "by twelve
men on a jury."

Crabbe's superiority to the Lakers lies for Jeffrey
chiefly in the fact that he has no idiosyncrasies
though he has many mannerisms ; he expresses no new
theories and no peculiar emotions in his portrayal of
common life. Hence his choice of vulgar subjects is
endurable — even highly commendable. His peasants
are the well-known peasants of every-day England, with
whose hard lot it behoves an enlightened Whig to sympathize — from a distance. But a realism that, like
Wordsworth's, professes to find in these poor peasants
the deepest spiritual insight and the purest springs of
moral life is simply for Jeffrey grotesque in its mala-
droitness and its confusion of values. Sydney Smith
used to say, "If I am doomed to be a slave at all, I
would rather be the slave of a king than a cobbler."
And this same prejudice against any topsy-turvy re-
assignment of values was largely responsible for Jeffrey's
dislike of Wordsworth's peasants and of his treatment of
common life. If peasants keep their places, as Crabbe's
peasants do, they may perfectly well be brought into the
precincts of poetry ; but to exalt them into types of moral
virtue and into heavenly messengers of divine truth, is to
"make tyrants of cobblers." Jacobinism in art as in
politics is to Jeffrey detestable.

In fact, all the pretensions of the new school to
illustrate by its art a new gospel of life were intensely
disagreeable to Jeffrey. Just so long as Romanticism
showed itself purely decorative, as in Scott or Keats,

Jeffrey could tolerate it or even delight in it. But the moment it begins, whether in Byron or Wordsworth, to take itself seriously and to struggle to express new moral and spiritual ideals, Jeffrey protests. Just here lies the key to what some critics have found rather a perplexing problem, — the reasons for the precise degree of Jeffrey's sympathy with Romanticism. Keats's luxuriant pictures of Greek life in *Endymion*, Jeffrey finds irresistible in " the intoxication of their sweetness" and in the " enchantments which they so lavishly present."[1] Let the poet remain a mere master of the revels, or a mere magician calling up by his incantations in verse a gorgeous phantasmagoria of sights and sounds for the delectation of idle readers, and Jeffrey will admire his fertility of invention, his wealth of imagination, his " rich lights of fancy" and " his flowers of poetry." For these reasons Moore and Campbell seem to Jeffrey the most admirable of the Romanticists, and their works the very best of the somewhat extravagant modern school. Writing in 1829, he arranges recent poets in the following order according to the probable duration of their fame : — " The tuneful quartos of Southey are already little better than lumber : — and the rich melodies of Keats and Shelley, — and the fantastical emphasis of Wordsworth, — and the plebeian pathos of Crabbe, are melting fast from the field of our view. The novels of Scott have put out his poetry. Even the splendid strains of Moore are fading into distance and dimness . . . and the blazing star of Byron himself is receding from its place of pride. . . . The two who have the longest withstood this rapid withering of the laurel . . . are Rogers and Campbell ; neither of them, it may be remarked, voluminous writers, and both distinguished rather for the fine taste and consummate

[1] *Selections*, p. 88.

elegance of their writings, than for that fiery passion, and disdainful vehemence, which seemed for a time to be so much more in favour with the public." [1] Now a glance at Jeffrey's list of poets makes it clear that those for whom he prophesies lasting fame are either pseudo-classicists or decorative Romanticists, and that those whose day he declares to be over are for the most part poets whose Romanticism was a vital principle. Rogers is, of course, a genuine representative of the psuedo-classical tradition, with all its devotion to form, its self-restraint, its poverty of imagination, and its distrust of passion. Moore, whom Jeffrey places late in his list of fading luminaries, and Campbell, whom he finds most nearly unchanging in lustre, are both in a way Romanticists; but they are alike in seeking chiefly for decorative effects and in not taking their art too seriously. So long, then, as the fire and the heat of Romanticism spent themselves merely in giving imaginative splendor to style, Jeffrey could tolerate the movement, and could even regard it with favor, as a return to that power and fervor and wild beauty that he had taught himself to admire in Elizabethan poetry. But the moment the new energy was suffered to penetrate life itself and to convert the conventional world of dead fact, through the vitalizing power of passion, into a genuinely new poetic material, then Jeffrey stood aghast at what seemed to him a return to chaos. Byron with his fiery bursts of selfish passion, Wordsworth with his steadily glowing consciousness of the infinite, and Shelley with his "white heat of transcendentalism," were all alike for Jeffrey portentously dangerous forces and unhealthy phenomena.

In the preceding discussion of Jeffrey's relation to

---

[1] Jeffrey's review of Mrs. Hemans's *Records of Women.*

Romanticism, the most noteworthy characteristics of his taste in literature and art have been suggested. It is useless to search his writings for an attempt to justify these likes and dislikes, in any other way than by an appeal to common sense, or to the consensus of the best instructed opinion. His famous review of *Alison on Taste* would be the most natural place for a formal argument in behalf of certain favorite principles of art. In this review, which in a somewhat altered form stood for many years in the *Encyclopædia Britannica* as the standard discussion of *Beauty*, Jeffrey considers the nature of taste, the origin of the feelings of the Sublime and the Beautiful, and sundry kindred questions ; but the outcome of the long discussion is wholly negative so far as concerns the suggestion of any criterion of beauty or satisfactory test of the claims of conflicting schools in literature or in art.

Jeffrey's arguments in the essay on *Beauty* cannot be analyzed here in detail ; analyses and comments will be found in the *Notes.* His conclusion is that the beauty of an object is merely the power of that object to set vibrating in a human heart certain subtle chords of past pleasure and pain ; that for any individual observer the object that touches his heart in this subtly conjuring fashion is unquestionably beautiful ; and that there are therefore as many kinds of real beauty as there are individuals with varying past experiences. This seems to make hopeless the attempt to set up any standard of taste, to say of any object, this is beautiful by divine right and should be so accepted by all judges. Yet Jeffrey seems to assert that there are such preëminently beautiful objects ; they are the objects which by virtue of " universal and indestructible " associations, do, as a matter of fact, set vibrating in the hearts of " the greater part of mankind," chords of past pleasure and pain. The unerring recognition of these objects is the characteristic of the *best taste*. Unfortunately, Jeffrey suggests no rule for determining abstractly what associations are "universal and indestructible," and no standard by which the clashing judgments of rival judges can be tested. Hence, his famous discussion offers very little practical guidance to those who are trying to train their tastes, throws very little light on Jeffrey's own likes and dislikes, and suggests hardly any principles of criticism. .

In one way, however, the discussion is serviceable to students of Jeffrey's critical methods; it makes clearer the line of thought that led him to value so highly the ethical interpretation of literature. Throughout the essay he insists on the intimate connection between a man's sense of beauty and his moral feelings. Beauty, he teaches, is the disguised suggestion of past passions,—of love, and pity, and fear, and hate. Now these emotions can be faintly re-awakened only in temperaments that have experienced them richly and intensely at first-hand; hence a keen sense of beauty can exist only in a nature that has sympathized widely and generously with its fellows. Moreover, the character of these past moral emotions will condition the character of a man's feeling for beauty, and will determine the kind of objects that stimulate him æsthetically. For all these reasons, then, the ethical value of literature was closely connected in Jeffrey's thought with its æsthetic value, and the ethical interpretation of literature seemed to him one of the most important duties of the critic.

Accordingly, in the preface to his collected essays Jeffrey claims special credit for his frequent use of the ethical point of view. " If I might be permitted farther to state, in what particular department, and generally, on account of what, I should most wish to claim a share of those merits, I should certainly say, that it was by having constantly endeavoured to combine Ethical precepts with Literary Criticism, and earnestly sought to impress my readers with a sense, both of the close connection between sound Intellectual attainments and the higher elements of Duty and Enjoyment ; and of the just and ultimate subordination of the former to the latter. The praise in short to which I aspire, and to merit which I am conscious that my efforts were most constantly directed, is, that I have, more uniformly and earnestly than any preceding critic, made the Moral tendencies of the works under consideration a leading subject of discussion."

This "proud claim," as Jeffrey calls it, seems amply justified when we compare Jeffrey's essays either with the critical essays in the earlier Reviews or with the more formal and elaborate critical essays of the eighteenth century.   Even Dr. Johnson with all his didacticism had little notion of extracting from a piece of literature the subtle spirit of good or of evil by which it draws men this way or that way in conduct.   An obvious infringe-ment of good morals in speech or in plot he was sure to condemn, and a formal inculcation of moral truth he was sure to recognize and approve.   But neither in Johnson nor anywhere else before Jeffrey do we find a critic con-stantly attempting to detect and define the moral atmos-phere that pervades the whole work of an author, and to determine the relation between this moral atmosphere and the author's personality as man and as author.   To have perceived the value of this ethical criticism, to have practised it skilfully, and to have fostered a taste for it, these are true claims to distinction ; and Jeffrey's services in these directions have been too often forgotten.   The

greater breadth of view of later critics and their surer
appreciation of ethical values should not be allowed to
deprive Jeffrey of his honor as a pioneer in ethical
criticism.

Of the modern historical method of criticism Jeffrey
never made thorough and consistent use. His grasp on
the principles of the method and his ability to apply them
are best illustrated in the essays on Ford's *Dramatic
Works* (August, 1811), on Mme. de Staël's *De la
Littérature* (November, 1812), and on *Wilhelm Meister's
Apprenticeship* (August, 1825). The essay on *Ford* contains, in the rapid survey of English poetry from the
earliest times, a piece of work that is very characteristic
of Jeffrey; the readiness of handling, the sure eye for
structure, the just distribution of emphasis, the aptness
of phrasing and briskness of style are such as no other
critic in 1811 could have reached. But even more noteworthy is the breadth of view ; the attempt to generalize
the qualities of the literature of the Restoration period,
and to explain them as resulting from the social life of
the time is a courageous and fairly effective application
of the historical method, and must have seemed to
Jeffrey's contemporaries startlingly original. Except
for this essay we might have supposed that Jeffrey's
introduction to the historical method came through
Mme. de Staël's work on the relations between literature
and social institutions. But this work was not published
till 1812, whereas Jeffrey's essay on *Ford* dates from
1811.

The most interesting of all the passages, however,
where Jeffrey applies or discusses the historical method
is the introduction to the essay on *Wilhelm Meister*,
written in 1825. Here Jeffrey comes surprisingly near
anticipating Taine in a formal statement of the *race*,

milieu, and *moment* theory of literature. The passage
will be found on pages 159–164 of this volume. It will
be seen that in this essay Jeffrey totally disregards race
as a modifying force ; he takes it for granted that
"human nature is everywhere fundamentally the same."
Taine's other two forces, — *moment* and *milieu*, — Jeffrey
defines in words which Taine would have accepted with
very little alteration. "The circumstances which have
distinguished [literature] into so many local varieties
. . . may be divided into two great classes, — the one
embracing all that relates to the newness or antiquity
of the society to which they belong, or, in other words,
to the stage which any particular nation has attained
in that progress from rudeness to refinement, in which
all are engaged ; — the other comprehending what may
be termed the accidental causes by which the character
and condition of communities may be affected ; such as
their government, their relative position as to power and
civilization to neighboring countries, their prevailing
occupations, determined in some degree by the capabilities of their soil and climate."[1]   This is to all intents
and purposes the classification that Taine makes in the
famous *Introduction* to his *Histoire de la littérature
anglaise*.[2]

   Despite, however, his clear perception of the principles
on which the use of the historical method rests, Jeffrey
is never to be trusted to make intelligent and effective
use of the method, or to be faithful to the point of view
it presupposes.   He is specially apt to be unhistorical
when he treats of the beginnings either of literature or
of institutions.   He lacked the knowledge of facts
which alone could render possible a fruitful historical

---

[1] *Selections*, p. 159.
[2] Cf. *Notes*, pp. 211–15.

conception. His construction of early periods is always
a priori in terms of a cheap psychology. His accóunt,
in the essay on *Leckie*, of the origin of government,
should be compared with his description of the earliest
attempts at poetic composition. In both cases he has
a great deal to say about what "it was natural" for the
earliest experimenters in each kind of work to aim at
and to effect, and he has substantially nothing to say
of the actual facts as determined by investigation.
Moreover, these earliest experimenters are for Jeffrey
marvellously like eighteenth-century *connoisseurs*, con-
fronting consciously, and trying to solve reflectively,
intricate problems in art or in politics. This view is, of
course, unhistorical, and illustrates the difficulty Jeffrey
had in escaping from old ways of thought.

Finally, Jeffrey never applies the historical method
successfully to the study of any contemporary piece of
literature ; almost his sole attempt so to use the historical method is in his essay on *Wilhelm Meister*, and
the inadequacy of his treatment there is such as to make
the reader admire his discretion in not oftener trying to
interpret historically the life and art of his own day.
His failure to appreciate the mad revolt of Byron and
Shelley against the conventionalism and poverty of
eighteenth-century moral ideals has already been noted,
as well as his corresponding failure to comprehend
Wordsworth's high conservatism. Perhaps the most
damaging accusation, that can be made against Jeffrey,
as a critic, is inability to read and interpret the age in
which he lived.

Jeffrey's imperfect grasp of the historical method is
shown in one other way ; he never realized that there
was any conflict between his work as a dogmatic critic
and his work as a scientific student of literature, and

apparently he never had a premonition of the blighting effect the historical method was ultimately to have on the prestige of the dogmatic critic. The history of criticism since Jeffrey's day has been largely the history of the decline in power of the dogmatic critic. Critics to-day explain and interpret, or else they translate for their readers by means of beautiful symbols their dim and obscure sensations of pleasure and pain in reading a piece of literature. They are scientific or they are impressionistic; they rarely dogmatize; and when they dogmatize, they speak with a fine consciousness of their human fallibility, which is curiously unlike the confidence of Jeffrey and his compeers. This change has been brought about partly by the Romantic movement with its fostering of individualism in art, and partly by the spread of historical conceptions in all departments of thought. Both these forces were in full play during Jeffrey's life, and of neither did he at all measure the scope or significance.

III.

It remains to speak of the new venture in literature with which Jeffrey's name and fame are always connected, the *Edinburgh Review*, and to consider what causes, apart from Jeffrey's personality, can be suggested to account for its prompt and unexampled success.

The story of the foundation of the *Review* has been told so often that it will hardly bear repeating. The classical account is Sydney Smith's and is to be found in the *Preface* of his collected *Works;* it has been reproduced in Lord Cockburn's *Life of Jeffrey*[1] and in the *Life*

---

[1] Ed. Philadelphia, 1852, I, 101.

and Times of Lord Brougham.[1]   With his usual crabbed-
ness Brougham disputes a few minor details, but he
leaves the substantial accuracy of "Sydney's" story unim-
peached.   The main facts may be briefly set together.
The idea of the new Review was Sydney Smith's.   The
most important conspirators were Sydney, Jeffrey, Francis
Horner, and Brougham.   The plot was discussed and
matured in Jeffrey's house in Buccleuch Place, Edinburgh.   Sydney Smith's famous proposal of a motto,
Tenui musam meditamur avena, "We cultivate literature
on a little oatmeal," was rejected ; the "sage Horner's"
suggestion was adopted, — a line from Publius Syrus,
Judex damnatur cum nocens absolvitur, which foretold the
righteous severity of tone that was to characterize the
Review.   The first number was to have appeared in June,
1802, but owing to dilatory contributors and Jeffrey's faint-
heartedness was seriously delayed ; it finally appeared in
October, 1802, under the supervision of Sydney Smith.
After the publication of the first number Jeffrey was
formally appointed editor, and with some hesitation
accepted the post.

The success of the *Review* was from the start beyond
all expectation.   "The effect," says Lord Cockburn,
"was electrical.   And instead of expiring, as many wished,
in their first effort, the force of the shock was increased
on each subsequent discharge.   It is impossible for those
who did not live at the time, and in the heart of the
scene, to feel, or almost to understand the impression
made by the new luminary, or the anxieties with which
its motions were observed."[2]   Lord Brougham's account
of the matter is no less emphatic.   "The success was
far beyond any of our expectations.   It was so great that

---

[1] Ed. New York, 1871, I, 176.
[2] Lord Cockburn's *Life of Lord Jeffrey,* I, 106.

Jeffrey was utterly dumbfounded, for he had predicted for our journal the fate of the original 'Edinburgh Review,' which, born in 1755, died in 1756, having produced only two numbers ! The truth is, the most sanguine among us, even Smith himself, could not have foreseen the greatness of the first triumph, any more than we could have imagined the long and successful career the *Review* was afterwards to run, or the vast reforms and improvements in all our institutions, social as well as political, it was destined to effect." [1]

The subscription list of the *Review* grew within six years from 750 to 9000 ; and by 1813 it numbered more than 12,000. The importance of these figures is better understood when the reader recollects that in 1816 the London *Times* sold only 8000 copies daily. Moreover, it should be remembered that one copy of a magazine went much further then than it goes now, and did service in more than a single household. In 1809 Jeffrey boasted that the *Review* was read by 50,000 thinking people within a month after it was printed ; doubtless this was a perfectly sound estimate.

Various causes have been suggested as contributing to the instant and phenomenal success of the *Review*, — the puzzling anonymity of its articles, its magisterial tone, the audacity of its attacks, what Horner calls its "scurrility," the novelty of its Scotch origin. All these causes doubtless had their influence. More important still, however, were the wit and knowledge and originality of the brilliant contributors that Jeffrey rallied round him. Writing to his brother in July, 1803, Jeffrey thus describes his fellow-workers : " I do not think you know any of my associates. There is the sage Horner, however, whom you have seen, and who has gone to the English bar with

---

[1] *The Life and Times of Lord Brougham*, I, 180.

the resolution of being Lord Chancellor ; Brougham, a
great mathematician, who has just published a book upon
the Colonial Policy of Europe, which all you Americans
should read ; Rev. Sydney Smith and P. Elmsley, two
Oxonian priests, full of jokes and erudition; my excellent
little Sanscrit Hamilton, who is also in the hands of
Bonaparte at Fontainebleau ; Thomas Thomson and
John Murray, two ingenious advocates ; and some dozen
of occasional contributors, among whom the most illustrious, I think, are young Watt of Birmingham, and Davy
of the Royal Institution."[1] Many of these names are
now forgotten, but those of Sydney Smith, Brougham,
Horner and Davy speak for themselves and are guaran-
tees of brilliancy of style, originality of treatment, and
vigorous thought.

The editor and the contributors, then, must receive
their full share of credit for the success of the new
Review; but their ability alone can hardly account for a
success that converted the "blue and yellow" into a
national institution. To explain a success so permanent
and far-reaching, we must look beyond editor and contributors and consider the relation of the *Review* to its
social environment. The *Edinburgh Review* came into
being in answer to a popular need ; it developed a new
literary form to meet this need ; and its business arrangements were such as enabled the cleverest and most
suggestive writers to adapt their work to the requirements of the reading public more readily and more
effectively than ever before. The meaning of these
assertions will grow clearer as we consider the difference between the *Edinburgh Review* and earlier English
Reviews.

[1] Lord Cockburn's *Life of Jeffrey,* II, 64.

IV.

Prior to 1802 there were two standard Reviews in Great Britain, — the *Monthly Review* and the *Critical Review*. Minor Reviews there had been in plenty, of longer or shorter life ; but these two periodicals had pushed beyond their rivals and were regarded as the best of their kind. The *Monthly Review* had been founded in 1749 by Ralph Griffiths, a bookseller ; it was Whig in politics and Low Church in religion. Its rival, the *Critical Review*, of which Smollett was for many years editor, had been founded in 1756, and was Tory and High Church. These Reviews were alike in form and were hardly to be distinguished in externals and in ostensible aim from the later *Edinburgh Review*. They were made up of short articles on current publications and professed to give trustworthy opinions of the merits of all new books.

When we push beyond form and outside, however, and consider the contents, the scope and tone of the articles, the policy of the manager, and the character of the contributors, we find these earlier Reviews totally unlike the *Edinburgh*. They were booksellers' organs, under the strict supervision of booksellers, and often edited by booksellers. They were used persistently and systematically, though, of course, discreetly, to further the bookseller's business schemes, to quicken the sale in case of a slow market, and to damage the publications of rivals. They were written for the most part by drudges and penny-a-liners, who worked under the orders of the bookseller like slaves under the lash of the slave-driver. All these points are well illustrated in the history of the relations between Dr. Griffiths, editor of the *Monthly*, and his subordinates.

Griffiths was originally a bookseller; and though he was able later to retire from this business and to devote himself wholly to the management of his *Review*, he retained still the instincts of a petty tradesman, and kept his eye on the state of the market like a skilful seller of perishable wares. Of scholarship, of genuine taste and literary ability he had next to nothing; but he had shrewd common sense, sound business instincts, tact in dealing with men, readiness to bully or to fawn as might be needful, and unlimited patience in scheming for the commercial success of his venture.

His dealings with Goldsmith between 1755 and 1765 and with William Taylor of Norwich between 1790 and 1800 illustrate perfectly his policy in conducting the *Monthly* and the light in which he regarded his contributors. Goldsmith he by turns bullied and bribed according as poor Goldsmith was more or less in need of money. On one occasion he became Goldsmith's security with his tailor for a new suit of clothes on condition that Goldsmith at once write four articles for the *Review;* these articles were turned out to order, and appeared in December, 1758. On Goldsmith's failing to pay his tailor's bill in the specified time, Griffiths demanded the return of the suit and also of the books; and when he found that Goldsmith had pawned the books, he wrote him abusively, terming him sharper and villain, and threatening him with jail. In 1759 on the appearance of Goldsmith's first book, Griffiths ordered one of his hacks, the notorious Kenrick, to ridicule the work, and to make a personal attack on the author. These orders were faithfully carried out in the next number of the *Monthly Review*.[1]

With William Taylor of Norwich Griffiths took a very

---

[1] Forster's *Goldsmith*, London, 1848, bk. ii, p. 170.

different tone. Taylor was one of the few men of
breeding and of parts who before 1802 condescended
to write for Reviews, and he was moreover for many
years the great English authority on German literature.
For these reasons Griffiths always handled him with the
utmost tenderness, and, even when giving him orders or
refusing his articles, took a flattering tone of deference
and admiration. On one occasion Taylor demanded an
increase of pay; Griffiths's answer gives a very instructive
glimpse of the relations between the bookseller-editor
and his hack-writers. The "gratuity" for review-work,
Griffiths assures Taylor, had been settled fifty years
before at two guineas a sheet of sixteen printed pages,
"a sum not then deemed altogether puny," and in the
case of most writers had since remained unchanged,
although there had been certain " allowed exceptions in
favour of the more difficult branches of the business."
These exceptions, however, had tended to cause much
jealousy and heart-burning among the contributors; for
"it could not be expected that those labourers in the
vineyard, who customarily executed the less difficult
branches of the culture, would ever be cordially convinced that *their* merits and importance were inferior to
any." After these laborious explanations Griffiths agrees
to raise Taylor's compensation to three guineas per sheet
of sixteen printed pages, though he expressly points out
that by so doing he risks "exciting jealousy in the corps,
similar, perhaps, to what happened among the vine-
dressers, Matt. chap. xx." " If objections arise," he
shrewdly continues, "we must resort for consolation to
a list of candidates for the next vacancy, for in the
literary harvest there is never any want of reapers." [1]
Griffiths's slave-driving propensities show clearly through

[1] J. W. Robberd's *Life of William Taylor*, I, 130–132.

the thin disguise of politic words. Plainly he feels himself absolute master of the minds and wills of an indefinite number of penny-a-liners ; and it is on these penny-a-liners that he resolves to depend for the great mass of his articles.

This, then, was the character of a typical editor-publisher of the old-fashioned Review, and such in its general outlines was the policy he pursued. The results were deplorable. The editor-publisher prescribed to his hacks what treatment a book should receive. Sometimes this was with a view to the market. "I send also the 'Horae Biblicae' at a venture," writes Griffiths to Taylor, ". . . it signifies not much whether we notice it or not, as it is not *on sale*." [1] The Italics are Griffiths's own. Sometimes, the publisher-editor merely wanted to favor a friend or injure an enemy. Griffiths's dictation in the case of Goldsmith's first book has already been noted. On another occasion Griffiths sent a copy of Murphy's *Tacitus* to Taylor with the following significant suggestion : "One thing I have to mention, *entre nous*, that Mr. M. is *one of us*, and that it is a rule in our society for the members to behave with due decorum toward each other, whenever they appear at their own bar as *authors*, out of their own critical province. If a kingdom (like poor France at present) be divided against itself, 'how shall that kingdom stand?'" [2] If Griffiths ventured on this dictation with a man of Taylor's standing and independence, his tyranny over his regular dependents must have been complete and relentless.

As a result, review-writing became purely hack-work. The reviewer had no voice of his own in his criticism ; what little individuality he might, in his feebleness, have

1 J. W. Robberd's *Life of William Taylor*, I, 139.
2 *Ibid.*, I, 122.

put into his work, had he been left to himself, disappeared under the eye of his task-master. He became a mere machine, praising and blaming perfunctorily and conventionally, at the bidding of the editor-publisher. Mawkish adulation or random abuse became the staple of critical articles; and in neither kind of work did the critic rise above the dead level of hopeless mediocrity.

A final result of this whole system of review-managing and hack-writing was unwillingness on the part of men of position to have anything to do with review-writing. If a man criticised books in a Review, he felt that he was putting himself on a level with Kenrick, Griffiths's notorious hireling who had been imprisoned for libel, with Kit Smart, who had bound himself to a bookseller for ninety-nine years, and with other like wretches. William Taylor of Norwich was one of the few gentlemen who, before 1802, ventured to write for Reviews.

With the establishment of the *Edinburgh Review* all this was changed. The prime principle of the new Review was independence of booksellers. The plan was not a bookseller's scheme, but was hatched in the fervid brains of half-a-dozen young adventurers in law and literature and politics. From the start the bookseller was a "mere instrument," as Brougham specially notes. The management of the Review was at first in the hands of Sydney Smith. When he set out for London his last words to the publisher Constable were, "If you will give £200 per annum to your editor and ten guineas a sheet, you will soon have the best Review in Europe."[1] Accordingly, the editorship was at once offered to Jeffrey, at even a higher salary, £300, than Sydney Smith had named. Jeffrey hesitated because of "the risk of general

[1] Lord Cockburn's *Life of Lord Jeffrey*, I, 108.

degradation."[1]   But he found the £300 "a monstrous bribe "; moreover, the other contributors were all planning to take their ten guineas a sheet; accordingly, after many qualms he swallowed his scruples and became a paid editor. " The publication," he wrote to his brother, in July 1803, "is in the highest degree respectable as yet, as there are none but gentlemen connected with it. If it ever sink into the state of an ordinary bookseller's journal, I have done with it."[2]

So began Jeffrey's " reign " of twenty-six years; and so ended the despotism of booksellers. Henceforth the editor, not the publisher, was master. It was Jeffrey who decided what books should be handled or rather what subjects should be discussed; it was Jeffrey who determined the price to be paid for each article, — "I had," he declares, "an unlimited discretion in this respect";[3] it was Jeffrey who pleaded with the dilatory, mollified the refractory, and reached out here and there after new contributors; in short, it was Jeffrey who shaped the policy of the *Review* and impressed on it its distinctive character. "The sage Horner's" nickname for Jeffrey, "King Jamfray," was certainly apt.

But there were several other hardly less important points in which the business policy of the *Edinburgh* was a new departure. The compensation for reviewing was greatly increased. The old price had been two guineas a sheet of sixteen printed pages; the *Edinburgh Review*, after the first three numbers, paid ten guineas a sheet, and very soon sixteen guineas. Moreover, this was the minimum rate; over two-thirds of the articles were, according to Jeffrey, " paid much higher, averaging

---

[1] Lord Cockburn's *Life of Jeffrey*, II, 63.
[2] *Ibid.*, II, 65.
[3] *Ibid.*, I, 110.

from twenty to twenty-five guineas a sheet on the whole number." [1]

Again, every contributor was forced to take pay ; no contributor, however nice his honor, was suffered to refuse compensation. This change was of the utmost importance ; the rule salved the consciences of many brilliant young professional men, who were glad of pay, but ashamed to write for it, and afraid of being dubbed penny-a-liners. By Jeffrey's clever arrangement they could write for fame or for simple amusement, and then have money "thrust upon them." With high prices and enforced compensation the new Review at once drew into its service men of a totally different stamp from the old hack-writers.

Finally, the *Edinburgh* was published quarterly, whereas the old Reviews were published monthly. This change was for two reasons important : in the first place, writers had more time in which to prepare their articles and led less of a hand-to-mouth life intellectually ; and, in the second place, the *Review* made no attempt to notice all publications and chose for discussion only books of real significance. Coleridge particularly commends this part of the *Review's* policy : " It has a claim upon the gratitude of the literary republic, and indeed of the reading public at large, for having originated the scheme of reviewing those books only, which are susceptible and deserving of argumentative criticism." [2]

V.

These, then, were the principal points in which the organization and policy of the *Edinburgh Review*

---

[1] Lord Cockburn's *Life of Jeffrey*, I, 110.
[2] Coleridge, *Biographia Literaria*, chap. 21.

contrasted with those of its predecessors ; and the influence of these changes on the tone and spirit of the articles in the new Review cannot well be exaggerated. The *Edinburgh Review* was not to be a catch-all for waste information ; it was to become an organ of thought, a busy intellectual center, from which the newest ideas were sent out in a perpetual stream through the minds of sympathetic readers. The *Review* had opinions of its own on all public questions. In politics, it advocated the principles of the Constitutional Whigs, at first in a non-partisan spirit, after 1808, fiercely and aggressively ; it pleaded for reform of the representation, for Catholic emancipation, for a wise recognition of the just discontent of the lower classes and for judicious measures to allay this discontent without violent Constitutional changes. In social matters, it urged reforms of all kinds, the repeal of the game laws, the improvement of prisons, the protection of chimney-sweeps and other social unfortunates. In religion, it argued for toleration. In education, it attacked pedantry and tradition, ridiculed the narrowness of university ideals, and contended for the .adoption of practical methods and utilitarian aims. In all these departments it criticised the existing order of things, always brilliantly and suggestively, and sometimes fiercely and radically, and stirred the public into a keener consciousness and more intelligent appreciation of the questions of the hour, social, political and religious.

Now it is plain that, to accomplish all this, writers would find it necessary to go far outside of the old limits of book-reviewing, and to make their articles express their own independent ideas on various important topics rather than simply their critical opinions of the merits of new publications. And this is precisely what happened. A book-review became in most cases merely a mask for the writer's own ideas on some burning question of the hour. In other words, the establishment of the *Edinburgh Review* really led to the evolution of a new literary form ; the old-fashioned review-article was converted into a brief argumentative essay discussing some living topic, political or social, in the light of the very latest ideas. This kind of essay had been unknown in the eighteenth century, and was developed at the opening of the nineteenth century in response to the needs of the moment.

Nor was this change in the nature of the review-article unremarked at the time ; Hazlitt noted it and with his usual sourness protested against it. "If [the critic] recurs," he says, "to the stipulated subject in the end, it is not till after he has exhausted his budget of general knowledge ; and he establishes his own claims first in an elaborate inaugural dissertation *de omni scibili et quibusdam aliis*, before he deigns to bring forward the pretensions of the original candidate for praise, who is only the second figure in the piece. We may sometimes see articles of this sort, in which no allusion whatever is made to the work under sentence of death, after the first announcement of the title-page."[1] Coleridge, on the other hand, approved of the change, and commended the "plan of supplying the vacant place of the trash or mediocrity wisely left to sink into oblivion by their own weight, with original essays on the most interesting subjects of the time, religious or political ; in which the titles of the books or pamphlets prefixed furnish only the name and occasion of the disquisition."[2] The reviewers themselves recognized, of course, the change they were working, though they did not altogether realize its

[1] Hazlitt's *Table Talk*, series ii, essay 6.
[2] Coleridge's *Biographia Literaria*, chap. 21.

significance. In 1807, Horner writes Jeffrey, "Have you any good subjects in view for your nineteenth? There are two I wish you, *yourself*, would undertake, if you can pick up books that would admit of them."[1] This quotation illustrates the fact that the important question in the minds of the reviewers was always, not "What new books have appeared?" but "What topics just now have the greatest actuality and are best worth discussing?"

This, then, was largely the cause of the success of the *Review* : it offered, in its articles, a literary form by means of which the most active and original minds could at once come into communication with "the intelligent public" on all vital topics ; it made the best thought and the newest knowledge more readily available than ever before for readers who were every day becoming more alive to their value.

The times were plainly favorable. The French Revolution had stirred men's imaginations as they had not been stirred for a century, and had shaken portentously in all directions the foundations of belief. Traditions in politics, in social organization, in religion were violently assailed by men like Godwin, Horne Tooke, and Holcroft, and loyally defended by enthusiastic conservatives. The fever of Romanticism was already making itself felt and was quickening men's hearts to new passions and firing their imaginations with new visions of possible bliss. The air was full of questions and doubts, of eager forecasts and of ominous warnings. All this ferment of life and feeling demanded freer utterance than could be found through old literary forms and with old methods of publication.

Moreover, the increasing importance of the middle class and the spread of popular education were favorable to the development of the new literary form. The number

---

[1] *Memoirs and Correspondence of Horner*, I, 419.

of men who read and thought for themselves, had been rapidly growing. These men were not scholars or deep thinkers, and had no leisure to puzzle out learned treatises. They were over-worked professional men or business men, who were alive to the questions of the hour, who had thought over them and discussed them wherever and whenever they could, and who were anxious for guidance from "men of light and leading." The essays of the new Review gave them just what they wanted, — brief, clear, yet original and suggestive dissertations by the best-trained minds on the most important current topics.

These, then, are some of the causes, over and beyond Jeffrey's editorial skill, and the brilliancy and originality of his co-workers, that led to the unprecedented success of the *Edinburgh Review.* Their importance and their significance are shown by the fact that within a few years several other Reviews were founded on precisely the same plan with the *Edinburgh*, and soon rivalled it in popular favor. In 1809 the Tory *Quarterly Review* was started with William Gifford as editor, and Scott, Southey, Canning, Ellis, and Croker among its contributors. In 1820 the *Retrospective Review* was established, and in 1824 the *Westminster Review*, the organ of the Radicals; Bentham was its patron, Bowring its editor, and James Mill and John Stuart Mill were constant contributors. These Reviews were all quarterlies, and in the details of their organization were modeled after the famous *Edinburgh*. They all found a ready welcome and, with the exception of the *Retrospective*, have continued to thrive down to our own day.

In the sixties, however, there came a still further development of the Review ; the *Fortnightly Review* and the *Contemporary Review* were established, — periodicals

that retain of the original Review nothing but the title.
They have thrown away the mask of the review-article,
and publish directly, over the author's name, brief discussions of whatever serious topics the public most care
to hear about. The discussions appear monthly, and
are somewhat less elaborate than the articles of the old
Quarterlies, but are fully as thoughtful and suggestive
and stimulating. These so-called *Reviews* evidently
represent one step forward in the process of adaptation
by means of which the writings of serious authors are
enabled to respond quickly and completely to the needs
of the public ; the establishment of the *Edinburgh Review*
was merely one of the earlier steps in the same process
of adaptation.

Chief Characteristics of
Elizabethans — Mark pas
sages where traits are seen

Charact. of Continental
Classical School

[illegible]
– [illegible]
[illegible]
[illegible]
[illegible] Short Stories

Romantic [illegible]
[illegible]

DRAMATIC WORKS OF JOHN FORD.

With an Introduction and Explanatory Notes. By Henry Weber,
Esq. 2 vols. 8vo, pp. 950. Edinburgh and London, 1811.

ALL true lovers of English poetry have been long in
love with the dramatists of the time of Elizabeth and
James ; and must have been sensibly comforted by their
late restoration to some degree of favour and notoriety.
If there was any good reason, indeed, to believe that the 5
notice which they have recently attracted proceeded from
any thing but that indiscriminate rage for editing and
annotating by which the present times are so happily
distinguished, we should be disposed to hail it as the
most unequivocal symptom of improvement in public 10
taste that has yet occurred to reward and animate our
labours. At all events, however, it gives us a chance for
such an improvement ; by placing in the hands of many,
who would not otherwise have heard of them, some of
those beautiful performances which we have always 15
regarded as among the most pleasing and characteristic
productions of our native genius.

Ford certainly is not the best of those neglected
writers, — nor Mr. Weber by any means the best of
their recent editors. But we cannot resist the oppor- 20
tunity which this publication seems to afford, of saying
a word or two of a class of writers, whom we have long
worshipped in secret with a sort of idolatrous veneration,
and now find once more brought forward as candidates
for public applause. The æra to which they belong, ·

indeed, has always appeared to us by far the brightest in
the history of English literature, — or indeed of human
intellect and capacity.   There never was, any where,
any thing like the sixty or seventy years that elapsed
5 from the middle of Elizabeth's reign to the period of the
Restoration.   In point of real force and originality of
genius, neither the age of Pericles, nor the age of
Augustus, nor the times of Leo X., nor of Louis XIV.,
can come at all into comparison : For, in that short
10 period, we shall find the names of almost all the very
great men that this nation has ever produced, — the
names of Shakespeare, and Bacon, and Spenser, and
Sydney, — and Hooker, and Taylor, and Barrow, and
Raleigh, — and Napier, and Milton, and Cudworth,
15 and Hobbes, and many others ; — men, all of them, not
merely of great talents and accomplishments, but of vast
compass and reach of understanding, and of minds truly
creative and original ; — not perfecting art by the delicacy of their taste, or digesting knowledge by the
20 justness of their reasonings ; but making vast and
substantial additions to the materials upon which taste
and reason must hereafter be employed, — and enlarging
to an incredible and unparalleled extent, both the stores
and the resources of the human faculties.
25 Whether the brisk concussion which was given to
men's minds by the force of the Reformation had much
effect in producing this sudden development of British
genius, we cannot undertake to determine.   For our own
part, we should be rather inclined to hold, that the
30 Reformation itself was but one symptom or effect of
that great spirit of progression and improvement which
had been set in operation by deeper and more general
causes ; and which afterwards blossomed out into this
splendid harvest of authorship.   But whatever may have

been the causes that determined the appearance of those
great works, the fact is certain, not only that they
appeared together in great numbers, but that they
possessed a common character, which, in spite of the
great diversity of their subjects and designs, would have 5
made them be classed together as the works of the same
order or description of·men, even if they had appeared
at the most distant intervals of time. They are the
works of Giants, in short, — and of Giants of one nation
and family ; — and their characteristics are, great force, 10
boldness, and originality ; together with a certain raci-
ness of English peculiarity, which distinguishes them
from all those performances that have since been
produced among ourselves, upon a more vague and
general idea of European excellence. Their sudden 15
appearance, indeed, in all this splendour of native
luxuriance, can only be compared to what happens on
the breaking up of a virgin soil, — where all the
indigenous plants spring up at once with a rank and
irrepressible fertility, and display whatever is peculiar or 20
excellent in their nature, on a scale the most conspicuous
and magnificent. The crops are not indeed so clean, as
where a more exhausted mould has been stimulated by
systematic cultivation ; nor so profitable, as where their
quality has been varied by a judicious admixture of 25
exotics, and accommodated to the demands of the
universe by the combinations of an unlimited trade.
But to those whose chief object of admiration is the
living power and energy of vegetation, and who take
delight in contemplating the various forms of her 30
unforced and natural perfection, · no spectacle can be
more rich, splendid, or attractive.

In the times of which we are speaking, classical
learning, though it had made great progress, had by no

means become an exclusive study ; and the ancients had
not yet been permitted to subdue men's minds to a sense
of hopeless inferiority, or to condemn the moderns to the
lot of humble imitators. They were resorted to, rather
5 to furnish materials and occasional ornaments, than as
models for the general style of composition ; and, while
they enriched the imagination, and insensibly improved
the taste of their successors, they did not at all restrain
their freedom, or impair their originality. No common
10 standard had yet been erected, to which all the works of
European genius were required to conform ; and no
general authority was acknowledged, by which all private
or local ideas of excellence must submit to be corrected.
Both readers and authors were comparatively few in
15 number. The former were infinitely less critical and
difficult than they have since become ; and the latter, if
they were not less solicitous about fame, were at least
much less jealous and timid as to the hazards which
attended its pursuit. Men, indeed, seldom took to
20 writing in those days, unless they had a great deal of
matter to communicate ; and neither imagined that they
could make a reputation by delivering commonplaces in
an elegant manner, or that the substantial value of their
sentiments would be disregarded for a little rudeness or
25 negligence in the finishing. They were habituated,
therefore, both to depend upon their own resources, and
to draw upon them without fear or anxiety ; and followed
the dictates of their own taste and judgment, without
standing much in awe of the ancients, of their readers,
30 or of each other.   .

The achievements of Bacon, and those who set free
°our understandings from the shackles of Papal and of
tyrannical imposition, afford sufficient evidence of the
benefit which resulted to the reasoning faculties from

this happy independence of the first great writers of this
nation. But its advantages were, if possible, still more
conspicuous in the mere literary character of their productions. The quantity of bright thoughts, of original
images, and splendid expressions, which they poured 5
forth upon every occasion, and by which they illuminated
and adorned the darkest and most rugged topics to
which they had happened to turn themselves, is such as
has never been equalled in any other age or country;
and places them at least as high, in point of fancy and 10
imagination, as of force of reason, or comprehensiveness
of understanding. In this highest and most comprehensive sense of the word, a great proportion of the writers
we have alluded to were *Poets:* and, without going to
those who composed in metre, and chiefly for purposes 15
of delight, we will venture to assert, that there is in any
one of the prose folios of Jeremy Taylor more fine
fancy and original imagery — more brilliant conceptions
and glowing expressions — more new figures, and new
applications of old figures — more, in short, of the body 20
and the soul of poetry, than in all the odes and .the epics
that have since been produced in Europe. There are
large portions of Barrow, and of Hooker and Bacon, of
which we may say nearly as much : nor can any one
have a tolerably adequate idea of the riches of our 25
language and our native genius, who has not made
himself acquainted with the prose writers, as well as the
poets, of this memorable period.

The civil wars, and the fanaticism by which they were
fostered, checked all this fine bloom of the imagination, 30
and gave a different and less attractive character to the
energies which they could not extinguish. Yet, those
were the times that matured and drew forth the dark, but
powerful genius of such men as Cromwell, and Harrison,

and Fleetwood, &c. — the milder and more generous
enthusiasm of Blake, and Hutchison, and Hampden —
and the stirring and indefatigable spirit of Pym, and
Hollis, and Vane — and the chivalrous and accomplished
5 loyalty of Strafford and Falkland ; at the same time that
they stimulated and repaid the severer studies of Coke,
and Selden, and Milton. The Drama, however, was
entirely destroyed, and has never since regained its
honours ; and Poetry, in general, lost its ease, and its
10 majesty and force, along with its copiousness and
originality.

The Restoration made things still worse : for it broke
down the barriers of our literary independence, and
reduced us to a province of the great republic of Europe.
15 The genius and fancy which lingered through the usurpation, though soured and blighted by the severities of
that inclement season, were still genuine English genius
and fancy ; and owned no allegiance to any foreign
authorities. But the Restoration brought in a French
20 taste upon us, and what was called a classical and a
polite taste ; and the wings of our English Muses were
clipped and trimmed, and their flights regulated at the
expense of all that was peculiar, and much of what was
brightest in their beauty. The King and his courtiers,
25 during their long exile, had, of course, imbibed the taste
of their protectors ; and, coming from the gay court of
France, with something of that additional profligacy that
belonged to their outcast and adventurer character, were
likely enough to be revolted by the peculiarities, and by
30 the very excellences, of our native literature. The grand
and sublime tone of our greater poets, appeared to them
dull, morose, and gloomy ; and the fine play of their rich
and unrestrained fancy, mere childishness and folly :
while their frequent lapses and perpetual irregularity

were set down as clear indications of barbarity and
ignorance. Such sentiments, too, were natural, we must
admit, for a few dissipated and witty men, accustomed
all their days to the regulated splendour of a court — to
the gay and heartless gallantry of French manners — 5
and to the imposing pomp and brilliant regularity of
French poetry. But, it may appear somewhat more
unaccountable that they should have been able to impose
their sentiments upon the great body of the nation.
A court, indeed, never has so much influence as at the 10
moment of a restoration : but the influence of an English
court has been but rarely discernible in the literature of
the country ; and had it not been for the peculiar
circumstances in which the nation was then placed, we
believe it would have resisted this attempt to naturalise 15
foreign notions, as sturdily as it was done on almost
every other occasion.

At this particular moment, however, the native literature
of the country had been sunk into a very low and feeble
state by the rigours of the usurpation, — the best written 20
recent models laboured under the reproach of republi-
canism, — and the courtiers were not only disposed to
see all its peculiarities with an eye of scorn and aversion,
but had even a good deal to say in favour of that very
opposite style to which they had been habituated. It was 25
a witty, and a grand, and a splendid style. It showed
more scholarship and art, than the luxuriant negligence of
the old English school ; and was not only free from many
of its hazards and some of its faults, but possessed
merits of its own, of a character more likely to please 30
those who had then the power of conferring celebrity, or
condemning to derision. Then it was a style which it
was peculiarly easy to justify by argument ; and in
support of which great authorities, as well as imposing

reasons, were always ready to be produced. It came upon us with the air and the pretension of being the style of cultivated Europe, and a true copy of the style of polished antiquity.   England, on the other hand, had
5 had but little intercourse with the rest of the world for a considerable period of time : Her language was not at all studied on the Continent, and her native authors had not been taken into account in forming those ideal standards of excellence which had been recently
10 constructed in France and Italy upon the authority of the Roman classics, and of their own most celebrated writers. When the comparison came to be made, therefore, it is easy to imagine that it should generally be thought to be very much to our disadvantage, and to understand how
15 the great multitude, even among ourselves, should be dazzled with the pretensions of the fashionable style of writing, and actually feel ashamed of their own richer and more varied productions.

It would greatly exceed our limits to describe accurately
20 the particulars in which this new Continental style differed from our old insular one : But, for our present purpose, it may be enough perhaps to say, that it was more worldly, and more townish, — holding more of reason, and ridicule, and authority — more elaborate and more
25 assuming — addressed more to the judgment than to the feelings, and somewhat ostentatiously accommodated to the habits, or supposed habits, of persons in fashionable life.   Instead of tenderness and fancy, we had satire and sophistry — artificial declamation, in place of the
30 spontaneous animation of genius — and for the universal language of Shakespeare, the personalities, the party politics, and the brutal obscenities of Dryden.   Nothing, indeed, can better characterize the change which had taken place in our national taste, than the alterations and

additions which this eminent person presumed — and thought it necessary — to make on the productions of Shakespeare and Milton. The heaviness, the coarseness, and the bombast of that abominable travestie, in which he has exhibited the Paradise Lost in the form of an 5 opera, and the atrocious indelicacy and compassionable stupidity of the new characters with which he has polluted the enchanted solitude of Miranda and Prospero in the Tempest, are such instances of degeneracy as we would be apt to impute rather to some transient hallucination 10 in the author himself, than to the general prevalence of any systematic bad taste in the public, did we not know that Wycherly and his coadjutors were in the habit of converting the neglected dramas of Beaumont and Fletcher into popular plays, merely by leaving out all the romantic 15 sweetness of their characters — turning their melodious blank verse into vulgar prose — and aggravating the indelicacy of their lower characters, by lending a more disgusting indecency to the whole *dramatis personæ.*

Dryden was, beyond all comparison, the greatest poet 20 of his own day ; and, endued as he was with a vigorous and discursive imagination, and possessing a mastery over his language which no later writer has attained, if he had known nothing of foreign literature, and been left to form himself on the models of Shakespeare, Spenser, and 25 Milton ; or if he had lived in.the country, at a distance from the pollutions of courts, factions, and playhouses, there is reason to think that he would have built up the pure and original school of English poetry so firmly, as to have made it impossible for fashion, or caprice, or 30 prejudice of any sort, ever to have rendered any other popular among our own inhabitants. As it is, he has not written one line that is pathetic, and very few that can be considered as sublime.

Addison, however, was the consummation of this Continental style ; and if it had not been redeemed about the same time by the fine talents of Pope, would probably have so far discredited it, as to have brought us back 5 to our original faith half a century ago. The extreme caution, timidity, and flatness of this author in his poetical compositions — the narrowness of his range in poetical sentiment and diction, and the utter want either of passion or of brilliancy, render it difficult to believe that 10 he was born under the same sun with Shakespeare, and wrote but a century after him. His fame, at this day stands solely upon the delicacy, the modest gaiety, and ingenious purity of his prose style ; — for the occasional elegance and small ingenuity of his poems can never 15 redeem the poverty of their diction, and the tameness of their conception. Pope has incomparably more spirit and taste and animation : but Pope is a satirist, and a moralist, and a wit, and a critic, and a fine writer, much more than he is a poet. He has all the delicacies and 20 proprieties and felicities of diction — but he has not a great deal of fancy, and scarcely ever touches any of the greater passions. He is much the best, we think, of the classical Continental school ; but he is not to be compared with the masters — nor with the pupils — of that Old 25 English one from which there had been so lamentable an apostacy. There are no pictures of nature or of simple emotion in all his writings. He is the poet of town life, and of high life, and of literary life ; and seems so much afraid of incurring ridicule by the display of natural 30 feeling or unregulated fancy, that it is difficult not to imagine that he would have thought such ridicule very well directed.

The best of what we copied from the Continental poets, on this desertion of our own great originals, is to be

found, perhaps, in the lighter pieces of Prior. That tone
of polite raillery — that airy, rapid, picturesque narrative,
mixed up with wit and *naïveté* — that style, in short, of
good conversation concentrated into flowing and polished
verses, was not within the vein of our native poets ; and 5
probably never would have been known among us, if we
had been left to our own resources. It is lamentable
that this, which alone was worth borrowing, is the only
thing which has not been retained. The tales and little
apologues of Prior are still the only examples of this 10
style in our language.

With the wits of Queen Anne this foreign school
attained the summit of its reputation ; and has ever
since, we think, been declining, though by slow and
almost imperceptible gradations. Thomson was the first 15
writer of any eminence who seceded from it, and made
some steps back to the force and animation of our
original poetry. Thomson, however, was educated in
Scotland, where the new style, we believe, had not yet
become familiar ; and lived, for a long time, a retired and 20
unambitious life, with very little intercourse with those
who gave the tone in literature at the period of his first
appearance. Thomson, accordingly, has always been
popular with a much wider circle of readers, than either
Pope or Addison ; and, in spite of considerable vulgarity 25
and signal cumbrousness of diction, has drawn, even from
the fastidious, a much deeper and more heartfelt
admiration.

Young exhibits, we think, a curious combination, or
contrast rather, of the two styles of which we have been 30
speaking. Though incapable either of tenderness or
passion, he had a richness and activity of fancy that
belonged rather to the days of James and Elizabeth, than
to those of George and Anne : — But then, instead of

indulging it, as the older writers would have done, in easy and playful inventions, in splendid descriptions, or glowing illustrations, he was led, by the restraints and established taste of his age, to work it up into strange
5 and fantastical epigrams, or into cold and revolting hyperboles. Instead of letting it flow gracefully on, in an easy and sparkling current, he perpetually forces it out in jets, or makes it stagnate in formal canals ; and thinking it necessary to write like Pope, when the bent of
10 his genius led him rather to copy what was best in Cowley and most fantastic in Shakespeare, he has produced something which excites wonder instead of admiration, and is felt by every one to be at once ingenious, incongruous, and unnatural.

15   After Young, there was a plentiful lack of poetical talent, down to a period comparatively recent. Akenside and Gray, indeed, in the interval, discovered a new way of imitating the ancients ; — and Collins and Goldsmith produced some small specimens of exquisite and original
20 poetry. At last, Cowper threw off the whole trammels of French criticism and artificial refinement ; and, setting at defiance all the imaginary requisites of poetical diction and classical imagery — dignity of style, and politeness of phraseology — ventured to write again with the force
25 and the freedom which had characterised the old school of English literature, and been so unhappily sacrificed, upwards of a century before. Cowper had many faults, and some radical deficiencies ; — but this atoned for all. There was something so delightfully refreshing, in seeing
30 natural phrases and natural images again displaying their unforced graces, and waving their unpruned heads in the enchanted gardens of poetry, that no one complained of the taste displayed in the selection ; — and Cowper is, and is likely to continue, the most popular

of all who have written for the present or the last generation.

Of the poets who have come after him, we cannot,
indeed, say that they have attached themselves to the
school of Pope and Addison ; or that they have even 5
failed to show a much stronger predilection for the native
beauties of their great predecessors. Southey, and
Wordsworth, and Coleridge, and Miss Baillie, have all of
them copied the manner of our older poets ; and, along
with this indication of good taste, have given great 10
proofs of original genius. The misfortune is, that their
copies of those great originals are liable to the charge of
extreme affectation. They do not write as those great
poets would have written : they merely mimic their
manner, and ape their peculiarities ; — and consequently, 15
though they profess to imitate the freest and most careless
of all versifiers, their style is more remarkably and
offensively artificial than that of any other class of
writers. They have mixed in, too, so much of the
mawkish tone of pastoral innocence and babyish 20
simplicity, with a sort of pedantic emphasis and ostentatious glitter, that it is difficult not to be disgusted with
their perversity, and with the solemn self-complacency,
and keen and vindictive jealousy, with which they have
put in their claims on public admiration. But we have 25
said enough elsewhere of the faults of those authors ;
and shall only add, at present, that, notwithstanding all
these faults, there is a fertility and a force, a warmth of
feeling and an exaltation of imagination about them,
which classes them, in our estimation, with a much higher 30
order of poets than the followers of Dryden and Addison ;
and justifies an anxiety for their fame, in all the admirers
of Milton and Shakespeare.

Of Scott, or of Campbell, we need scarcely say any

thing, with reference to our present object, after the very copious accounts we have given of them on former occasions. The former professes to copy something a good deal older than what we consider as the golden age
5 of English poetry, — and, in reality, has copied every style, and borrowed from every manner that has prevailed, from the times of Chaucer to his own ; — illuminating and uniting, if not harmonizing them all, by a force of colouring, and a rapidity of succession, which is not to
10 be met with in any of his many models. The latter, we think, can scarcely be said to have copied his pathos, or his energy, from any models whatever, either recent or early. The exquisite harmony of his versification is elaborated, perhaps, from the Castle of Indolence of
15 Thomson, and the serious pieces of Goldsmith ; — and it seems to be his misfortune, not to be able to reconcile himself to any thing which he cannot reduce within the limits of this elaborate harmony. This extreme fastidiousness, and the limitation of his efforts to themes of
20 unbroken tenderness or sublimity, distinguish him from the careless, prolific, and miscellaneous authors of our primitive poetry ; — while the enchanting softness of his pathetic passages, and the power and originality of his more sublime conceptions, place him at a still greater
25 distance from the wits, as they truly called themselves, of Charles II. and Queen Anne.

We do not know what other apology to offer for this hasty, and, we fear, tedious sketch of the history of our poetry, but that it appeared to us to be necessary, in
30 order to explain the peculiar merit of that class of writers to which the author before us belongs ; and that it will very greatly shorten what we have still to say on the characteristics of our older dramatists. An opinion prevails very generally on the Continent, and with

foreign-bred scholars among ourselves, that our national taste has been corrupted chiefly by our idolatry of Shakespeare ; — and that it is our patriotic and traditional admiration of that singular writer, that reconciles us to the monstrous compound of faults and beauties that occur in his performances, and must to all impartial judges appear quite absurd and unnatural. Before entering upon the character of a contemporary dramatist, it was of some importance, therefore, to show that there was a distinct, original, and independent school of literature in England in the time of Shakespeare ; to the general tone of whose productions his works were sufficiently conformable ; and that it was owing to circumstances in a great measure accidental, that this native school was superseded about the time of the Restoration, and a foreign standard of excellence intruded on us, not in the drama only, but in every other department of poetry. This new style of composition, however, though adorned and recommended by the splendid talents of many of its followers, was never perfectly naturalised, we think, in this country ; and has ceased, in a great measure, to be cultivated by those who have lately aimed with the greatest success at the higher honours of poetry. Our love of Shakespeare, therefore, is not a *monomania* or solitary and unaccountable infatuation ; but is merely the natural love which all men bear to those forms of excellence that are accommodated to their peculiar character, temperament, and situation ; and which will always return, and assert its power over their affections, long after authority has lost its reverence, fashions been antiquated, and artificial tastes passed away. In endeavouring, therefore, to bespeak some share of favour for such of his contemporaries as had fallen out of notice, during the prevalence of an imported literature, we con-

ceive that we are only enlarging that foundation of native
genius on which alone any lasting superstructure can be
raised, and invigorating that deep-rooted stock upon
which all the perennial blossoms of our literature must
5 still be engrafted.

_ The notoriety of Shakespeare may seem to make it
superfluous to speak of the peculiarities of those old
dramatists, of whom he will be admitted to be so worthy
a representative.   Nor shall we venture to say anything
10 of the confusion of their plots, the disorders of their
chronology, their contempt of the unities, or their imperfect discrimination between the provinces of Tragedy
and Comedy.   Yet there are characteristics which the
lovers of literature may not be displeased to find enu-
15 merated, and which may constitute no dishonourable
distinction for the whole fraternity, independent of the
splendid talents and incommunicable graces of their
great chieftain.

Of the old English dramatists, then, including under
20 this name (besides Shakespeare), Beaumont and Fletcher,
Massinger, Jonson, Ford, Shirley, Webster, Dekkar,
Field, and Rowley, it may be said, in general, that they
are more poetical, and more original in their diction, than
the dramatists of any other age or country.   Their scenes
25 abound more in varied images, and gratuitous excursions
of fancy.   Their illustrations, and figures of speech, are
more borrowed from rural life, and from the simple occupations or universal feelings of mankind.   They are not
confined to a certain range of dignified expressions, nor
30 restricted to a particular assortment of imagery, beyond
which it is not lawful to look for embellishments.   Let
any one compare the prodigious variety, and wide-ranging
freedom of Shakespeare, with the narrow round of flames,
tempests, treasons, victims, and tyrants, that scantily

adorn the sententious pomp of the French drama, and
he will not fail to recognise the vast superiority of the
former, in the excitement of the imagination, and all the
diversities of poetical delight. That very mixture of
styles, of which the French critics have so fastidiously 5
complained, forms, when not carried to any height of
extravagance, one of the greatest charms of our ancient
dramatists. It is equally sweet and natural for personages toiling on the barren heights of life, to be occasionally recalled to some vision of pastoral innocence and 10
tranquillity, as for the victims or votaries of ambition to
cast a glance of envy and agony on the joys of humble
content.

Those charming old writers, however, have a still more
striking peculiarity in their conduct of the dialogue. On 15
the modern stage, every scene is *visibly* studied and
digested beforehand, — and every thing from beginning
to end, whether it be description, or argument, or vitu-
peration, is very obviously and ostentatiously set forth in
the most advantageous light, and with all the decorations 20
of the most elaborate rhetoric. Now, for mere rhetoric,
and fine composition, this is very right ; — but, for an
imitation of nature, it is not quite so well : And however
we may admire the skill of the artist, we are not very
likely to be moved with any very lively sympathy in the 25
emotions of those very rhetorical interlocutors. When we
come to any important part of the play, on the Continental or modern stage, we are sure to have a most
complete, formal, and exhausting discussion of it, in long
flourishing orations , — argument after argument pro- 30
pounded and answered with infinite ingenuity, and topic
after topic brought forward in well-digested method,
without any deviation that the most industrious and
practised pleader would not approve of, — till nothing

more remains to be said, and a new scene introduces
us to a new set of gladiators, as expert and persevering
as the former. It is exactly the same when a story is to
be told,—a tyrant to be bullied,—or a princess to be
5 wooed. On the old English stage, however, the proceed-
ings were by no means so regular. There the discussions
always appear to be casual, and the argument quite
artless and disorderly. The persons of the drama, in
short, are made to speak like men and women who meet
10 without preparation, in real life. Their reasonings are
perpetually broken by passion, or left imperfect for want
of skill. They constantly wander from the point in hand,
in the most unbusinesslike manner in the world;—and
after hitting upon a topic that would afford a judicious
15 playwright room for a magnificent seesaw of pompous
declamation, they have generally the awkwardness to let
it slip, as if perfectly unconscious of its value; and uniformly leave the scene without exhausting the controversy, or stating half the plausible things for themselves
20 that any ordinary advisers might have suggested — after
a few weeks' reflection. As specimens of eloquent argu-
mentation, we must admit the signal inferiority of our
native favourites; but as true copies of nature,—as
vehicles of passion, and representations of character, we
25 confess we are tempted to give them the preference.
When a dramatist brings his chief characters on the
stage, we readily admit that he must give them something
to say,—and that this something must be interesting
and characteristic;—but he should recollect also, that
30 they are supposed to come there without having anticipated all they were to hear, or meditated on all they were
to deliver; and that it cannot be characteristic, therefore,
because it must be glaringly unnatural, that they should
proceed regularly through every possible view of the

subject, and exhaust, in set order, the whole magazine of reflections that can be brought to bear upon their situation.

It would not be fair, however, to leave this view of the matter, without observing, that this unsteadiness and 5 irregularity of dialogue, which gives such an air of nature to our older plays, and keeps the curiosity and attention so perpetually awake, is frequently carried to a most blamable excess ; and that, independent of their passion for verbal quibbles, there *is* an inequality and a capri- 10 cious uncertainty in the taste and judgment of these good old writers, which excites at once our amazement and our compassion. If it be true, that no other man has ever written so finely as Shakespeare has done in his happier passages, it is no less true that there is not a 15 scribbler now alive who could possibly write worse than he has sometimes written, — who could, on occasion, devise more contemptible ideas, or misplace them so abominably, by the side of such incomparable excellence. That there were no critics, and no critical readers in 20 those days, appears to us but an imperfect solution of the difficulty. He who could write so admirably, must have been a critic to himself. *Children*, indeed, may play with the most precious gems, and the most worth- less pebbles, without being aware of any difference in 25 their value ; but the fiery powers which are necessary to the production of intellectual excellence, must enable the possessor to recognise it as excellence ; and he who knows when he succeeds, can scarcely be unconscious of his failures. Unaccountable, however, as it is, the fact 30 is certain, that almost all the dramatic writers of this age appear to be alternately inspired, and bereft of understanding ; and pass, apparently without being conscious of the change, from the most beautiful displays

of genius to the most melancholy exemplifications of
stupidity.

There is only one other peculiarity which we shall
notice in those ancient dramas ; and that is, the singular,
5 though very beautiful style, in which the greater part of
them are composed,—a style which we think must be
felt as peculiar by all who peruse them, though it is by
no means easy to describe in what its peculiarity consists.
It is not, for the most part, a lofty or sonorous style,—
10 nor can it be said generally to be finical or affected, —or
strained, quaint, or pedantic :—But it is, at the same
time, a style full of turn and contrivance,—with some
little degree of constraint and involution,—very often
characterised by a studied briefness and simplicity of
15 diction, yet relieved by a certain indirect and figurative
cast of expression,—and almost always coloured with a
modest tinge of ingenuity, and fashioned, rather too
visibly, upon a particular model of elegance and purity.
In scenes of powerful passion, this sort of artificial pret-
20 tiness is commonly shaken off ; and, in Shakespeare, it
disappears under all his forms of animation : But it sticks
closer to most of his contemporaries. In Massinger (who
has no passion), it is almost always discernible ; and, in
the author before us, it gives a peculiar tone to almost
25 all the estimable parts of his productions.

CHARACTERS OF SHAKESPEARE'S PLAYS.

By William Hazlitt. 8vo, pp. 352. London, 1817.[1]

THIS is not a book of black-letter learning, or historical
elucidation ; — neither is it a metaphysical dissertation,
full of wise perplexities and elaborate reconcilements.   It
is, in truth, rather an encomium on Shakespeare, than a
commentary or critique on him — and is written, more to   5
show extraordinary love, than extraordinary knowledge of
his productions.   Nevertheless, it is a very pleasing book
— and, we do not hesitate to say, a book of very considerable originality and genius.   The author is not merely
an admirer of our great'dramatist, but an Idolator of him; 10
and openly professes his idolatry.   We have ourselves
too great a leaning to the same superstition, to blame him .
very much for his error, and though we think, of course,
that our own admiration is, on the whole, more discriminating and judicious, there are not many points on which, 15
especially after reading his eloquent exposition of them,
we should be much inclined to disagree with him.

[1] It may be thought that enough had been said of our early
dramatists, in the immediately preceding article ; and it probably is
so.   But I could not resist the temptation of thus renewing, in my
own name, that vow of allegiance, which I had so often taken
anonymously to the only true and lawful King of our English Poetry!
and now venture, therefore, fondly to replace this slight and perishable wreath on his august and undecaying shrine : with no farther
apology than that it presumes to direct attention but to one, and
that, as I think, a comparatively neglected aspect of his universal
genius.

The book, as we have already intimated, is written less
to tell the reader what Mr. H. *knows* about Shakespeare
or his writings, than to explain to them what he *feels* about
them — and *why* he feels so — and thinks that all who
5 profess to love poetry should feel so likewise.   What we
chiefly look for in such a work, accordingly, is a fine sense
of the beauties of the author, and an eloquent exposition
of them ; and all this, and more, we think, may be found
in the volume before us.   There is nothing niggardly in
10 Mr. H.'s praises, and nothing affected in his raptures.
He seems animated throughout with a full and hearty
sympathy with the delight which his author should inspire,
and pours himself gladly out in explanation of it, with a
fluency and ardour, obviously much more akin to enthu-
15 siasm than affectation.   He seems pretty generally, indeed, in a state of happy intoxication — and has borrowed
from his great original, not indeed the force or brilliancy
of his fancy, but something of its playfulness, and a large
share of his apparent joyousness and self-indulgence in
20 its exercise.   It is evidently a great pleasure to him to be
fully possessed with the beauties of his author, and to
follow the impulse of his unrestrained eagerness to impress them upon his readers.

When we have said that his observations are generally
25 right, we have said, in substance, that they are not
generally original ; for the beauties of Shakespeare are
not of so dim or equivocal a nature as to be visible only
to learned eyes — and undoubtedly his finest passages
are those which please all classes of readers, and are ad-
30 mired for the same qualities by judges from every school
of criticism.   Even with regard to those passages, however, a skilful commentator will find something worth
hearing to tell.   Many persons are very sensible of the
effect of fine poetry on their feelings, who do not well

know how to refer these feelings to their causes ; and it is always a delightful thing to be made to see clearly the sources from which our delight has proceeded — and to trace back the mingled stream that has flowed upon our hearts, to the remoter fountains from which it has been gathered. And when this is done with warmth as well as precision, and embodied in an eloquent description of the beauty which is explained, it forms one of the most attractive, and not the least instructive, of literary exercises. In all works of merit, however, and especially in all works of original genius, there are a thousand retiring and less obtrusive graces, which escape hasty and superficial observers, and only give out their beauties to fond and patient contemplation ; a thousand slight and harmonising touches, the merit and the effect of which are equally imperceptible to vulgar eyes ; and a thousand indications of the continual presence of that poetical spirit, which can only be recognised by those who are in some measure under its influence, or have prepared themselves to receive it, by worshipping meekly at the shrines which it inhabits.

In the exposition of these, there is room enough for originality, — and more room than Mr. H. has yet filled. In many points, however, he has acquitted himself excellently ; — partly in the development of the principal characters with which Shakespeare has peopled the fancies of all English readers — but principally, we think, in the delicate sensibility with which he has traced, and the natural eloquence with which he has pointed out that fond familiarity with beautiful forms and images — that eternal recurrence to what is sweet or majestic in the simple aspects of nature — that indestructible love of flowers and odours, and dews and clear waters, and soft airs and sounds, and bright skies, and woodland solitudes,

and moonlight bowers, which are the Material elements
of Poetry — and that fine sense of their undefinable
relation to mental emotion, which is its essence and
vivifying Soul — and which, in the midst of Shakespeare's
5 most busy and atrocious scenes, falls like gleams of sun-
shine on rocks and ruins — contrasting with all that is
rugged and repulsive, and reminding us of the existence
of purer and brighter elements! — which HE ALONE has
poured out from the richness of his own mind, without
10 effort or restraint ; and contrived to intermingle with the
play of all the passions, and the vulgar course of this
world's affairs, without deserting for an instant the proper
business of the scene, or appearing to pause or digress,
from the love of ornament or need of repose! — HE ALONE,
15 who, when the object requires it, is always keen and
worldly and practical — and who yet, without changing
his hand, or stopping his course, scatters around him, as
he goes, all sounds and shapes of sweetness — and con-
jures up landscapes of immortal fragrance and freshness,
20 and peoples them with Spirits of glorious aspect and
attractive grace — and is a thousand times more full of
fancy and imagery, and splendour, than those who, in
pursuit of such enchantments, have shrunk back from the
delineation of character or passion, and declined the dis-
25 cussion of human duties and cares.   More full of wisdom
and ridicule and sagacity, than all the moralists and
satirists that ever existed — he is more wild, airy, and inventive, and more pathetic and fantastic, than all the
poets of all regions and ages of the world : — and has all
30 those elements so happily mixed up in him, and bears his
high faculties so temperately, that the most severe reader
cannot complain of him for want of strength or of reason
— nor the most sensitive for defect of ornament or
ingenuity.   Every thing in him is in unmeasured abund-

ance, and unequalled perfection — but every thing so
balanced and kept in subordination, as not to jostle or
disturb or take the place of another. The most exquisite
poetical conceptions, images, and descriptions, are given
with such brevity, and introduced with such skill, as 5
merely to adorn, without loading the sense they accompany. Although his sails are purple and perfumed, and
his prow of beaten gold, they waft him on his voyage, not
less, but more rapidly and directly than if they had been
composed of baser materials. All his excellences, like 10
those of Nature herself, are thrown out together ; and,
instead of interfering with, support and recommend each
other. His flowers are not tied up in garlands, nor his
fruits crushed into baskets — but spring living from the
soil, in all the dew and freshness of youth ; while the 15
graceful foliage in which they lurk, and the ample
branches, the rough and vigorous stem, and the wide-
spreading roots on which they depend, are present along
with them, and share, in their places, the equal care of
their Creator. 20

RELIQUES OF ROBERT BURNS.

*Consisting chiefly of Original Letters, Poems, and Critical Observa-
tions on Scottish Songs. Collected and published by R. H. Cromek.
8vo, pp. 450. London, 1808.*

BURNS is certainly by far the greatest of our poetical
prodigies — from Stephen Duck down to Thomas Dermody. *They* are forgotten already; or only remembered
for derision. But the name of Burns, if we are not
5 mistaken, has not yet "gathered all its fame"; and will
endure long after those circumstances are forgotten
which contributed to its first notoriety. So much indeed
are we impressed with a sense of his merits, that we
cannot help thinking it a derogation from them to
10 consider him as a prodigy at all; and are convinced that
he will never be rightly estimated as a poet, till that
vulgar wonder be entirely repressed which was raised on
his having been a ploughman. It is true, no doubt, that
he was born in an humble station; and that much of his
15 early life was devoted to severe labour, and to the
society of his fellow-labourers. But he was not himself
either uneducated or illiterate; and was placed in a
situation more favourable, perhaps, to the development
of great poetical talents, than any other which could
20 have been assigned him. He was taught, at a very early
age, to read and write; and soon after acquired a
competent knowledge of French, together with the
elements of Latin and Geometry. His taste for reading

was encouraged by his parents and many of his associates ; and, before he had ever composed a single
stanza, he was not only familiar with many prose writers,
but far more intimately acquainted with Pope, Shakespeare, and Thomson, than nine tenths of the youth that 5
now leave our schools for the university. Those authors,
indeed, with some old collections of songs, and the lives
of Hannibal and of Sir William Wallace, were his
habitual study from the first days of his childhood ; and
co-operating with the solitude of his rural occupations, 10
were sufficient to rouse his ardent and ambitious mind to
the love and the practice of poetry. He had about as
much scholarship, in short, we imagine, as Shakespeare ;
and far better models to form his ear to harmony, and
train his fancy to graceful invention. 15

We ventured, on a former occasion, to say something
of the effects of regular education, and of the general
diffusion of literature, in repressing the vigour and
originality of all kinds of mental exertion. That speculation was perhaps carried somewhat too far ; but if the 20
paradox have proof any where, it is in its application to
poetry. Among well educated people, the standard
writers of this description are at once so venerated and
so familiar, that it is thought equally impossible to rival
them, as to write verses without attempting it. If there 25
be one degree of fame which excites emulation, there is
another which leads to despair : Nor can we conceive
any one less likely to be added to the short list of original
poets, than a young man of fine fancy and delicate taste,
who has acquired a high relish for poetry, by perusing 30
the most celebrated writers, and conversing with the
most intelligent judges. The head of such a person is
filled, of course, with all the splendid passages of ancient
and modern authors, and with the fine and fastidious

remarks which have been made even on those passages.
When he turns his eyes, therefore, on his own conceptions
or designs, they can scarcely fail to appear rude and
contemptible. He is perpetually haunted and depressed
5 by the ideal presence of those great masters, and their
exacting critics. He is·aware to what comparisons his
productions will be subjected among his own friends and
associates ; and recollects the derision with which so
many rash adventurers have been chased back to their
10 obscurity.   Thus, the merit of his great predecessors
chills, instead of encouraging his ardour ; and the
illustrious names which have already reached to the
summit of excellence, act like the tall and spreading
trees of the forest, which overshadow and strangle the
15 saplings which may have struck root in the soil below —
and afford efficient shelter to nothing but creepers and
parasites.

There is, no doubt, in some few individuals, " that
strong divinity of soul " — that decided and irresistible
20 vocation to glory, which, in spite of all these obstructions,
calls out, perhaps once or twice in a century, a bold and
original poet from the herd of scholars and academical
literati. But the natural tendency of their studies, and
by far their most common effect, is to repress originality,
25 and discourage enterprise ; and either to change those
whom nature meant for poets, into mere readers of
poetry, or to bring them out in the form of witty
parodists, or ingenious imitators. Independent of the
reasons which have been already suggested, it will perhaps
30 be found, too, that necessity is the mother of invention,
in this as well as in the more vulgar arts ; or, at least,
that inventive genius will frequently slumber in inaction,
where the preceding ingenuity has in part supplied the
wants of the owner. A solitary and uninstructed man,

with lively feelings and an inflammable imagination, will often be irresistibly led to exercise those gifts, and to occupy and relieve his mind in poetical composition : But if his education, his reading, and his society supply him with an abundant store of images and emotions, he 5 will probably think but little of those internal resources, and feed his mind contentedly with what has been provided by the industry of others.

To say nothing, therefore, of the distractions and the dissipation of mind that belong to the commerce of the 10 world, nor of the cares of minute accuracy and high finishing which are imposed on the professed scholar, there seem to be deeper reasons for the separation of originality and accomplishment ; and for the partiality which has led poetry to choose almost all her prime 15 favourites among the recluse and uninstructed. A youth of quick parts, in short, and creative fancy — with just so much reading as to guide his ambition, and roughhew his notions of excellence — if his lot be thrown in humble retirement, where he has no reputation to lose, and 20 where he can easily hope to excel all that he sees around him, is much more likely, we think, to give himself up to poetry, and to train himself to habits of invention, than if he had been encumbered by the pretended helps of extended study and literary society. 25

If these observations should fail to strike of themselves, they may perhaps derive additional weight from considering the very remarkable fact, that almost all the great poets of every country have appeared in an early stage of their history, and in a period comparatively rude and un- 30 lettered. Homer went forth, like the morning star, before the dawn of literature in Greece, and almost all the great and sublime poets of modern Europe are already between two and three hundred years old. Since that time,

although books and readers, and opportunities of reading, are multiplied a thousand fold, we have improved chiefly in point and terseness of expression, in the art of raillery, and in clearness and simplicity of thought.   Force, rich-
5 ness, and variety of invention, are now at least as rare as ever.   But the literature and refinement of the age does not exist at all for a rustic and illiterate individual ; and, consequently, the present time is to him what the rude times of old were to the vigorous writers which adorned
10 them.

But though, for these and for other reasons, we can see no propriety in regarding the poetry of Burns chiefly as the wonderful work of a peasant, and thus admiring it much in the same way as if it had been written with his
15 toes ; yet there are peculiarities in his works which remind us of the lowness of his origin, and faults for which the defects of his education afford an obvious cause, if not a legitimate apology.   In forming a correct estimate of these works, it is necessary to take into
20 account those peculiarities.

The first is, the undiciplined harshness and acrimony of his invective.   The great boast of polished life is the delicacy, and even the generosity of its hostility—that quality which is still the characteristic, as it furnishes
25 the denomination, of a gentleman — that principle which forbids us to attack the defenceless, to strike the fallen, or to mangle the slain—and enjoins us, in forging the shafts of satire, to increase the polish exactly as we add to their keenness or their weight.   For this, as well as
30 for other things, we are indebted to chivalry ; and of this Burns had none.   His ingenious and amiable biographer has spoken repeatedly in praise of his talents for satire—we think, with a most unhappy partiality.   His epigrams and lampoons appear to us, one and all,

unworthy of him ; — offensive from their extreme coarseness and violence — and contemptible from their want of
wit or brilliancy. They seem to have been written, not
out of playful malice or virtuous indignation, but out of
fierce and ungovernable anger. His whole raillery con- 5
sists in railing; and his satirical vein displays itself
chiefly in calling names and in swearing. We say this
mainly with a reference to his personalities. In many of
his more general representations of life and manners,
there is no doubt much that may be called satirical, 10
mixed up with admirable humour, and description of
inimitable vivacity.

There is a similar want of polish, or at least of respect-
fulness, in the general tone of his gallantry. He has
written with more passion, perhaps, and more variety of 15
natural feeling, on the subject of love, than any other
poet whatever — but with a fervour that is sometimes
indelicate, and seldom accommodated to the timidity and
" sweet austere composure " of women of refinement. He
has expressed admirably the feelings of an enamoured 20
peasant, who, however refined or eloquent he may be,
always approaches his mistress on a footing of equality ;
but has never caught that tone of chivalrous gallantry
which uniformly abases itself in the presence of the
object of its devotion. Accordingly, instead of suing for 25
a smile, or melting in a tear, his muse deals in nothing
but locked embraces and midnight rencontres ; and, even
in his complimentary effusions to ladies of the highest
rank, is for straining them to the bosom of her impetuous
votary. It is easy, accordingly, to see from his corres- 30
pondence, that many of his female patronesses shrunk
from the vehement familiarity of his admiration ; and
there are even some traits in the volumes before us, from
which we can gather, that he resented the shyness and

estrangement to which those feelings gave rise, with at
least as little chivalry as he had shown in producing them.

But the leading vice in Burns's character, and the
cardinal deformity, indeed, of all his productions, was his
5 contempt, or affectation of contempt, for prudence,
decency, and regularity ; and his admiration of thoughtlessness, oddity, and vehement sensibility ; — his belief,
in short, in *the dispensing power* of genius and social
feeling, in all matters of morality and common sense.
10 This is the very slang of the worst German plays, and
the lowest of our town-made novels ; nor can any thing
be more lamentable, than that it should have found a
patron in such a man as Burns, and communicated to
many of his productions a character of immorality, at
15 once contemptible and hateful.   It is but too true, that
men of the highest genius have frequently been hurried
by their passions into a violation of prudence and duty ;
and there is something generous, at least, in the apology
which their admirers may make for them, on the score of
20 their keener feelings and habitual want of reflection.
But this apology, which is quite unsatisfactory in the
mouth of another, becomes an insult and an absurdity
whenever it proceeds from their own.   A man may say
of his friend, that he is a noble-hearted fellow — too
25 generous to be just, and with too much spirit to be
always prudent and regular.   But he cannot be allowed
to say even this of himself ; and still less to represent
himself as a hairbrained sentimental soul, constantly
carried away by fine fancies and visions of love and
30 philanthropy, and born to confound and despise the cold-
blooded sons of prudence and sobriety.   This apology,
indeed, evidently destroys itself : For it shows that conduct to be the result of deliberate system, which it affects
at the same time to justify as the fruit of mere thought-

lessness and casual impulse. Such protestations, therefore, will always be treated, as they deserve, not only
with contempt, but with incredulity; and their magnani-
mous authors set down as determined profligates, who
seek to disguise their selfishness under a name somewhat 5
less revolting. That profligacy is almost always selfishness, and that the excuse of impetuous feeling can hardly
ever be justly pleaded for those who neglect the ordinary
duties of life, must be apparent, we think, even to the
least reflecting of those sons of fancy and song. It 10
requires no habit of deep thinking, nor any thing more,
indeed, than the information of an honest heart, to perceive that it is cruel and base to. spend, in vain super-
fluities, that money which belongs of right to the pale
industrious tradesman and his famishing infants; or that 15
it is a vile prostitution of language, to talk of that man's
generosity or goodness of heart, who sits raving about
friendship and philanthropy in a tavern, while his wife's
heart is breaking at her cheerless fireside, and his children pining in solitary poverty.   20

This pitiful cant of careless feeling and eccentric
genius, accordingly, has never found much favour in the
eyes of English sense and morality. The most signal
effect which it ever produced, was on the muddy brains
of some German youth, who are said to have left college 25
in a body to rob on the highway: because Schiller had
represented the captain of a gang as so very noble a
creature. — But in this country, we believe, a predilection
for that honourable profession must have preceded this
admiration of the character. The style we have been 30
speaking of, accordingly, is now the heroics only of the
hulks and the house of correction; and has no chance, we
suppose, of being greatly admired, except in the farewell
speech of a young gentleman preparing for Botany Bay.

It is humiliating to think how deeply Burns has fallen into this debasing error. He is perpetually making a parade of his thoughtlessness, inflammability, and imprudence, and talking with much complacency and exultation 5 of the offence he has occasioned to the sober and correct part of mankind. This odious slang infects almost all his prose, and a very great proportion of his poetry ; and is, we are persuaded, the chief, if not the only source of disgust with which, in spite of his genius, we know that 10 he is regarded by many very competent and liberal judges. His apology, too, we are willing to believe, is to be found in the original lowness of his situation, and the slightness of his acquaintance with the world. With his talents and powers of observation, he could not have 15 seen *much* of the beings who echoed this raving, without feeling for them that distrust and contempt which would have made him blush to think he had ever stretched over them the protecting shield of his genius.

Akin to this most lamentable trait of vulgarity, and 20 indeed in some measure arising out of it, is that perpetual boast of his own independence, which is obtruded upon the readers of Burns in almost every page of his writings. The sentiment itself is noble, and it is often finely expressed ;—but a gentleman would only have expressed 25 it when he was insulted or provoked ; and would never have made it a spontaneous theme to those friends in whose estimation he felt that his honour stood clear. It is mixed up, too, in Burns with too fierce a tone of defiance, and indicates rather the pride of a sturdy 30 peasant, than the calm and natural elevation of a generous mind.

The last of the symptoms of rusticity which we think it necessary to notice in the works of this extraordinary man, is that frequent mistake of mere exaggeration and violence, for force and sublimity, which has defaced so much of his prose composition, and given an air of heaviness and labour to a good deal of his serious poetry. The truth is, that his *forte* was in humour and in pathos —or rather in tenderness of feeling ; and that he has 5 very seldom succeeded, either where mere wit and sprightliness, or where great energy and weight of sentiment were requisite. He had evidently a very false and crude notion of what constituted *strength* of writing ; and instead of that simple and brief directness which stamps 10 the character of vigour upon every syllable, has generally had recourse to a mere accumulation of hyperbolical expressions, which encumber the diction instead of exalting it, and show the determination to be impressive, without the power of executing it. This error also we 15 are inclined to ascribe entirely to the defects of his education. The value of simplicity in the expression of passion, is a lesson, we believe, of nature and of genius ; —but its importance in mere grave and impressive writing, is one of the latest discoveries of rhetorical experience. 20

With the allowances and exceptions we have now stated, we think Burns entitled to the rank of a great and original genius. He has in all his compositions great force of conception ; and great spirit and animation in its expression. He has taken a large range through the 25 region of Fancy, and naturalized himself in almost all her climates. He has great humour—great powers of description—great pathos — and great discrimination of character. Almost every thing that he says has spirit and originality ; and every thing that he says well, is 30 characterized by a charming facility, which gives a grace even to occasional rudeness, and communicates to the reader a delightful sympathy with the spontaneous soaring and conscious inspiration of the poet.

Considering the reception which these works have met
with from the public, and the long period during which
the greater part of them have been in their possession, it
may appear superfluous to say any thing as to their
5 characteristic or peculiar merit. Though the ultimate
judgment of the public, however, be always sound, or at
least decisive as to its general result, it is not always
very apparent upon what grounds it has proceeded ; nor
in consequence of what, or in spite of what, it has been
10 obtained. In Burns's works there is much to censure, as
well as much to praise ; and as time has not yet separated
his ore from its dross, it may be worth while to state, in
a very general way, what we presume to anticipate as the
result of this separation.   Without pretending to enter at
15 all into the comparative merit of particular passages, we
may venture to lay it down as our opinion — that his
poetry is far superior to his prose ; that his Scottish
compositions are greatly to be preferred to his English
ones ; and that his Songs will probably outlive all his
20 other productions.   A very few remarks on each of these
subjects will comprehend almost all that we have to say
of the volumes now before us.

THE LADY OF THE LAKE.

A Poem by Walter Scott. Second Edition. 8vo, pp. 434. 1810.

MR. SCOTT, though living in an age unusually prolific
of original poetry, has manifestly outstripped all his
competitors in the race of popularity ; and stands
already upon a height to which no other writer has
attained in the memory of any one now alive. We   5
doubt, indeed, whether any English poet *ever* had so
many of his books sold, or so many of his verses read
and admired by such a multitude of persons in so short
a time. We are credibly informed that nearly thirty
thousand copies of " The Lay " have been already   10
disposed of in this country ; and that the demand for
Marmion, and the poem now before us, has been still
more considerable, — a circulation we believe, altogether
without example, in the case of a bulky work, not
addressed to the bigotry of the mere mob, either religious 15
or political.

A popularity so universal is a pretty sure proof of
extraordinary merit, — a far surer one, we readily admit,
than would be afforded by any praises of ours : and,
therefore, though we pretend to be privileged, in ordinary 20
cases, to foretell the ultimate reception of all claims on
public admiration, our function may be thought to cease,
where the event is already so certain and conspicuous.
As it is a sore thing, however, to be deprived of our
privileges on so important an occasion, we hope to be   25

pardoned for insinuating, that, even in such a case, the
office of the critic may not be altogether superfluous.
Though the success of the author be decisive, and even
likely to be permanent, it still may not be without its use
5 to point out, in consequence of what, and in spite of
what, he has succeeded ; nor altogether uninstructive to
trace the precise limits of the connection which, even in
this dull world, indisputably subsists between success and
desert, and to ascertain how far unexampled popularity
10 does really imply unrivalled talent.

As it is the object of poetry to give pleasure, it would
seem to be a pretty safe conclusion, that that poetry
must be the best which gives the greatest pleasure to the
greatest number of persons.   Yet we must pause a little,
15 before we give our assent to so plausible a proposition.
It would not be quite correct, we fear, to say that those
are invariably the best judges who are most easily
pleased.   The great multitude, even of the reading world,
must necessarily be uninstructed and injudicious ; and
20 will frequently be found, not only to derive pleasure from
what is worthless in finer eyes, but to be quite insensible
to those beauties which afford the most exquisite delight
to more cultivated understandings.   True pathos and
sublimity will indeed charm every one : but, out of this
25 lofty sphere, we are pretty well convinced, that the poetry
which appears most perfect to a very refined taste, will
not often turn out to be very popular poetry.

This, indeed, is saying nothing more, than that the
ordinary readers of poetry have not a very refined taste ;
30 and that they are often insensible to many of its highest
beauties, while they still more frequently mistake its
imperfections for excellence.   The fact, when stated in
this simple way, commonly excites neither opposition nor
surprise : and yet, if it be asked, why the taste of a few

individuals, who do not perceive beauty where many others
perceive it, should be exclusively dignified with the name
of a good taste ; or why poetry, which gives pleasure to
a very great number of readers, should be thought
inferior to that which* pleases a much smaller number, — 5
the answer, perhaps, may not be quite so ready as might
have been expected from the alacrity of our assent to the
first proposition. That there is a good answer to be
given, however, we entertain no doubt : and if that
which we are about to offer should not appear very clear 10
or satisfactory, we must submit to have it thought, that
the fault is not altogether in the subject.

In the first place, then, it should be remembered, that
though the taste of very good judges is necessarily the
taste of a few, it is implied, in their description, that they 15
are persons eminently qualified, by natural sensibility,
and long experience and reflection, to perceive all beauties
that really exist, as well as to settle the relative value and
importance of all the different sorts of beauty ; — they
are in that very state, in short, to which all who are in 20
any degree capable of tasting those refined pleasures
would certainly arrive, if their sensibility were increased,
and their experience and reflection enlarged. It is
difficult, therefore, in following out the ordinary analogies
of language, to avoid considering them as in the right, 25
and calling their taste the true and the just one ; when
it appears that it is such as is uniformly produced by
the cultivation of those faculties upon which all our
perceptions of taste so obviously depend.

It is to be considered also, that though it be the end 30
of poetry to please, one of the parties whose pleasure,.
and whose notions of excellence, will always be primarily
consulted in its composition, is the poet himself ; and as
he must necessarily be more cultivated than the great

body of his readers, the presumption is, that he will always belong, comparatively speaking, to the class of good judges, and endeavour, consequently, to produce that sort of excellence which is likely to meet with *their* 5 approbation.   When authors, therefore, and those of whose suffrages authors are most ambitious, thus conspire to fix upon the same standard of what is good in taste and composition, it is easy to see how it should come to bear this name in society, in preference to what might 10 afford more pleasure to individuals of less influence. Besides all this, it is obvious that it must be infinitely more *difficult* to produce any thing comformable to this exalted standard, than merely to fall in with the current of popular taste.   To attain the former object, it is 15 necessary, for the most part, to understand thoroughly all the feelings and associations that are modified or created by cultivation : — To accomplish the latter, it will often be sufficient merely to have observed the course of familiar preferences.   Success, however, is rare, in 20 proportion as it is difficult ; and it is needless to say, what a vast addition rarity makes to value, — or how exactly our admiration at success is proportioned to our sense of the difficulty of the undertaking.

Such seem to be the most general and immediate 25 causes of the apparent paradox, of reckoning that which pleases the greatest number as inferior to that which pleases the few ; and such the leading grounds for fixing the standard of excellence, in a question of mere feeling and gratification, by a different rule than that of the 30 quantity of gratification produced.   With regard to some of the fine arts — for the distinction between popular and actual merit obtains in them all — there are no other reasons, perhaps, to be assigned ; and, in Music for example, when we have said that it is the *authority* of those who are best qualified by nature and study, and the *difficulty* and *rarity* of the attainment, that entitles certain exquisite performances to rank higher than others that give far more general delight, we have probably said all that can be said in explanation of this mode of 5 speaking and judging. In poetry, however, and in some other departments, this familiar, though somewhat extraordinary rule of estimation, is justified by other considerations.

As it is the cultivation of natural and perhaps universal 10 capacities, that produces that refined taste which takes away our pleasure in vulgar excellence, so, it is to be considered, that there is an universal tendency to the propagation of such a taste ; and that, in times tolerably favourable to human happiness, there is a continual 15 progress and improvement in this, as in the other faculties of nations and large assemblages of men. The number of intelligent judges may therefore be regarded as perpetually on the increase. The inner circle, to which the poet delights chiefly to pitch his voice, is perpetually 20 enlarging ; and, looking to that great futurity to which his ambition is constantly directed, it may be found, that the most refined style of composition to which he can attain, will be, at the last, the most extensively and permanently popular. This holds true, we think, with 25 regard to all the productions of art that are open to the inspection of any considerable part of the community ; . but, with regard to poetry in particular, there is one circumstance to be attended to, that renders this conclu-sion peculiarly safe, and goes far indeed to reconcile the 30 taste of the multitude with that of more cultivated judges.

As it seems difficult to conceive that mere cultivation should either absolutely create or utterly destroy any

natural capacity of enjoyment, it is not easy to suppose, that the qualities which delight the uninstructed should be *substantially* different from those which give pleasure to the enlightened. They may be arranged according to
5 a different scale, — and certain shades and accompaniments may be more or less indispensable ; but the qualities in a poem that give most pleasure to the refined and fastidious critic, are in substance, we believe, the very same that delight the most injudicious of its admirers: —
10 and the very wide difference which exists between their usual estimates, may be in a great degree accounted for, by considering, that the one judges absolutely, and the other relatively — that the one attends only to the intrinsic qualities of the *work*, while the other refers more
15 immediately to the merit of the *author*. The most popular passages in popular poetry, are in fact, for the most part, very beautiful and striking ; yet they are very often such passages as could never be ventured on by any writer who aimed at the praise of the judicious ; and this, for
20 the obvious reason, that they are trite and hackneyed, — that they have been repeated till they have lost all grace and propriety, — and, instead of exalting the imagination by the impression of original genius or creative fancy, only nauseate and offend, by the association of paltry
25 plagiarism and impudent inanity. It is only, however, on those who have read and remembered the original passages, and their better imitations, that this effect is produced. To the ignorant and the careless, the twentieth imitation has all the charm of an original ; and
30 that which oppresses the more experienced reader with weariness and disgust, rouses them with all the force and vivacity of novelty. It is not then, because the ornaments of popular poetry are deficient in intrinsic worth and beauty, that they are slighted by the critical reader,

but because he at once recognises them to be stolen, and perceives that they are arranged without taste or congruity. In his indignation at the dishonesty, and his contempt for the poverty of the collector, he overlooks altogether the value of what he has collected, or remem- 5 bers it only as an aggravation of his offence, — as converting larceny into sacrilege, and adding the guilt of profanation to the folly of unsuitable finery. There are other features, no doubt, that distinguish the idols of vulgar admiration from the beautiful exemplars of pure 10 taste ; but this is so much the most characteristic and remarkable, that we know no way in which we could so shortly describe the poetry that pleases the multitude, and displeases the select few, as by saying that it consisted of all the most known and most brilliant parts of 15 the most celebrated authors, — of a splendid and unmeaning accumulation of those images and phrases which had long charmed every reader in the works of their original inventors.

The justice of these remarks will probably be at once 20 admitted by all who have attended to the history and effects of what may be called *Poetical diction* in general, or even of such particular phrases and epithets as have been indebted to their beauty for too great a notoriety. Our associations with all this class of expressions, which 25 have become trite only in consequence of their intrinsic excellence, now suggest to us no ideas but those of schoolboy imbecility and childish affectation. We look upon them merely as the common, hired, and tawdry trappings of all who wish to put on, for the hour, the 30 masquerade habit of poetry; and, instead of receiving from them any kind of delight or emotion, do not even distinguish or attend to the signification of the words of which they consist. The ear is so palled with their

repetition, and so accustomed to meet with them as the
habitual expletives of the lowest class of versifiers, that
they come at last to pass over it without exciting any
sort of conception whatever, and are not even so much
5 attended to as to expose their most gross incoherence or
inconsistency to detection.   It is of this quality that
Swift has availed himself in so remarkable a manner, in
his famous "Song by a person of quality," which consists
entirely in a selection of some of the most trite and well-
10 sounding phrases and epithets in the poetical lexicon of
the time, strung together without any kind of meaning or
consistency, and yet so disposed, as to have been perused,
perhaps by one half of their readers, without any suspicion of the deception.   Most of those phrases, however,
15 which had thus become sickening, and almost insignificant,
to the intelligent readers of poetry in the days of Queen
Anne, are in themselves beautiful and expressive, and, no
doubt, retain much of their native grace in those ears
that have not been alienated by their repetition.

20   But it is not merely from the use of much excellent
diction, that a modern poet is thus debarred by the
lavishness of his predecessors.   There is a certain range
of subjects and characters, and a certain manner and
tone, which were probably, in their origin, as graceful
25 and attractive, which have been proscribed by the same
dread of imitation.   It would be too long to enter, in this .
place, into any detailed examination of the peculiarities
— originating chiefly in this source — which distinguish
ancient from modern poetry.   It may be enough just to
30 remark, that, as the elements of poetical emotion are
necessarily limited, so it was natural for those who first
sought to excite it, to avail themselves of those subjects,
situations, and images, that were most obviously calculated to produce that effect ; and to assist them by the

use of all those aggravating circumstances that most
readily occurred as likely to heighten their operation. In
this way, they may be said to have got possession of all
the choice materials of their art ; and, working without
fear of comparisons, fell naturally into a free and grace- 5
ful style of execution, at the same time that the profusion
of their resources made them somewhat careless and
inexpert in their application. After-poets were in a very
different situation. They could neither take the most
natural and general topics of interest, nor treat them 10
with the ease and indifference of those who had the whole
store at their command — because this was precisely what'
had been already done by those who had gone before
them : And they were therefore put upon various expedi-
ents for attaining their object, and yet preserving their 15
claim to originality. Some of them accordingly set themselves to observe and delineate both characters and
external objects with greater minuteness and fidelity, —
and others to analyse more carefully the mingling
passions of the heart, and to feed and cherish a more 20
limited train of emotion, through a longer and more
artful succession of incidents, — while a third sort dis-
torted both nature and passion, according to some fantastical theory of their own ; or took such a narrow
corner of each, and dissected it with such curious and 25
microscopic accuracy, that its original form was no longer
discernible by the eyes of the uninstructed. In this way
we think that modern poetry has both been enriched with
more exquisite pictures and deeper and more sustained
strains of pathetic, than were known to the less elaborate 30
artists of antiquity ; at the same time that it has been
defaced with more affectation, and loaded with far more
intricacy. But whether they failed or succeeded, — and
whether they distinguished themselves from their prede-

cessors by faults or by excellences, the later poets, we
conceive, must be admitted to have almost always written
in a more constrained and narrow manner than their
originals, and to have departed farther from what was
5 obvious, easy, and natural. Modern poetry, in this
respect, may be compared, perhaps, without any great
impropriety, to modern sculpture. It is greatly inferior
to the ancient in freedom, grace, and simplicity; but, in
return, it frequently possesses a more decided expression ;
10 and more fine finishing of less suitable embellishments.

Whatever may be gained or lost, however, by this
change of manner, it is obvious, that poetry must become
less popular by means of it : For the most natural and
obvious manner, is always the most taking ; — and what-
15 ever costs the author much pains and labour, is usually
found to require a corresponding effort on the part of the
reader, — which all readers are not disposed to make.
That they who seek to be original by means of affectation, should revolt more by their affectation than they
20 attract by their originality, is just and natural; but even
the nobler devices that win the suffrages of the judicious
by their intrinsic beauty, as well as their novelty, are apt
to repel the multitude, and to obstruct the popularity of
some of the most exquisite productions of genius. The
25 beautiful but minute delineations of such admirable
observers as Crabbe or Cowper, are apt to appear tedious .
to those who take little interest in their subjects, and
have no concern about their art ; — and the refined, deep,
and sustained pathetic of Campbell, is still more apt to
30 be mistaken for monotony and languor by those who are
either devoid of sensibility, or impatient of quiet reflection. The most popular style undoubtedly is that which
has great variety and brilliancy, rather than exquisite
finish in its images and descriptions; and which touches

lightly on many passions, without raising any so high as
to transcend the comprehension of ordinary mortals —
or dwelling on it so long as to exhaust their patience.

Whether Mr. Scott holds the same opinion with us
upon these matters, and has intentionally conformed his 5
practice to this theory, — or whether the peculiarities in
his compositions have been produced merely by following
out the natural bent of his genius, we do not presume to
determine : But, that he has actually made use of all our
recipes for popularity, we think very evident ; and con- 10
ceive, that few things are more curious than the singular
skill, or good fortune, with which he has reconciled his
claims on the favour of the multitude, with his pretensions to more select admiration.   Confident in the force
and originality of his own genius, he has not been afraid 15
to avail himself of common-places both of diction and of
sentiment, whenever they appeared to be beautiful or
impressive, — using them, however, at all times, with the
skill and spirit of an inventor ; and, quite certain that he
could not be mistaken for a plagiarist or imitator, he has 20
made free use of that great treasury of characters, images,
and expressions, which had been accumulated by the
most celebrated of his predecessors, — at the same time
that the rapidity of his transitions, the novelty of his
combinations, and the spirit and variety of his own 25
thoughts and inventions, show plainly that he was a
borrower from anything but poverty, and *took* only what
he would have *given*, if he had been born in an earlier
generation.   The great secret of his popularity, however,
and the leading characteristic of his poetry, appear to us 30
to consist evidently in this, that he has made more use
of common topics, images, and expressions, than any
original poet of later times ; and, at the same time, displayed more genius and originality than any recent

author who has worked in the same materials. By the
latter peculiarity, he has entitled himself to the admiration of every description of readers ; — by the former, he
is recommended in an especial manner to the inexperi-
5 enced — at the hazard of some little offence to the more
cultivated and fastidious.

In the choice of his subjects, for example, he does
not attempt to interest merely by fine observations or
pathetic sentiment, but takes the assistance of a story,
10 and enlists the reader's curiosity among his motives for
attention. Then his characters are all selected from the
most common *dramatis personæ* of poetry ; — kings, warriors, knights, outlaws, nuns, minstrels, secluded damsels,
wizards, and true lovers. He never ventures to carry us
15 into the cottage of the modern peasant, like Crabbe or
Cowper ; nor into the bosom of domestic privacy, like
Campbell ; nor among creatures of the imagination, like
Southey or Darwin. Such personages, we readily admit,
are not in themselves so interesting or striking as those
20 to whom Mr. Scott has devoted himself ; but they are
far less familiar in poetry — and are therefore more likely,
perhaps, to engage the attention of those to whom poetry
is familiar. In the management of the passions, again,
Mr. Scott appears to us to have pursued the same
25 popular, and comparatively easy course. He has raised
all the most familiar and poetical emotions, by the most
obvious aggravations, and in the most compendious and
judicious ways. He has dazzled the reader with the
splendour, and even warmed him with the transient heat
30 of various affections ; but he has nowhere fairly kindled
him with enthusiasm, or melted him into tenderness.
Writing for the world at large, he has wisely abstained
from attempting to raise any passion to a height to which
worldly people could not be transported ; and contented

himself with giving his reader the chance of feeling, as a
brave, kind, and affectionate gentlemen must often feel
in the ordinary course of his existence, without trying to
breathe into him either that lofty enthusiasm which dis-
dains the ordinary business and amusements of life, or 5
that quiet and deep sensibility which unfits for most of
its pursuits. With regard to diction and imagery, too, it
is quite obvious that Mr. Scott has not aimed at writing
either in a very pure or a very consistent style. He
seems to have been anxious only to strike, and to be 10
easily and universally understood ; and, for this purpose,
to have culled the most glittering and conspicuous expressions of the most popular authors, and to have
interwoven them in splendid confusion with his own nervous diction and irregular versification. Indifferent 15
whether he coins or borrows, and drawing with equal
freedom on his memory and his imagination, he goes
boldly forward, in full reliance on a never-failing
abundance ; and dazzles, with his richness and variety,
even those who are most apt to be offended with his 20
glare and irregularity. There is nothing, in Mr. Scott, of
the severe and majestic style of Milton — or of the terse
and fine composition of Pope — or of the elaborate
elegance and melody of Campbell — or even of the
flowing and redundant diction of Southey. — But there is 25
a medley of bright images and glowing words, set care-
lessly and loosely together — a diction, tinged succes-
sively with the careless richness of Shakespeare, the
harshness and antique simplicity of the old romances,
the homeliness of vulgar ballads and anecdotes, and 30
the sentimental glitter of the most modern poetry, —
passing from the borders of the ludicrous to those of the
sublime — alternately minute and energetic — sometimes
artificial, and frequently negligent — but always full of

spirit and vivacity, — abounding in images that are
striking, at first sight, to minds of every contexture —
and never expressing a sentiment which it can cost the
most ordinary reader any exertion to comprehend.

5   Such seem to be the leading qualities that have contributed to Mr. Scott's popularity ; and as some of them
are obviously of a kind to diminish his merit in the eyes
of more fastidious judges, it is but fair to complete this
view of his peculiarities by a hasty notice of such of them
10 as entitle him to unqualified admiration ; — and here it is
impossible not to be struck with that vivifying spirit of
strength and animation which pervades all the inequali-
ties of his composition, and keeps constantly on the mind
of the reader the impression of great power, spirit and
15 intrepidity.   There is nothing cold, creeping, or feeble,
in all Mr. Scott's poetry ; — no laborious littleness, or
puling classical affectation.   He has his failures, indeed,
like other people ; but he always attempts vigorously :
and never fails in his immediate object, without accom-
20 plishing something far beyond the reach of an ordinary
writer.   Even when he wanders from the paths of pure
taste, he leaves behind him the footsteps of a powerful
genius ; and moulds the most humble of his materials
into a form worthy of a nobler substance.   Allied to this
25 inherent vigour and animation, and in a great degree
derived from it, is that air of facility and freedom which
adds so peculiar a grace to most of Mr. Scott's compositions.   There is certainly no living poet whose works
seem to come from him with so much ease, or who so
30 seldom appears to labour, even in the most burdensome
parts of his performance.   He seems, indeed, never to
think either of himself or his reader, but to be completely
identified and lost in the personages with whom he is
occupied ; and the attention of the reader is consequently

either transferred, unbroken, to their adventures, or, if it glance back for a moment to the author, it is only to think how much more might be done, by putting forth that strength at full, which has, without effort, accomplished so many wonders. It is owing partly to these 5 qualities, and partly to the great variety of his style, that Mr. Scott is much less frequently tedious than any other bulky poet with whom we are acquainted. His store of images is so copious, that he never dwells upon one long enough to produce weariness in the reader ; and, even 10 where he deals in borrowed or in tawdry wares, the rapidity of his transitions, and the transient glance with which he is satisfied as to each, leave the critic no time to be offended, and hurry him forward, along with the multitude, enchanted with the brilliancy of the exhibition. 15 Thus, the very frequency of his deviations from pure taste, comes, in some sort, to constitute their apology ; and the profusion and variety of his faults to afford a new proof of his genius.

These, we think, are the general characteristics of Mr. 20 Scott's poetry. Among his minor peculiarities, we might notice his singular talent for description, and especially for the description of scenes abounding in *motion* or *action* of any kind. In this department, indeed, we conceive him to be almost without a rival, either among 25 modern or ancient poets ; and the character and process of his descriptions are as extraordinary as their effect is astonishing. He places before the eyes of his readers a more distinct and complete picture, perhaps, than any other artist ever presented by mere words ; and yet he 30 does not (like Crabbe) enumerate all the visible parts of the subjects with any degree of minuteness, nor confine himself, by any means, to what is visible. The singular merit of his delineations, on the contrary, consists in

this, that, with a few bold and abrupt strokes, he finishes
a most spirited outline, — and then instantly kindles it
by the sudden light and colour of some moral affection.
There are none of his fine descriptions, accordingly,
5 which do not derive a great part of their clearness and
picturesque effect, as well as their interest, from the
quantity of character and moral expression which is thus
blended with their details, and which, so far from inter-
rupting the conception of the external object, very power-
10 fully stimulate the fancy of the reader to complete it ;
and give a grace and a spirit to the whole representation,
of which we do not know where to look for any other
example.

Another very striking peculiarity in Mr. Scott's poetry,
15 is the air of freedom and nature which he has contrived
to impart to most of his distinguished characters ; and
with which no poet more modern than Shakespeare has
ventured to represent personages of such dignity. We
do not allude here merely to the genuine familiarity and
20 homeliness of many of his scenes and dialogues, but to
that air of gaiety and playfulness in which persons of
high rank seem, from time immemorial, to have thought
it necessary to array, not their courtesy only, but their
generosity and their hostility. This tone of good society,
25 Mr. Scott has shed over his higher characters with great
grace and effect ; and has, in this way, not only made his
representations much more faithful and true to nature,
but has very agreeably relieved the monotony of that
tragic solemnity which ordinary writers appear to think
30 indispensable to the dignity of poetical heroes and
heroines. We are not sure, however, whether he has not
occasionally exceeded a little in the use of this ornament ;
and given, now and then, too coquettish and trifling a
tone to discussions of weight and moment.

POEMS.

By the Reverend George Crabbe. 8vo, pp. 260. London, 1807.[1]

WE receive the proofs of Mr. Crabbe's poetical existence, which are contained in this volume, with the same
sort of feeling that would be excited by tidings of an
ancient friend, whom we no longer expected to hear of in
this world. We rejoice in his resurrection, both for his   5
sake and for our own: But we feel also a certain movement of self-condemnation, for having been remiss in our
inquiries after him, and somewhat too negligent of the
honours which ought, at any rate, to have been paid to
his memory.   10

---

[1] I have given a larger space to Crabbe in this republication than
to any of his contemporary poets ; not merely because I think more
highly of him than of most of them, but also because I fancy that
he has had less justice done him. The nature of his subjects was
not such as to attract either imitators or admirers, from among the
ambitious or fanciful lovers of poetry ; or, consequently, to set him
at the head of a School, or let him surround himself with the
zealots of a Sect: And it must also be admitted, that his claims to
distinction depend fully as much on his great powers of observation,
his skill in touching the deeper sympathies of our nature, and his
power of inculcating, by their means, the most impressive lessons of
humanity, as on any fine play of fancy, or grace and beauty in his
delineations. I have great faith, however, in the intrinsic worth and
ultimate success of those more substantial attributes ; and have,
accordingly, the strongest impression that the citations I have here
given from Crabbe will strike more, and sink deeper into the minds
of readers to whom they are new (or by whom they may have been
partially forgotten), than any I have been able to present from other

It is now, we are afraid, upwards of twenty years since
we were first struck with the vigour, originality, and truth
of description of "The Village"; and since, we regretted
that an author, who could write so well, should have
5 written so little. From that time to the present, we have
heard little of Mr. Crabbe; and fear that he has been in
a great measure lost sight of by the public, as well as by
us. With a singular, and scarcely pardonable indifference
to fame, he has remained, during this long interval, in
10 patient or indolent repose; and, without making a single
movement to maintain or advance the reputation he had
acquired, has permitted others to usurp the attention
which he was sure of commanding, and allowed himself
to be nearly forgotten by a public, which reckons upon
15 being reminded of all the claims which the living have
on its favour. His former publications, though of distinguished merit, were perhaps too small in volume to
remain long the objects of general attention, and seem,
by some accident, to have been jostled aside in the
20 crowd of more clamorous competitors.

Yet, though the name of Crabbe has not hitherto been
very common in the mouths of our poetical critics, we
believe there are few real lovers of poetry to whom some
of his sentiments and descriptions are not secretly

writers. It probably is idle enough (as well as a little presumptuous)
to suppose that a publication like this will afford many opportunities
of testing the truth of this prediction. But, as the experiment is to
be made, there can be no harm in mentioning this as one of its
objects.

It is but candid, however, after all, to add, that my concern for
Mr. Crabbe's reputation would scarcely have led me to devote near
one hundred pages to the estimate of his poetical merits, had I not
set some value on the speculations as to the elements of poetical
excellence in general, and its moral bearings and affinities—for the
introduction of which this estimate seemed to present an occasion,
or apology.

familiar. There is a truth and force in many of his delineations of rustic life, which is calculated to sink deep into the memory; and, being confirmed by daily observation, they are recalled upon innumerable occasions—when the ideal pictures of more fanciful authors 5 have lost all their interest. For ourselves at least, we profess to be indebted to Mr. Crabbe for many of these strong impressions; and have known more than one of our unpoetical acquaintances, who declared they could never pass by a parish workhouse without thinking of the 10 description of it they had read at school in the Poetical Extracts. The volume before us will renew, we trust, and extend many such impressions. It contains all the former productions of the author, with about double their bulk of new matter; most of it in the same taste and 15 manner of composition with the former; and some of a kind, of which we have had no previous example in this author. The whole, however, is of no ordinary merit, and will be found, we have little doubt, a sufficient warrant for Mr. Crabbe to take his place as one of the 20 most original, nervous, and pathetic poets of the present century.

His characteristic, certainly, is force, and truth of description, joined for the most part to great selection and condensation of expression;—that kind of strength 25 and originality which we meet with in Cowper, and that sort of diction and versification which we admire in "The Deserted Village" of Goldsmith, or "The Vanity of Human Wishes" of Johnson. If he can be said to have imitated the manner of any author, it is Goldsmith, 30 indeed, who has been the object of his imitation; and yet his general train of thinking, and his views of society, are so extremely opposite, that, when "The Village" was first published, it was commonly considered as an anti-

dote or an answer to the more captivating representations
of "The Deserted Village." Compared with this celebrated author, he will be found, we think, to have more
vigour and less delicacy; and while he must be admitted
5 to be inferior in the fine finish and uniform beauty of his
composition, we cannot help considering him superior,
both in the variety and the truth of his pictures. Instead
of that uniform tint of pensive tenderness which over-
spreads the whole poetry of Goldsmith, we find in Mr.
10 Crabbe many gleams of gaiety and humour. Though
his habitual views of life are more gloomy than those of
his rival, his poetical temperament seems far more cheerful; and when the occasions of sorrow and rebuke are
gone by, he can collect himself for sarcastic pleasantry,
15 or unbend in innocent playfulness. His diction, though
generally pure and powerful, is sometimes harsh, and
sometimes quaint; and he has occasionally admitted a
couplet or two in a state so unfinished, as to give a character of inelegance to the passages in which they occur.
20 With a taste less disciplined and less fastidious than that
of Goldsmith, he has, in our apprehension, a keener eye
for observation, and a readier hand for the delineation of
what he has observed. There is less poetical keeping in
his whole performance; but the groups of which it con-
25 sists are conceived, we think, with equal genius, and
drawn with greater spirit as well as far greater fidelity.

It is not quite fair, perhaps, thus to draw a detailed
parallel between a living poet, and one whose reputation
has been sealed by death, and by the immutable sentence
30 of a surviving generation. Yet there are so few of his
contemporaries to whom Mr. Crabbe bears any resemblance, that we can scarcely explain our opinion of his
merit, without comparing him to some of his predecessors.
There is one set of writers, indeed, from whose works

those of Mr. Crabbe might receive all that elucidation
which results from contrast, and from an entire opposition
in all points of taste and opinion. We allude now to the
Wordsworths, and the Southeys, and Coleridges, and all
that ambitious fraternity, that, with good intentions and 5
extraordinary talents, are labouring to bring back our
poetry to the fantastical oddity and puling childishness of
Withers, Quarles, or Marvel. These gentlemen write a
great deal about rustic life, as well as Mr. Crabbe ; and
they even agree with him in dwelling much on its dis- 10
comforts ; but nothing can be more opposite than the
views they take of the subject, or the manner in which
they execute their representations of them.

Mr. Crabbe exhibits the common people of England
pretty much as they are, and as they must appear to 15
every one who will take the trouble of examining into
their condition ; at the same time that he renders his
sketches in a very high degree interesting and beautiful
— by selecting what is most fit for description — by
grouping them into such forms as must catch the attention 20
or awake the memory — and by scattering over the whole
such traits of moral sensibility, of sarcasm, and of deep
reflection, as every one must feel to be natural, and own
to be powerful. The gentlemen of the new school, on
the other hand, scarcely ever condescend to take their 25
subjects from any description of persons at all known to
the common inhabitants of the world ; but invent for
themselves certain whimsical and unheard-of beings, to
whom they impute some fantastical combination of feelings, and then labour to excite our sympathy for them, 30
either by placing them in incredible situations, or by
some strained and exaggerated moralisation of a vague
and tragical description. Mr. Crabbe, in short, shows us
something which we have all seen, or may see, in real life;

and draws from it such feelings and such reflections as
every human being must acknowledge that it is calculated
to excite. He delights us by the truth, and vivid and
picturesque beauty of his representations, and by the
5 force and pathos of the sensations with which we feel that
they are connected. Mr. Wordsworth and his associates,
on the other hand, introduce us to beings whose existence
was not previously suspected by the acutest observers of
nature ; and excite an interest for them — where they do
10 excite any interest— more by an eloquent and refined
analysis of their own capricious feelings, than by any obvious or intelligible ground of sympathy in their situation.

Those who are acquainted with the Lyrical Ballads, or
the more recent publications of Mr. Wordsworth, will
15 scarcely deny the justice of this representation ; but in
order to vindicate it to such as do not enjoy that advantage, we must beg leave to make a few hasty references
to the former, and by far the least exceptionable of those
productions.

20   A village schoolmaster, for instance, is a pretty common
poetical character. Goldsmith has drawn him inimitably;
so has Shenstone, with the slight change of sex; and Mr.
Crabbe, in two passages, has followed their footsteps.
Now, Mr. Wordsworth has a village schoolmaster also —
25 a personage who makes no small figure in three or four of
his poems. But by what traits is this worthy old gentleman delineated by the new poet ? No pedantry — no
innocent vanity of 'learning — no mixture of indulgence
with the pride of power, and of poverty with the conscious-
30 ness of rare acquirements. Every feature which belongs
to the situation, or marks the character in common apprehension, is scornfully discarded by Mr. Wordsworth; who
represents his grey-haired rustic pedagogue as a sort of
half crazy, sentimental person, overrun with fine feelings,

constitutional merriment, and a most humorous melancholy. Here are the two stanzas in which this consistent
and intelligible character is pourtrayed. The diction is
at least as new as the conception.

> " The sighs which Matthew heav'd were sighs 5
>   Of one tir'd out with *fun* and *madness ;*
> The tears which came to Matthew's eyes
>   Were tears of light — *the oil of gladness.*
>
> " Yet sometimes, when the secret cup
>   Of still and serious thought went round 10
> He seem'd as if he *drank it up,*
>   He felt with spirit so profound.
> Thou *soul* of God's best *earthly mould,*" &c.

A frail damsel again is a character common enough in
all poems ; and one upon which many fine and pathetic 15
lines have been expended. Mr. Wordsworth has written
more than three hundred on the subject ; but, instead of
new images of tenderness, or delicate representation of
intelligible feelings, he has contrived to tell us nothing
whatever of the unfortunate fair one, but that her name 20
is Martha Ray; and that she goes up to the top of a hill,
in a red cloak, and cries " O misery! " All the rest of
the poem is filled with a description of an old thorn and
a pond, and of the silly stories which the neighbouring
old women told about them. 25

The sports of childhood, and the untimely death of
promising youth, is also a common topic of poetry. Mr.
Wordsworth has made some blank verse about it ; but,
instead of the delightful and picturesque sketches with
which so many authors of modern talents have presented 30
us on this inviting subject, all that he is pleased to communicate of *his* rustic child, is, that he used to amuse
himself with shouting to the owls, and hearing them
answer. To make amends for this brevity, the process
of his mimicry is most accurately described. 35

———— " With fingers interwoven, both hands
Press'd closely palm to palm, and to his mouth
Uplifted, he, as through an instrument,
Blew mimic hootings to the silent owls,
5   That they might answer him."——

This is all we hear of him ; and for the sake of this one accomplishment, we are told, that the author has frequently stood mute, and gazed on his grave for half an hour together!

10   Love, and the fantasies of lovers, have afforded an ample theme to poets of all ages. Mr. Wordsworth, however, has thought fit to compose a piece, illustrating this copious subject by one single thought. A lover trots away to see his mistress one fine evening, gazing all the 15 way on the moon ; when he comes to her door,

    " O mercy! to myself I cried,
    If Lucy should be dead! "

And there the poem ends!

    Now, we leave it to any reader of common candour 20 and discernment to say, whether these representations of character and sentiment are drawn from that eternal and universal standard of truth and nature, which every one is knowing enough to recognise, and no one great enough to depart from with impunity; or whether they are not 25 formed, as we have ventured to allege, upon certain fantastic and affected peculiarities in the mind or fancy of the author, into which it is most improbable that many of his readers will enter, and which cannot, in some cases, be comprehended without much effort and explanation. 30 Instead of multiplying instances of these wide and wilful aberrations from ordinary nature, it may be more satisfactory to produce the author's own admission of the narrowness of the plan upon which he writes, and of the very extraordinary circumstances which he himself sometimes thinks it necessary for his readers to keep in view, if they would wish to understand the beauty or propriety of his delineations.

A pathetic tale of guilt or superstition may be told, we are apt to fancy, by the poet himself, in his general character of poet, with full as much effect as by any other 5 person. An old nurse, at any rate, or a monk or parish clerk, is always at hand to give grace to such a narration. None of these, however, would satisfy Mr. Wordsworth. He has written a long poem of this sort, in which he thinks it indispensably necessary to apprise the reader, 10 that he has endeavoured to represent the language and sentiments of a particular character — of which character, he adds, "the reader will have a general notion, if he has ever known a man, *a captain of a small trading vessel,* for example, who being *past the middle age of life,* has retired 15 upon an *annuity, or small independent income,* to some *village* or country, of which he was *not a native,* or in which he had not been accustomed to live!"

Now, we must be permitted to doubt, whether, among all the readers of Mr. Wordsworth (few or many), there 20 is a single individual who has had the happiness of knowing a person of this very peculiar description ; or who is capable of forming any sort of conjecture of the particular disposition and turn of thinking which such a combination of attributes would be apt to produce. To us, we will 25 confess, the *annonce* appears as ludicrous and absurd as it would be in the author of an ode or an epic to say, "Of this piece the reader will necessarily form a very erroneous judgment, unless he is apprised, that it was written by a pale man in a green coat — sitting cross- 30 legged on an oaken stool — with a scratch on his nose, and a spelling dictionary on the table."[1]

[1] Some of our readers may have a curiosity to know in what manner this old annuitant captain does actually express himself in

From these childish and absurd affectations, we turn
with pleasure to the manly sense and correct picturing of
Mr. Crabbe ; and, after being dazzled and made giddy
with the elaborate raptures and obscure originalities of
5 these new artists, it is refreshing to meet again with the
spirit and nature of our old masters, in the nervous pages
of the author now before us.

the village of his adoption. For their gratification, we annex the
two first stanzas of his story; in which, with all the attention we
have been able to bestow, we have been utterly unable to detect
any traits that can be supposed to characterise either a seaman, an
annuitant, or a stranger in a country town. It is a style, on the
contrary, which we should ascribe, without hesitation, to a certain
poetical fraternity in the West of England ; and which, we verily
believe, never was, and never will be, used by any one out of that
fraternity.

> " There is a thorn — it looks so old,
>   In truth you 'd find it hard to say,
>   How it could ever have been young !
>   It looks so old and gray.
>   Not higher than a two-years' child
>   *It stands erect;* this aged thorn !
>   No leaves it has, no thorny points ;
>   It is a mass of knotted joints :
>   A wretched thing forlorn,
>   *It stands erect ;* and like a stone,
>   With lichens it is overgrown.
>
> " *Like rock or stone, it is o'ergrown*
>   *With lichens ;* — to the very top;
>   And hung with heavy tufts of moss
>   A melancholy crop.
>   Up from the earth these mosses creep.
>   And *this poor thorn*, they clasp it round
>   So close, you'd say that they were bent,
>   *With plain and manifest intent !*
>   To drag it to the ground ;
>   And all had join'd in one endeavour,
>   To bury *this poor thorn* for ever."

And this it seems, is Nature, and Pathos, and Poetry !

THE BOROUGH.

A Poem, in Twenty-four Letters. By the Rev. George Crabbe, LL.B.
8vo, pp. 344. London, 1810.

WE are very glad to meet with Mr. Crabbe so soon
again ; and particularly glad to find, that his early return
has been occasioned, in part, by the encouragement he
received on his last appearance. This late spring of
public favour, we hope, he will live to see ripen into 5
mature fame. We scarcely know any poet who deserves
it better ; and are quite certain there is none who is more
secure of keeping with posterity whatever he may win
from his contemporaries.

The present poem is precisely of the character of The 10
Village and The Parish Register: It has the same
peculiarities, and the same faults and beauties ; though a
severe critic might perhaps add, that its peculiarities are
more obtrusive, its faults greater, and its beauties less.
However that be, both faults and beauties are so plainly 15
produced by the peculiarity, that it may be worth while,
before giving any more particular account of it, to try if
we can ascertain in what that consists.

And here we shall very speedily discover, that Mr.
Crabbe is distinguished from all other poets, both by the 20
choice of his subjects, and by his manner of treating
them. All his persons are taken from the lower ranks of
life ; and all his scenery from the most ordinary and
familiar objects of nature or art. His characters and
incidents, too, are as common as the elements out of 25

which they are compounded are humble; and not only
has he nothing prodigious or astonishing in any of his
representations, but he has not even attempted to impart
any of the ordinary colours of poetry to those vulgar
5 materials.　He has no moralising swains or sentimental
tradesmen ; and scarcely ever seeks to charm us by the
artless graces or lowly virtues of his personages.　On the
contrary, he has represented his villagers and humble
burghers as altogether as dissipated, and ·more dishonest
10 and discontented, than the profligates of higher life ; and,
instead of conducting us through blooming groves and
pastoral meadows, has led us along filthy lanes and
crowded wharves, to hospitals, alms houses, and gin-
shops.　In some of these delineations, he may be con-
15 sidered the Satirist of low life — an occupation sufficiently
arduous, and, in a great degree, new and original in our
language.　But by far the greater part of his poetry is of
a different and a higher character ; and aims at moving
or delighting us by lively, touching, and finely contrasted
20 representations of the dispositions, sufferings, and occupations of those ordinary persons who form the far
greater part of our fellow-creatures.　This, too, he has
sought to effect, merely by placing before us the clearest,
most brief, and most striking sketches of their external
25 condition — the most sagacious and unexpected strokes
of character — and the truest and most pathetic pictures
of natural feeling and common suffering.　By the mere
force of his art, and the novelty of his style, he forces us
. to attend to objects that are usually neglected, and to
30 enter into feelings from which we are in general but too
eager to escape ; — and then trusts to nature for the
effect of the representation.

　　It is obvious, at first sight, that this is not a task for
an ordinary hand ; and that many ingenious writers, who

make a very good figure with battles, nymphs, and moonlight landscapes, would find themselves quite helpless, if
set down among streets, harbours, and taverns. The
difficulty of such subjects, in short, is sufficiently visible
— and some of the causes of that difficulty : But they 5
have their advantages also ; — and of these, and their
hazards, it seems natural to say a few words, before
entering more minutely into the merits of the work
before us.

The first great advantage of such familiar subjects is, 10
that every one is necessarily well acquainted with the
originals ; and is therefore sure to feel all that pleasure,
from a faithful representation of them, which results from
the perception of a perfect and successful imitation. In
the kindred art of painting, we find that this single con- 15
sideration has been sufficient to stamp a very high value
upon accurate and lively delineations of objects, in themselves uninteresting, and even disagreeable ; and no very
inconsiderable part of the pleasure which may be derived
from Mr. Crabbe's poetry may probably be referred to 20
its mere truth and fidelity; and to the brevity and clearness with which he sets before his readers, objects and
characters with which they have been all their days
familiar.

In his happier passages, however, he has a higher 25
merit, and imparts a far higher gratification. The chief
delight of poetry consists, not so much in what it directly
supplies to the imagination, as in what it enables it to
supply to itself ; — not in warming the heart by its passing brightness, but in kindling its own latent stores of 30
light and heat ; — not in hurrying the fancy along by a
foreign and accidental impulse, but in setting it agoing,
by touching its internal springs and principles of activity.
Now, this highest and most delightful effect can only be

produced by the poet's striking a note to which the heart
and the affections naturally vibrate in unison ; — by rous-
ing one of a large family of kindred impressions ; — by
dropping the rich seed of his fancy upon the fertile and
5 sheltered places of the imagination. But it is evident,
that the emotions connected with common and familiar
objects — with objects which fill every man's memory,
and are necessarily associated with all that he has ever
really felt or fancied, are of all others the most likely to
10 answer this description, and to produce, where they can
be raised to a sufficient height, this great effect in its
utmost perfection. It is for this reason that the images
and affections that belong to our *universal* nature, are
always, if tolerably represented, infinitely more captivat-
15 ing, in spite of their apparent commonness and simplicity,
than those that are peculiar to certain situations, however
they may come recommended by novelty or grandeur.
The familiar feeling of maternal tenderness and anxiety,
which is every day before our eyes, even in the brute
20 creation — and the enchantment of youthful love, which
is nearly the same in all characters, ranks, and situations
— still contribute far more to the beauty and interest of
poetry than all the misfortunes of princes, the jealousies
of heroes, and the feats of giants, magicians, or ladies
25 in armour. Every one can enter into the former set of
feelings ; and but a few into the latter. The one calls
up a thousand familiar and long-remembered emotions —
which are answered and reflected on every side by the
kindred impressions which experience or observation
30 have traced upon every memory: while the other lights up
but a transient and unfruitful blaze, and passes away without perpetuating itself in any kindred and native sensation.

Now, the delineation of all that concerns the lower
and most numerous classes of society, is, in this respect,

on a footing with the pictures of our primary affections
— that their originals are necessarily familiar to all men,
and are inseparably associated with their own most interesting impressions. Whatever may be our own condition,
we all live surrounded with the poor, from infancy to 5
age ; — we hear daily of their sufferings and misfortunes ;
— and their toils, their crimes, or their pastimes, are our
hourly spectacle. Many diligent readers of poetry know
little, by their own experience, of palaces, castles, or
camps ; and still less of tyrants, warriors and banditti ; 10
but every one understands about cottages, streets, and
villages ; and conceives, pretty correctly, the character
and condition of sailors, ploughmen, and artificers. If
the poet can contrive, therefore, to create a sufficient
interest in subjects like these, they will infallibly sink 15
deeper into the mind, and be more prolific of kindred
trains of emotion, than subjects of greater dignity. Nor
is the difficulty of exciting such an interest by any means
so great as is generally imagined. For it is common
human nature, and common human feelings, after all, 20
that form the true source of interest in poetry of every
description ; — and the splendour and the marvels by
which it is sometimes surrounded, serve no other purpose
than to fix our attention on those workings of the heart,
and those energies of the understanding, which alone 25
command all the genuine sympathies of human beings —
and which may be found as abundantly in the breasts of
cottagers as of kings. Wherever there are human beings,
therefore, with feelings and characters to be represented,
our attention may be fixed by the art of the poet — by 30
his judicious selection of circumstances — by the force
and vivacity of his style, and the clearness and brevity of
his representations.

In point of fact, we are all touched more deeply, as

well as more frequently, in real life, with the sufferings of
peasants than of princes ; and sympathise much oftener,
and more heartily, with the successes of the poor, than of
the rich and distinguished.   The occasions of such feel-
5 ings are indeed so many, and so common, that they do
not often leave any very permanent traces behind them,
but pass away, and are effaced by the very rapidity of
their succession.   The business and the cares, and the
pride of the world, obstruct the development of the
10 emotions to which they would naturally give rise ; and
press so close and thick upon the mind, as to shut it, at
most seasons, against the reflections that are perpetually
seeking for admission.   When we have leisure, however,
to look quietly into our hearts, we shall find in them an
15 infinite multitude of little fragments of sympathy with our
brethren in humble life — abortive movements of compassion, and embryos of kindness and concern, which
had once fairly begun to live and germinate within them,
though withered and broken off by the selfish bustle and
20 fever of our daily occupations.   Now, all these may be
revived and carried on to maturity by the art of the poet ;
— and, therefore, a powerful effort to interest us in the
feelings of the humble and obscure, will usually call forth
more deep, more numerous, and more permanent emo-
25 tions, than can ever be excited by the fate of princesses
and heroes.   Independent of the circumstances to which
we have already alluded, there are causes which make us
at all times more ready to enter into the feelings of the
humble, than of the exalted part of our species.   Our
30 sympathy with their enjoyments is enhanced by a certain
mixture of pity for their general condition, which, by
purifying it from that taint of envy which almost always
adheres to our admiration of the great, renders it more
welcome and satisfactory to our bosoms ; while our con-

cern for their sufferings is at once softened and endeared
to us, by the recollection of our own exemption from
them, and by the feeling, that we frequently have it in
our power to relieve them.

From these, and from other causes, it appears to us to 5
be certain, that where subjects, taken from humble life,
can be made sufficiently interesting to overcome the
distaste and the prejudices with which the usages of
polished society too generally lead us to regard them,
the interest which they excite will commonly be more 10
profound and more lasting than any that can be raised
upon loftier themes ; and the poet of the Village and the
Borough be oftener, and longer read, than the poet of
the Court or the Camp. The most popular passages of
Shakespeare and Cowper, we think, are of this description: 15
and there is much, both in the volume before us, and in
Mr. Crabbe's former publications, to which we might
now venture to refer, as proofs of the same doctrine.
When such representations have once made an impression on the imagination, they are remembered daily, and 20
for ever. We can neither look around, nor within us,
without being reminded of their truth and their importance ; and, while the more brilliant effusions of romantic
fancy are recalled only at long intervals, and in rare
situations, we feel that we cannot walk a step from our 25
own doors, nor cast a glance back on our departed years,
without being indebted to the poet of vulgar life for some
striking image or touching reflection, of which the occasions were always before us, but — till he taught us how
to improve them — were almost always allowed to escape. 30

Such, we conceive, are some of the advantages of the
subjects which Mr. Crabbe has in a great measure introduced into modern poetry ; — and such the grounds upon
which we venture to perdict the durability of the reputa-

tion which he is in the course of acquiring. That they
have their disadvantages also, is obvious ; and it is no
less obvious, that it is to these we must ascribe the
greater part of the faults and deformities with which this
5 author is fairly chargeable. The two great errors into
which he has fallen, are — that he has described many
things not worth describing ; — and that he has frequently
excited disgust, instead of pity or indignation, in the
breasts of his readers. These faults are obvious — and,
10 we believe, are popularly laid to his charge : Yet there is,
in so far as we have observed, a degree of misconception
as to the true grounds and limits of the charge, which
we think it worth while to take this opportunity of cor-
recting.

15　　The poet of humble life *must* describe a great deal —
and must even describe, minutely, many things which
possess in themselves no beauty or grandeur. The
reader's fancy must be awaked — and the power of his
own pencil displayed ; — a distinct locality and imaginary
20 reality must be given to his characters and agents : and
the ground colour of their common condition must be
laid in, before his peculiar and selected groups can be
presented with any effect or advantage. In the same
way, he must study characters with a minute and ana-
25 tomical precision ; and must make both himself and his
readers familiar with the ordinary traits and general
family features of the beings among whom they are to
move, before they can either understand, or take much
interest in the individuals who are to engross their atten-
30 tion. Thus far, there is no excess or unnecessary minuteness. But this faculty of observation, and this power of
description, hold out great temptations to go further.
There is a pride and a delight in the exercise of all
peculiar power ; and the poet, who has learned to de-

scribe external objects exquisitely, with a view to heighten
the effect of his moral designs, and to draw characters
with accuracy, to help forward the interest or the pathos
of the picture, will be in great danger of describing
scenes, and drawing characters, for no other purpose, but 5
to indulge his taste, and to display his talents. It cannot
be denied, we think, that Mr. Crabbe has, on many
occasions, yielded to this temptation. He is led away,
every now and then, by his lively conception of external
objects, and by his nice and sagacious observation of 10
human character ; and wantons and luxuriates in descriptions and moral portrait painting, while his readers are
left to wonder to what end so much industry has been
exerted.

His chief fault, however, is his frequent lapse into 15
disgusting representations ; and this, we will confess, is
an error for which we find it far more difficult either to
account or to apologise. We are not, however, of the
opinion which we have often heard stated, that he has
represented human nature under too unfavourable an 20
aspect ; or that the distaste which his poetry sometimes
produces, is owing merely to the painful nature of the
scenes and subjects with which it abounds. On the
contrary, we think he has given a juster, as well as a
more striking picture, of the true character and situation 25
of the lower orders of this country, than any other writer,
whether in verse or in prose ; and that he has made no
more use of painful emotions than was necessary to the
production of a pathetic effect.

All powerful and pathetic poetry, it is obvious, abounds 30
in images of distress. The delight which it bestows
partakes strongly of pain ; and, by a sort of contradic-
tion, which has long engaged the attention of the reflecting, the compositions that attract us most powerfully,

and detain us the longest, are those that produce in us most of the effects of actual suffering and wretchedness. The solution of this paradox is to be found, we think, in the simple fact, that pain is a far stronger sensation than
5 pleasure, in human existence ; and that the cardinal virtue of all things that are intended to delight the mind, is to produce a strong sensation. Life itself appears to consist in sensation ; and the universal passion of all beings that have life, seems to be, that they should be
10 made intensely conscious of it, by a succession of powerful and engrossing emotions. All the mere gratifications or natural· pleasures that are in the power even of the most fortunate, are quite insufficient to fill this vast craving for sensation : And accordingly, we see every
15 day, that a more violent stimulus is sought for by those who have attained the vulgar heights of life, in the pains and dangers of war — the agonies of gaming — or the feverish toils of ambition. To those who have tasted of those potent cups, where the bitter, however, so
20 obviously predominates, the security, the comforts, and what are called the enjoyments of common life, are intolerably insipid and disgusting. Nay, we think we have observed, that even those who, without any effort or exertion, have experienced unusual misery, frequently
25 appear, in like manner, to acquire a sort of taste or craving for it ; and come to look on the tranquillity of ordinary life with a kind of indifference not unmingled with contempt. It is certain, at least, that they dwell with most apparent satisfaction on the memory of those
30 days, which have been marked by the deepest and most agonising sorrows ; and derive a certain delight from the recollections of those overwhelming sensations which once occasioned so fierce a throb in the languishing pulse of their existence.

If any thing of this kind, however, can be traced in real life — if the passion for emotion be so strong as to carry us, not in imagination, but in reality, over the rough edge of present pain — it will not be difficult to explain, why it should be so attractive in the copies and fictions 5 of poetry. There, as in real life, the great demand is for emotion ; while the pain with which it may be attended, can scarcely, by any possibility, exceed the limits of endurance. The recollection, that it is but a copy and a fiction, is quite sufficient to keep it down to a moderate 10 temperature, and to make it welcome as the sign or the harbinger of that agitation of which the soul is avaricious. It is not, then, from any peculiar quality in painful emotions that they become capable of affording the delight which attends them in tragic or pathetic poetry 15 — but merely from the circumstance of their being more intense and powerful than any other emotions of which the mind is susceptible. If it was the constitution of our nature to feel joy as keenly, or to sympathise with it as heartily as we do with sorrow, we have no doubt that no 20 other sensation would ever be intentionally excited by the artists that minister to delight. But the fact is, that *the pleasures* of which we are capable are slight and feeble compared with *the pains* that we may endure ; and that, feeble as they are, the sympathy which they excite falls 25 much more short of the original emotion. When the object, therefore, is to obtain sensation, there can be no doubt to which of the two fountains we should repair ; and if there be but few pains in real life which are not, in some measure, endeared to us by the emotions 30 with which they are attended, we may be pretty sure, that the more distress we introduce into poetry, the more we shall rivet the attention and attract the admiration of the reader.

There is but one exception to this rule—and it brings us back from the apology of Mr. Crabbe, to his condemnation. Every form of distress, whether it proceed from passion or from fortune, and whether it fall upon vice or
5 virtue, adds to the interest and the charm of poetry— except only that which is connected with ideas of *Disgust* —the least taint of which disenchants the whole scene, and puts an end both to delight and sympathy. But what is it, it may be asked, that is the proper object of disgust?
10 and what is the precise description of things which we think Mr. Crabbe so inexcusable for admitting? It is not easy to define a term at once so simple and so significant; but it may not be without its use, to indicate, in a general way, our conception of its true force and
15 comprehension.

It is needless, we suppose, to explain what are the objects of disgust in physical or external existences. These are sufficiently plain and unequivocal ; and it is universally admitted, that all mention of them must be
20 carefully excluded from every poetical description. With regard, again, to human character, action, and feeling, we should be inclined to term every thing disgusting, which represented misery, without making any appeal to our love, respect, or admiration. If the suffering person be
25 amiable, the delightful feeling of love and affection tempers the pain which the contemplation of suffering has a tendency to excite, and enhances it into the stronger, and therefore more attractive, sensation of pity. If there be great power or energy, however, united
30 to guilt or wretchedness, the mixture of admiration exalts the emotion into something that is sublime and pleasing : and even in cases of mean and atrocious, but efficient guilt, our sympathy with the victims upon whom it is practised, and our active indignation and desire of

vengeance, reconcile us to the humiliating display, and make a compound that, upon the whole, is productive of pleasure.

The only sufferers, then, upon whom we cannot bear to look, are those that excite pain by their wretchedness, 5 while they are too depraved to be the objects of affection, and too weak and insignificant to be the causes of misery to others, or, consequently, of indignation to the spectators. Such are the depraved, abject, diseased, and neglected poor — creatures in whom every thing amiable 10 or respectable has been extinguished by sordid passions or brutal debauchery ; — who have no means of doing the mischief of which they are capable — whom every one despises, and no one can either love or fear. On the characters, the miseries, and the vices of such beings, we 15 look with *disgust* merely : and, though it may perhaps serve some *moral* purpose, occasionally to set before us this humiliating spectacle of human nature sunk to utter worthlessness and insignificance, it is altogether in vain to think of exciting pity or horror, by the truest and most 20 forcible representations of their sufferings or their enormities. They have no hold upon any of the feelings that lead us to take an interest in our fellow-creatures ; — we turn away from them, therefore, with loathing and dispassionate aversion ; — we feel our imaginations 25 polluted by the intrusion of any images connected with them ; and are offended and disgusted when we are forced to look closely upon those festering heaps of moral filth and corruption.

It is with concern we add, that we know no writer who 30 has sinned so deeply in this respect as Mr. Crabbe — who has so often presented us with spectacles which it is purely painful and degrading to contemplate, and bestowed such powers of conception and expression in giving us

distinct ideas of what we must ever abhor to remember.
If Mr. Crabbe had been a person of ordinary talents,
we might have accounted for his error, in some degree,
by supposing, that his frequent success in treating of
5 subjects which had been usually rejected by other poets,
had at length led him to disregard, altogether, the common
impressions of mankind as to what was allowable and
what inadmissible in poetry ; and to reckon the unalter-
able laws by which nature has regulated our sympathies,
10 among the prejudices by which they were shackled and
impaired.   It is difficult, however, to conceive how a
writer of his quick and exact observation should have
failed to perceive, that there is not a single instance of a
serious interest being excited by an object of disgust ;
15 and that Shakespeare himself, who has ventured every
thing, has never ventured to shock our feelings with the
crimes or the sufferings of beings absolutely without
power or principle.   Independent of universal practice,
too, it is still more difficult to conceive how he should
20 have overlooked the reason on which this practice is
founded ; for though it be generally true, that poetical
representations of suffering and of guilt produce emotion,
and consequently delight, yet it certainly did not require
the penetration of Mr. Crabbe to discover, that there is
25 a degree of depravity which counteracts our sympathy
with suffering, and a degree of insignificance which
extinguishes our interest in guilt.   We abstain from
giving any extracts in support of this accusation ; but
those who have perused the volume before us, will have
30 already recollected the story of Frederic Thompson, of
Abel Keene, of Blaney, of Benbow, and a good part
of those of Grimes and Ellen Orford — besides many
shorter passages.   It is now time, however, to give the
reader a more particular account of the work which
35 contains them.

TALES OF THE HALL.

By the Reverend George Crabbe. 2 vols. 8vo, pp. 670. London, 1819.

MR. CRABBE is the greatest *mannerist*, perhaps, of all
our living poets ; and it is rather unfortunate that the
most prominent features of his mannerism are not the
most pleasing. The homely, quaint, and prosaic style
— the flat, and often broken jingling versification — the 5
eternal full-lengths of low and worthless characters —
with their accustomed garnishings of sly jokes and familiar
moralising — are all on the surface of his writings ; and
are almost unavoidably the things by which we are
first reminded of him, when we take up any of his new 10
productions. Yet they are *not* the things that truly constitute his peculiar manner ; or give that character by
which he will, and ought to be, remembered with future
generations. It is plain enough, indeed, that these are
things that will make nobody remembered — and can 15
never, therefore, be really characteristic of some of the
most original and powerful poetry that the world has ever
seen.

Mr. C., accordingly, has other gifts ; and those not
less peculiar or less strongly marked than the blemishes 20
with which they are contrasted ; an unrivalled and almost
magical power of observation, resulting in descriptions so
true to nature as to strike us rather as transcripts than
imitations — an anatomy of character and feeling not less
exquisite and searching — an occasional touch of match- 25

less tenderness — and a deep and dreadful pathetic, interspersed by fits, and strangely interwoven with the most
minute and humble of his details.   Add to all this the
sure and profound sagacity of the remarks with which he
5 every now and then startles us in the midst of very
unambitious discussions ; — and the weight and terseness
of the maxims which he drops, like oracular responses,
on occasions that give no promise of such a revelation ;
— and last, though not least, that sweet and seldom
10 sounded chord of Lyrical inspiration, the lightest touch
of which instantly charms away all harshness from his
numbers, and all lowness from his themes — and at once
exalts him to a level with the most energetic and inventive poets of his age.

15   These, we think, are the true characteristics of the
genius of this great writer ; and it is in their mixture
with the oddities and defects to which we have already
alluded, that the peculiarity of his manner seems to us
substantially to consist.   The ingredients may all of them
20 be found, we suppose, in other writers ; but their combination — in such proportions at least as occur in this
instance — may safely be pronounced to be original.

Extraordinary, however, as this combination must
appear, it does not seem very difficult to conceive in what
25 way it may have arisen, and, so far from regarding it as
a proof of singular humorousness, caprice, or affectation
in the individual, we are rather inclined to hold that
something approaching to it must be the natural result of
a long habit of observation in a man of genius, possessed
30 of that temper and disposition which is the usual accompaniment of such a habit ; and that the same strangely
compounded and apparently incongruous assemblage of
themes and sentiments would be frequently produced
under such circumstances — if authors had oftener the

courage to write from their own impressions, and had less
fear of the laugh or wonder of the more shallow and
barren part of their readers.

A great talent for observation, and a delight in the
exercise of it — the power and the practice of dissecting 5
and disentangling that subtle and complicated tissue, of
habit, and self-love, and affection, which constitute human
character — seems to us, in all cases, to imply a contemplative, rather than an active disposition. It can only
exist, indeed, where there is a good deal of social 10
sympathy ; for, without this, the occupation could excite
no interest, and afford no satisfaction — but only such a
measure and sort of sympathy as is gratified by being a
spectator, and not an actor on the great theatre of life —
and leads its possessor rather to look with eagerness on 15
the feats and the fortunes of others, than to take a share
for himself in the game that is played before him. Some
stirring and vigorous spirits there are, no doubt, in which
this taste and talent is combined with a more thorough
and effective sympathy ; and leads to the study of men's 20
characters by an actual and hearty participation in their
various passions and pursuits ; — though it is to be
remarked, that when such persons embody their observations in writing, they will generally be found to exhibit
their characters in action, rather than to describe them in 25
the abstract ; and to let their various personages disclose
themselves and their peculiarities, as it were spontaneously, and without help or preparation, in their ordinary
conduct and speech — of all which we have a very
splendid and striking example in the Tales of My Land- 30
lord, and the other pieces of that extraordinary writer.
In the common case, however, a great observer, we
believe, will be found, pretty certainly, to be a person of
a shy and retiring temper — who does not mingle enough

with the people he surveys, to be heated with their
passions, or infected with their delusions — and who has
usually been led, indeed, to take up the office of a looker
on, from some little infirmity of nerves, or weakness of
5 spirits, which has unfitted him from playing a more
active part on the busy scene of existence.

Now, it is very obvious, we think, that this contemplative turn, and this alienation from the vulgar pursuits
of mankind, must in the first place, produce a great con-
10 tempt for most of those pursuits, and the objects they
seek to obtain — a levelling of the factitious distinctions
which human pride and vanity have established in the
world, and a mingled scorn and compassion for the lofty
pretensions under which men so often disguise the noth-
15 ingness of their chosen occupations. When the many-
coloured scene of life, with all its petty agitations, its
shifting pomps, and perishable passions, is surveyed by
one who does not mix in its business, it is impossible
that it should not appear a very pitiable and almost
20 ridiculous affair; or that the heart should not echo
back the brief and emphatic exclamation of the mighty
dramatist —

> ———— " Life's a poor player,
> Who frets and struts his hour upon the stage,
> 25   And then is heard no more ! " —

Or the more sarcastic amplification of it, in the words
of our great moral poet —

> "Behold the Child, by Nature's kindly law,
> Pleas'd with a rattle, tickl'd with a straw !
> 30   Some livelier plaything gives our Youth delight,
> A little louder, but as empty quite :
> Scarfs, garters, gold our riper years engage;
> And beads and prayer-books are the *toys* of Age !
> Pleas'd with this bauble still as that before,
> 35   Till tir'd we sleep — and *Life's poor play is o'er !* "

This is the more solemn view of the subject : — But the first fruits of observation are most commonly found to issue in Satire — the unmasking the vain pretenders to wisdom, and worth, and happiness, with whom society is infested, and holding up to the derision of mankind those 5 meannesses of the great, those miseries of the fortunate, and those

"Fears of the brave, and follies of the wise,"

which the eye of a dispassionate observer so quickly detects under the glittering exterior by which they would 10 fain be disguised — and which bring pretty much to a level the intellect, and morals, and enjoyments, of the great mass of mankind.

This misanthropic end has unquestionably been by far the most common result of a habit of observation ; and 15 that in which its effects have most generally terminated : Yet we cannot bring ourselves to think that it is their just or natural termination. Something, no doubt, will depend on the temper of the individual, and the proportions in which the gall and the milk of human kindness 20 have been originally mingled in his composition. — Yet satirists, we think, have not in general been ill-natured persons — and we are inclined rather to ascribe this limited and uncharitable application of their powers of observation to their love of fame and popularity, — which 25 are well known to be best secured by successful ridicule or invective — or, quite as probably, indeed, to the narrowness and insufficiency of the observations themselves, and the imperfection of their talents for their due conduct and extension. It is certain, at least, we think, 30 that the satirist makes use of but half the discoveries of the observer ; and teaches but half — the worser half – of the lessons which may be deduced from his occupa-

tion.   He puts down, indeed, the proud pretensions of
the great and arrogant, and levels the vain distinctions
which   human   ambition   has   established   among   the
brethren of mankind; he

5   " Bares the mean heart that lurks beneath a Star,"

— and destroyed the illusions which would limit our
sympathy to the forward and figuring persons of this
world — the favourites of fame and fortune.   But the
true result of observation should be, not so much to cast
10 down the proud, as to raise up the lowly; — not so
much to diminish our sympathy with the powerful and
renowned, as to extend it to all, who, in humbler conditions, have the same, or still higher claims on our esteem
or affection. — It is not surely the natural consequence
15 of learning to judge truly of the characters of men, that
we should despise or be indifferent about them all; —
and, though we have learned to see through the false
glare which plays round the envied summits of existence,
and to know how little dignity, or happiness, or worth, or
20 wisdom, may sometimes belong to the possessors of
power, and fortune, and learning and renown, — it does
not follow, by any means, that we should look upon the
whole of human life as a mere deceit and imposture,
or think the concerns of our species fit subjects only
25 for scorn and derision.   Our promptitude to admire and
to envy will indeed be corrected, our enthusiasm abated,
and our distrust of appearances increased ; — but the
sympathies and affections of our nature will continue, and
be better directed — our love of our kind will not be
30 diminished — and our indulgence for their faults and
follies, ˙if we read our lesson aright, will be signally
strengthened and confirmed.   The true and proper effect,
therefore, of a habit of observation, and a thorough and

penetrating knowledge of human character, will be, not
to extinguish our sympathy, but to extend it — to turn,
no doubt, many a throb of admiration, and many a sigh
of love into a smile of derison or of pity ; but at the
same time to reveal much that commands our homage   5
and excites our affection, in those humble and unexplored
regions of the heart and understanding, which never
engage the attention of the incurious, — and to bring the
whole family of mankind nearer to a level, by finding out
latent merits as well as latent defects in all its members, 10
and compensating the flaws that are detected in the
boasted ornaments of life, by bringing to light the richness and the lustre that sleep in the mines beneath its
surface.

We are afraid some of our readers may not at once 15
perceive the application of these profound remarks to
the subject immediately before us.   But there are others,
we doubt not, who do not need to be told that they are
intended to explain how Mr. Crabbe, and other persons
with the same gift of observation, should so often busy 20
themselves with what may be considered as low and
vulgar character ; and, declining all dealings with heroes
and heroic topics, should not only venture to seek for an
interest in the concerns of ordinary mortals, but actually
intersperse small pieces of ridicule with their undignified 25
pathos, and endeavour to make their readers look on their
book with the same mingled feelings of compassion and
amusement, with which — unnatural as it may appear to
the readers of poetry — they, and all judicious observers,
actually look upon human life and human nature.—This, 30
we are persuaded, is the true key to the greater part of
the peculiarities of the author before us ; and though we
have disserted upon it a little longer than was necessary,
we really think it may enable our readers to comprehend

him, and our remarks on him, something better than they could have done without it.

There is, as everybody must have felt, a strange satire and sympathy in all his productions—a great kindliness and compassion for the errors and sufferings of our poor human nature, but a strong distrust of its heroic virtues and high pretensions. His heart is always open to pity, and all the milder emotions—but there is little aspiration after the grand and sublime of character, nor very much encouragement for raptures and ecstasies of any description. These, he seems to think, are things rather too fine for the said poor human nature: and that, in our low and erring condition, it is a little ridiculous to pretend, either to very exalted and immaculate virtue, or very pure and exquisite happiness. He not only never meddles, therefore, with the delicate distresses and noble fires of the heroes and heroines of tragic and epic fable, but may generally be detected indulging in a lurking sneer at the pomp and vanity of all such superfine imaginations—and turning from them, to draw men in their true postures and dimensions, and with all the imperfections that actually belong to their condition:— the prosperous and happy overshadowed with passing clouds of *ennui,* and disturbed with little flaws of bad humour and discontent—the great and wise beset at times with strange weaknesses and meannesses and paltry vexations—and even the most virtuous and enlightened falling far below the standard of poetical perfection—and stooping every now and then to paltry jealousies and prejudices—or sinking into shabby sensualities—or meditating on their own excellence and importance, with a ludicrous and lamentable anxiety.

This is one side of the picture; and characterises sufficiently the satirical vein of our author: But the other

is the most extensive and important. In rejecting the
vulgar sources of interest in poetical narratives, and
reducing his ideal persons to the standard of reality,
Mr. C. does by no means seek to extinguish the sparks
of human sympathy within us, or to throw any damp on 5
the curiosity with which we naturally explore the characters of each other. On the contrary, he has afforded
new and more wholesome food for all those propensities
— and, by placing before us those details which our
pride or fastidiousness is so apt to overlook, has dis- 10
closed, in all their truth and simplicity, the native and
unadulterated workings of those affections which are at
the bottom of all social interest, and are really rendered
less touching by the exaggerations of more ambitious
artists — while he exhibits, with admirable force and 15
endless variety, all those combinations of passions and
opinions, and all that cross-play of selfishness and
vanity, and indolence and ambition, and habit and
reason, which make up the intellectual character of
individuals, and present to every one an instructive 20
picture of his neighbour or himself. Seeing, by the perfection of his art, the master passions in their springs,
and the high capacities in their rudiments — and having
acquired the gift of tracing all the propensities and
marking tendencies of our plastic nature, in their first 25
slight indications, or even from the aspect of the disguises they so often assume, he does not need, in order
to draw out his characters in all their life and distinct-
ness, the vulgar demonstration of those striking and
decided actions by which their maturity is proclaimed 30
even to the careless and inattentive ; — but delights to
point out to his readers, the seeds or tender filaments of
those talents and feelings which wait only for occasion
and opportunity to burst out and astonish the world —

and to accustom them to trace, in characters and actions
apparently of the most ordinary description, the self-same
attributes that, under other circumstances, would attract
universal attention, and furnish themes for the most
5 popular and impassioned descriptions.

That he should not be guided in the choice of his
subject by any regard to the rank or condition which his
persons hold in society, may easily be imagined; and,
with a view to the ends he aims at, might readily be
10 forgiven. But we fear that his passion for observation,
and the delight he takes in tracing out and analyzing all
the little traits that indicate character, and all the little
circumstances that influence it, have sometimes led him
to be careless about his selection of the instances in
15 which it was to be exhibited, or at least to select them
upon principles very different from those which give them
an interest in the eyes of ordinary readers. For the
purpose of mere anatomy, beauty of form or complexion
are things quite indifferent; and the physiologist, who
20 examines plants only to study their internal structure,
and to make himself master of the contrivances by which
their various functions are performed, pays no regard to
the brilliancy of their hues, the sweetness of their odours,
or the graces of their form. Those who come to him
25 for the sole purpose of acquiring knowledge may partici-
pate perhaps in this indifference; but the world at large
will wonder at them—and he will engage fewer pupils to
listen to his instructions, than if he had condescended in
some degree to consult their predilections in the begin-
30 ning. It is the same case, we think, in many respects,
with Mr. Crabbe. Relying for the interest he is to produce, on the curious expositions he is to make of the
elements of human character, or at least finding his own
chief gratification in those subtle investigations, he seems

to care very little upon what particular individuals he pitches for the purpose of these demonstrations. Almost every human mind, he seems to think, may serve to display that fine and mysterious mechanism which it is his delight to explore and explain; — and almost every 5 condition, and every history of life, afford occasions to show how it may be put into action, and pass through its various combinations. It seems, therefore, almost as if he had caught up the first dozen or two of persons that came across him in the ordinary walks of life, — and then 10 fitting in his little window in their breasts, and applying his tests and instruments of observation, had set himself about such a minute and curious scrutiny of their whole habits, history, adventures, and dispositions, as he · thought must ultimately create not only a familiarity, but 15 an interest, which the first aspect of the subject was far enough from leading any one to expect. That he succeeds more frequently than could have been antici- pated, we are very willing to allow. But we cannot help feeling, also, that a little more pains bestowed in the 20 selection of his characters, would have made his power of observation and description tell with tenfold effect; and that, in spite of the exquisite truth of his delinea- tions, and the fineness of the perceptions by which he was enabled to make them, it is impossible to take any 25 considerable interest in many of his personages, or to avoid feeling some degree of fatigue at the minute and patient exposition that is made of all that belongs to them.

ENDYMION.

A Poetic Romance. By John Keats. 8vo, pp. 207. London, 1818.

We had never happened to see either of these volumes
till very lately — and have been exceedingly struck with
the genius they display, and the spirit of poetry which
breathes through all their extravagance. That imitation
5 of our old writers, and especially of our older dramatists,
to which we cannot help flattering ourselves that we have
somewhat contributed, has brought on, as it were, a
second spring in our poetry ; — and few of its blossoms
are either more profuse of sweetness, or richer in promise,
10 than this which is now before us. Mr. Keats, we understand, is still a very young man ; and his whole works,
indeed, bear evidence enough of the fact. They are full
of extravagance and irregularity, rash attempts at originality, interminable wanderings, and excessive obscurity.
15 They manifestly require, therefore, all the indulgence
that can be claimed for a first attempt : — But we think
it no less plain that they deserve it : For they are flushed
all over with the rich lights of fancy ; and so coloured
and bestrewn with the flowers of poetry ; that even while
20 perplexed and bewildered in their labyrinths, it is impossible to resist the intoxication of their sweetness, or
to shut our hearts to the enchantments they so lavishly
present. The models upon which he has formed himself,
in the Endymion, the earliest and by much the most con-
25 siderable of his poems, are obviously The Faithful

Shepherdess of Fletcher, and the Sad Shepherd of Ben
Jonson ; — the exquisite metres and inspired diction of
which he has copied with great boldness and fidelity —
and, like his great originals, has also contrived to impart
to the whole piece that true rural and poetical air — 5
which breathes only in them, and in Theocritus — which
is at once homely and majestic, luxurious and rude, and
sets before us the genuine sights and sounds and smells
of the country, with all the magic and grace of Elysium.
His subject has the disadvantage of being Mythological ; 10
and in this respect, as well as on account of the raised
and rapturous tone it consequently assumes, his poem, it
may be thought, would be better compared to the Comus
and the Arcades of Milton, of which, also, there are
many traces of imitation. The great distinction, how- 15
ever, between him and these divine authors, is, that
imagination in them is subordinate to reason and judgment, while, with him, it is paramount and supreme —
that their ornaments and images are employed to em-
bellish and recommend just sentiments, engaging inci- 20
dents, and natural characters, while his are poured out
without measure or restraint, and with no apparent
design but to unburden the breast of the author, and give
vent to the overflowing vein of his fancy. The thin and
scanty tissue of his story is merely the light framework 25
on which his florid wreaths are suspended ; and while
his imaginations go rambling and entangling themselves
every where, like wild honeysuckles, all idea of sober
reason, and plan, and consistency, is utterly forgotten,
and "strangled in their waste fertility." A great part of 30
the work, indeed, is written in the strangest and most
fantastical manner that can be imagined. It seems as if
the author had ventured every thing that occured to him
in the shape of a glittering image or striking expression

—taken the first word that presented itself to make up a
rhyme, and then made that word the germ of a new
cluster of images — a hint for a new excursion of the
fancy — and so wandered on, equally forgetful whence he
5 came, and heedless whither he was going, till he had
covered his pages with an interminable arabesque of
connected and incongruous figures, that multiplied as
they extended, and were only harmonised by the brightness of their tints, and the graces of their forms.   In
10 this rash and headlong career he has of course many
lapses and failures.   There is no work, accordingly, from
which a malicious critic could cull more matter for
ridicule, or select more obscure, unnatural, or absurd
passages.   But we do not take *that* to be our office ; —
15 and must beg leave, on the contrary, to say, that any one
who, on this account, would represent the whole poem as
despicable, must either have no notion of poetry, or no
regard to truth.

It is, in truth, at least as full of genius as of absurdity ;
20 and he who does not find a great deal in it to admire and
to give delight, cannot in his heart see much beauty in
the two exquisite dramas to which we have already
alluded ; or find any great pleasure in some of the finest
creations of Milton and Shakespeare.   There are very
25 many such persons, we verily believe, even among the
reading and judicious part of the community — correct
scholars, we have no doubt, many of them, and, it may
be, very classical composers in prose and in verse — but
utterly ignorant, on our view of the matter, of the true
30 genius of English poetry, and incapable of estimating its
appropriate and most exquisite beauties.   With that
spirit we have no hesitation in saying that Mr. Keats is
deeply imbued — and of those beauties he has presented
us with many striking examples.   We are very much

inclined indeed to add, that we do not know any book which we would sooner employ as a test to ascertain whether any one had in him a native relish for poetry, and a genuine sensibility to its intrinsic charm. The greater and more distinguished poets of our country have 5 so much else in them, to gratify other tastes and propensities, that they are pretty sure to captivate and amuse those to whom their poetry may be but an hinderance and obstruction, as well as those to whom it constitutes their chief attraction. The interest of the 10 stories they tell — the vivacity of the characters they delineate — the weight and force of the maxims and sentiments in which they abound — the very pathos, and wit and humour they display, which may all and each of them exist apart from their poetry, and independent of it, 15 are quite sufficient to account for their popularity, without referring much to that still higher gift, by which they subdue to their enchantments those whose souls are truly attuned to the finer impulses of poetry. It is only, therefore, where those other recommendations are want- 20 ing, or exist in a weaker degree, that the true force of the attraction, exercised by the pure poetry with which they are so often combined, can be fairly appreciated : — where, without much incident or many characters, and with little wit, wisdom, or arrangement, a number of 25 bright pictures are presented to the imagination, and a fine feeling expressed of those mysterious relations by which visible external things are assimilated with inward thoughts and emotions, and become the images and exponents of all passions and affections. To an un- 30 poetical reader such passages will generally appear mere raving and absurdity — and to this censure a very great part of the volumes before us will certainly be exposed, with this class of readers. Even in the judgment of a

fitter audience, however, it must, we fear, be admitted,
that, besides the riot and extravagance of his fancy the
scope and substance of Mr. Keats's poetry is rather too
dreamy and abstracted to excite the strongest interest, or
5 to sustain the attention through a work of any great
compass or extent.   He deals too much with shadowy and
incomprehensible beings, and is too constantly rapt into
an extramundane Elysium, to command a lasting interest
with ordinary mortals — and must employ the agency of
10 more varied and coarser emotions, if he wishes to take
rank with the enduring poets of this or of former generations.   There is something very curious, too, we think,
in the way in which he, and Mr. Barry Cornwall also,
have dealt with the Pagan mythology, of which they have
15 made so much use in their poetry.   Instead of presenting
its imaginary persons under the trite and vulgar traits
that belong to them in the ordinary systems, little more
is borrowed from these than the general conception of
their condition and relations ; and an original character
20 and distinct individuality is then bestowed upon them,
which has all the merit of invention, and all the grace
and attraction of the fictions on which it is engrafted.
The ancients, though they probably did not stand in any
great awe of their deities, have yet abstained very much
25 from any minute or dramatic representation of their
feelings and affections.   In Hesiod and Homer, they
are broadly delineated by some of their actions and
adventures, and introduced to us merely as the agents in
those particular transactions ; while in the Hymns, from
30 those ascribed to Orpheus and Homer, down to those of
Callimachus, we have little but pompous epithets and
invocations, with a flattering commemoration of their
most famous exploits — and are never allowed to enter
into their bosoms, or follow out the train of their feelings,

with the presumption of our human sympathy. Except the love-song of the Cyclops to his Sea Nymph in Theocritus — the Lamentation of .Venus for Adonis in Moschus — and the more recent Legend of Apuleius, we scarcely recollect a passage in all the writings of anti- 5 quity in which the passions of an immortal are fairly disclosed to the scrutiny and observation of men. The author before us, however, and some of his contemporaries, have dealt differently with the subject ; — and, sheltering the violence of the fiction under the ancient 10 traditionary fable, have in reality created and imagined an entire new set of characters ; and brought closely and minutely before us the loves and sorrows and perplexities of beings, with whose names and supernatural attributes we had long been familiar, without any sense or feeling 15 of their personal character. We have more than doubts of the fitness of such personages to maintain a permanent interest with the modern public ; — but the way in which they are here managed certainly gives them the best chance that now remains for them ; and, at all events, it 20 cannot be denied that the effect is striking and graceful. But we must now proceed to our extracts.

CHILDE HAROLD'S PILGRIMAGE.

Canto the Third. By Lord Byron. 8vo, pp. 79. London, 1816.[1]

IF the finest poetry be that which leaves the deepest impression on the minds of its readers — and this is not the worst test of its excellence — Lord Byron, we think, must be allowed to take precedence of all his distin-
5 guished contemporaries. He has not the variety of Scott — nor the delicacy of Campbell — nor the absolute truth of Crabbe — nor the polished sparkling of Moore ; but in force of diction, and inextinguishable energy of sentiment, he clearly surpasses them all. " Words that
10 breathe, and thoughts that burn," are not merely the ornaments, but the common staple of his poetry ; and he is not inspired or impressive only in some happy passages, but through the whole body and tissue of his composition. It was an unavoidable condition, perhaps,
15 of this higher excellence, that his scene should be

[1] I have already said so much of Lord Byron with reference to his Dramatic productions, that I cannot now afford to republish more than one other paper on the subject of his poetry in general : And I select this, rather because it refers to a greater variety of these compositions, than because it deals with such as are either absolutely the best, or the most characteristic of his genius. The truth is, however, that all his writings are characteristic ; and lead, pretty much alike, to those views of the dark and the bright parts of his nature, which have led me, I fear (though almost irresistibly) into observations more personal to the character of the author, than should generally be permitted to a mere literary censor.

narrow, and his persons few. To compass such ends as
he had in view, it was necessary to reject all ordinary
agents, and all trivial combinations.   He could not
possibly be amusing, or ingenious or playful ; or hope to
maintain the requisite pitch of interest by the recitation 5
of sprightly adventures, or the opposition of common
characters. To produce great effects, in short, he felt
that it was necessary to deal only with the greater
passions — with the exaltations of a daring fancy, and
the errors of a lofty intellect — with the pride, the 10
terrors, and the agonies of strong emotion — the fire and
air alone of our human elements.

In this respect, and in his general notion of the end
and the means of poetry, we have sometimes thought
that his views fell more in with those of the Lake poets, 15
than of any other existing party in the poetical commonwealth : And, in some of his later productions especially,
it is impossible not to be struck with his occasional
approaches to the style and manner of this class of
writers. Lord Byron, however, it should be observed, 20
like all other persons of a quick sense of beauty, and
sure enough of their own originality to be in no fear
of paltry imputations, is a great mimic of styles and
manners, and a great borrower of external character.
He and Scott, accordingly, are full of imitations of all 25
the writers from whom they have ever derived gratification ; and the two most original writers of the age might
appear, to superficial observers, to be the most deeply
indebted to their predecessors.   In this particular instance,
we have no fault to find with Lord Byron.   For undoubt- 30
edly the finer passages of Wordsworth and Southey have
in them wherewithal to lend an impulse to the utmost
ambition of rival genius ; and their diction and manner
of writing is frequently both striking and original.   But

we must say, that it would afford us still greater pleasure
to find these tuneful gentlemen returning the compliment
which Lord Byron has here paid to their talents ; and
forming themselves on the model rather of his imitations,
5 than of their own originals. — In those imitations they
will find that, though he is sometimes abundantly mystical,
he never, or at least very rarely, indulges in absolute
nonsense — never takes his lofty flights upon mean or
ridiculous occasions — and, above all, never dilutes his
10 strong conceptions, and magnificent imaginations, with a
flood of oppressive verbosity.   On the contrary, he is, of
all living writers, the most concise and condensed ;
and, we would fain hope, may go far, by his example, to
redeem the great reproach of our modern literature — its
15 intolerable prolixity and redundance.   In his nervous
and manly lines, we find no elaborate amplification of
common sentiments — no ostentatious polishing of pretty
expressions ; and we really think that the brilliant success
which has rewarded his disdain of those paltry artifices,
20 should put to shame for ever that puling and self-admiring
race, who can live through half a volume on the stock of
a single thought, and expatiate over divers fair quarto
pages with the details of one tedious description.   In
Lord Byron, on the contrary, we have a perpetual stream
25 of thick-coming fancies — an eternal spring of fresh-
blown images, which seem called into existence by the
sudden flash of those glowing thoughts and overwhelming
emotions, that struggle for expression through the whole
flow of his poetry — and impart to a diction that is often
30 abrupt and irregular, a force and a charm which frequently
realize all that is said of inspiration.

   With all these undoubted claims to our admiration,
however, it is impossible to deny that the noble author
before us has still something to learn, and a good deal to

correct. He is frequently abrupt and careless, and sometimes obscure. There are marks, occasionally, of effort
and straining after an emphasis, which is generally
spontaneous; and, above all, there is far too great a
monotony in the moral colouring of his pictures, and too 5
much repetition of the same sentiments and maxims.
He delights too exclusively in the delineation of a
certain morbid exaltation of character and feeling — a
sort of demoniacal sublimity, not without some traits of
the ruined Archangel. He is haunted almost perpetually 10
with the image of a being feeding and fed upon by
violent passions, and the recollections of the catas-
trophes they have occasioned : And, though worn out
by their past indulgence, unable to sustain the burden
of an existence which they do not continue to animate : 15
— full of pride, and revenge, and obduracy — disdaining
life and death, and mankind and himself — and trampling,
in his scorn, not only upon the falsehood and formality
of polished life, but upon its tame virtues and slavish
devotion : Yet envying, by fits, the very beings he de- 20
spises, and melting into mere softness and compassion,
when the helplessness of childhood or the frailty of
woman make an appeal to his generosity. Such is the
person with whom we are called upon almost exclusively to sympathise in all the greater productions of 25
this distinguished writer : — In Childe Harold — in the
Corsair — in Lara — in the Siege of Corinth — in Parisina,
and in most of the smaller pieces.

It is impossible to represent such a character better
than Lord Byron has done in all these productions — or 30
indeed to represent any thing more terrible in its anger,
or more attractive in its relenting. In point of effect, we
readily admit, that no one character can be more poetical
or impressive : — But it is really too much to find the

scene perpetually filled by one character — not only in all the acts of each several drama, but in all the different dramas of the series ; — and, grand and impressive as it is, we feel at last that these very qualities make some
5 relief more indispensable, and oppress the spirits of ordinary mortals with too deep an impression of awe and repulsion. There is too much guilt in short, and too much gloom, in the leading character ; — and though it be a fine thing to gaze, now and then, on stormy seas,
10 and thunder-shaken mountains, we should prefer passing our days in sheltered valleys, and by the murmur of calmer waters.

We are aware that these metaphors may be turned against us — and that, without metaphor, it may be said
15 that men do not *pass their days* in reading poetry — and that, as they may look into Lord Byron only about as often as they look abroad upon tempests, they have no more reason to complain of him for being grand and gloomy, than to complain of the same qualities in the
20 glaciers and volcanoes which they go so far to visit. Painters, too, it may be said, have often gained great reputation by their representations of tigers and other ferocious animals, or of caverns and banditti — and poets should be allowed, without reproach, to indulge
25 in analogous exercises. We are far from thinking that there is no weight in these considerations ; and feel how plausibly it may be said, that we have no better reason for a great part of our complaint, than that an author, to whom we are already very greatly indebted, has chosen
30 rather to please himself, than us, in the use he makes of his talents.

This, no doubt, seems both unreasonable and ungrateful. But it is nevertheless true, that a public benefactor becomes a debtor to the public, and is, in some degree,

responsible for the employment of those gifts which seem
to be conferred upon him, not merely for his own delight,
but for the delight and improvement of his fellows through
all generations. Independent of this, however, we think
there is a reply to the apology. A great living poet is 5
not like a distant volcano, or an occasional tempest. He
is a volcano in the heart of our land, and a cloud that
hangs over our dwellings; and we have some reason
to complain, if, instead of genial warmth and grateful
shade, he voluntarily darkens and inflames our atmos- 10
phere with perpetual fiery explosions and pitchy vapours.
Lord Byron's poetry, in short, is too attractive and too
famous to lie dormant or inoperative ; and, therefore, if
it produce any painful or pernicious effects, there will
be murmurs, and ought to be suggestions of alteration. 15
Now, though an artist may draw fighting tigers and
hungry lions in as lively or natural a way as he can,
without giving any encouragement to human ferocity,
or even much alarm to human fear, the case is somewhat
different, when a poet represents men with tiger-like 20
dispositions : — and yet more so, when he exhausts the
resources of his genius to make this terrible being
interesting and attractive, and to represent all the lofty
virtues as the natural allies of his ferocity. It is still
worse when he proceeds to show, that all these precious 25
gifts of dauntless courage, strong affection, and high
imagination, are not only akin to guilt, but the parents
of misery ; — and that those only have any chance of
tranquillity or happiness in this world, whom it is the
object of his poetry to make us shun and despise. 30

These, it appears to us, are not merely errors in taste,
but perversions of morality ; and, as a great poet is
necessarily a moral teacher, and gives forth his ethical
lessons, in general with far more effect and authority

than any of his graver brethren, he is peculiarly liable
to the censures reserved for those who turn the means of
improvement to purposes of corruption.

It may no doubt be said, that poetry in general tends
5 less to the useful than the splendid qualities of our
nature — that a character poetically good has long been
distinguished from one that is morally so — and that,
ever since the time of Achilles, our sympathies, on such
occasions, have been chiefly engrossed by persons whose
10 deportment is by no means exemplary; and who in many
points approach to the temperament of Lord Byron's ideal
hero. There is some truth in this suggestion also. But
other poets, in the *first* place, do not allow their favourites
so outrageous a monopoly of the glory and interest of the
15 piece — and sin less therefore against the laws either of
poetical or distributive justice. In the *second* place, their
heroes are not, generally, either so bad or so good as
Lord Byron's — and do not indeed very much exceed the
standard of truth and nature, in either of the extremes.
20 His, however, are as monstrous and unnatural as centaurs,
and hippogriffs — and must ever figure in the eye of sober
reason as so many bright and hateful impossibilities. But
the most important distinction is, that the other poets
who deal in peccant heroes, neither feel nor express that
25 ardent affection for them, which is visible in the whole
of this author's delineations; but merely make use of
them as necessary agents in the extraordinary adventures
they have to detail, and persons whose minged vices and
virtues are requisite to bring about the catastrophe of
30 their story. In Lord Byron, however, the interest of the
story, where there happens to be one, which is not always
the case, is uniformly postponed to that of the character
itself — into which he enters so deeply, and with so
extraordinary a fondness, that he generally continues

to speak in its language, after it has been dismissed from the stage ; and to inculcate, on his own authority, the same sentiments which had been previously recommended by its example. We do not consider it as unfair, therefore, to say that Lord Byron appears to us to be 5 the zealous apostle of a certain fierce and magnificent misanthropy ; which has already saddened his poetry with too deep a shade, and not only led to a great misapplication of great talents, but contributed to render popular some very false estimates of the constituents of 10 human happiness and merit. It is irksome, however, to dwell upon observations so general — and we shall probably have better means of illustrating these remarks, if they are really well founded, when we come to speak of the particular publications by which they have now been 15 suggested.

We had the good fortune, we believe, to be among the first who proclaimed the rising of a new luminary, on the appearance of Childe Harold on the poetical horizon, — and we pursued his course with due attention through 20 several of the constellations. If we have lately omitted to record his progress with the same accuracy, it is by no means because we have regarded it with more indifference, or supposed that it would be less interesting to the public — but because it was so extremely conspicuous as 25 no longer to require the notices of an official observer. In general, we do not think it necessary, nor indeed quite fair, to oppress our readers with an account of works, which are as well known to them as to ourselves ; or with a repetition of sentiments in which all the world 30 is agreed. Wherever, a work, therefore, is very popular, and where the general opinion of its merits appears to be substantially right, we think ourselves at liberty to leave it out of our chronicle, without incurring the censure of

neglect or inattention. · A very rigorous application of
this maxim might have saved our readers the trouble of
reading what we now write — and, to confess the truth,
we write it rather to gratify ourselves, than with the hope
5 of giving them much information. At the same time,
some short notice of the progress of such a writer ought,
perhaps, to appear in his comtemporary journals, as a
tribute due to his eminence ; — and a zealous critic can
scarcely set about examining the merits of any work, or
10 the nature of its reception by the public, without speedily
discovering very urgent cause for his admonitions, both
to the author and his admirers.

*   *   *

The most considerable of [the author's recent publica-
15 tions,] is the Third Canto of Childe Harold ; a work
which has the disadvantage of all continuations, in
admitting of little absolute novelty in the plan of the
work or the cast of its character, and must, besides,
remind all Lord Byron's readers of the extraordinary
20 effect produced by the sudden blazing forth of his
genius, upon their first introduction to that title. In
spite of all this, however, we are persuaded that this
Third Part of the poem will not be pronounced inferior to either of the former ; and, we think, will prob-
25 ably be ranked above them by those who have been most
delighted with the whole. The great success of this
singular production, indeed, has always appeared to us
an extraordinary proof of its merits ; for, with all its
genius, it does not belong to a sort of poetry that rises
30 easily to popularity. — It has no story or action — very
little variety of character — and a great deal of reasoning
and reflection of no very attractive tenor. It is substantially a contemplative and ethical work, diversified
with fine description, and adorned or overshaded by the

perpetual presence of one emphatic person, who is sometimes the author, and sometimes the object, of the reflections on which the interest is chiefly rested. It required,
no doubt, great force of writing, and a decided tone of
originality to recommend a performance of this sort so 5
powerfully as this has been recommended to public notice
and admiration — and those high characteristics belong
perhaps still more eminently to the part that is now
before us, than to any of the former. There is the same
stern and lofty disdain of mankind, and their ordinary 10
pursuits and enjoyments; with the same bright gaze on
nature, and the same magic power of giving interest and
effect to her delineations — but mixed up, we think, with
deeper and more matured reflections, and a more intense
sensibility to all that is grand or lovely in the external 15
world. — Harold, in short, is somewhat older since he
last appeared upon the scene — and while the vigour of
his intellect has been confirmed, and his confidence in
his own opinions increased, his mind has also become
more sensitive; and his misanthropy, thus softened over 20
by habits of calmer contemplation, appears less active
and impatient, even although more deeply rooted than
before. Undoubtedly the finest parts of the poem before
us, are those which thus embody the weight of his moral
sentiments; or disclose the lofty sympathy which binds 25
the despiser of Man to the glorious aspects of Nature.
It is in these, we think, that the great attractions of the
work consist, and the strength of the author's genius is
seen. The narrative and mere description are of far
inferior interest. With reference to the sentiments and 30
opinions, however, which thus give its distinguishing
character to the piece, we must say, that it seems no
longer possible to ascribe them to the ideal person whose
name it bears, or to any other than the author himself. —

Lord Byron, we think, has formerly complained of those
who identified him with his hero, or supposed that Harold
was but the expositor of his own feelings and opinions;
— and in noticing the former portions of the work, we
5 thought it unbecoming to give any countenance to such
a supposition. — In this last part, however, it is really
impracticable to distinguish them. — Not only do the
author and his hero travel and reflect together, — but, in
truth, we scarcely ever have any distinct intimation to
10 which of them the sentiments so energetically expressed
are to be ascribed; and in those which are unequivocally
given as those of the noble author himself, there is the
very same tone of misanthropy, sadness, and scorn, which
we were formerly willing to regard as a part of the
15 assumed costume of the Childe. We are far from supposing, indeed, that Lord Byron would disavow any of
these sentiments; and though there are some which we
must ever think it most unfortunate to entertain, and
others which it appears improper to have published; the
20 greater part are admirable, and cannot be perused without emotion, even by those to whom they may appear
erroneous.

THE EXCURSION.

*Being a Portion of the Recluse, a Poem. By William Wordsworth.
4to, pp. 447.   London, 1814.*[1]

THIS will never do ! It bears no doubt the stamp of
the author's heart and fancy :   But unfortunately not half
so visibly as that of his peculiar system.   His former

[1] I have spoken in many places rather too bitterly and confidently
of the faults of Mr. Wordsworth's poetry : And forgetting that,
even on my own view of them, they were but faults of taste, or
venial self-partiality, have sometimes visited them, I fear, with an
asperity which should be reserved for objects of Moral reprobation.
If I were now to deal with the whole question of his poetical merits,
though my judgment might not be substantially different, I hope I
should repress the greater part of these *vivacités* of expression : and
indeed so strong has been my feeling in this way, that, considering
how much I have always loved many of the attributes of his Genius,
and how entirely I respect his Character, it did at first occur to me
whether it was quite fitting that, in my old age and his, I should
include in this publication any of those critiques which may have
formerly given pain or offence, to him or his admirers.   But, when
I reflected that the mischief, if there really ever was any, was long
ago done, and that I still retain, in substance, the opinions which I
should now like to have seen more gently expressed, I felt that to
omit all notice of them on the present occasion, might be held to
import a retractation which I am as far as possible from intending ;
or even be represented as a very shabby way of backing out of
sentiments which should either be manfully persisted in, or openly
renounced, and abandoned as untenable.
  I finally resolved, therefore, to reprint my review of " The Excursion " ; which contains a pretty full view of my griefs and charges
against Mr. Wordsworth ; set forth too, I believe, in a more

poems were intended to recommend that system, and to
bespeak favour for it by their individual merit ; — but
this, we suspect, must be recommended by the system —
and can only expect to succeed where it has been
5 previously established.   It is longer, weaker, and tamer, ⎰

temperate strain than most of my other inculpations, — and of
which I think I may now venture to say farther that if the faults are
unsparingly noted, the beauties are not penuriously or grudgingly
allowed ; but commended to the admiration of the reader with at
least as much heartiness and good-will.

But I have also reprinted a short paper on the same author's
" White Doe of Rylstone," — in which there certainly is no praise,
or notice of beauties, to set against the very unqualified censures of
which it is wholly made up.   I have done this, however, not merely
because I adhere to these censures, but chiefly because it seemed
necessary to bring me fairly to issue with those who may not concur
in them.   I can easily understand that many whose admiration of the
Excursion, or the Lyrical Ballads, rests substantially on the passages
which I too should join in admiring, may view with greater indul·
gence than I can do, the tedious and flat passages with which they
are interspersed, and may consequently think my censure of these
works a great deal too harsh and uncharitable.   Between such
persons and me, therefore, there may be no radical difference of
opinion, or contrariety as to principles of judgment.   But if there
be any who actually admire this White Doe of Rylstone, or Peter
Bell the Waggoner, or the Lamentations of Martha Rae, or the
Sonnets on the Punishment of Death, there can be no such
ambiguity, or means of reconcilement.   Now I have been assured
not only that there are such persons, but that almost all those who
seek to exalt Mr. Wordsworth as the founder of a new school of
poetry, consider these as by far his best and most characteristic
productions ; and would at once reject from their communion
any one who did not acknowledge in them the traces of a high
inspiration.   Now I wish it to be understood, that when I speak with
general intolerance or impatience of the school of Mr. Wordsworth,
it is to the school holding these tenets, and applying these tests,
that I refer : and I really do not see how I could better explain the
grounds of my dissent from their doctrines, than by republishing my
remarks on this " White Doe."

than any of Mr. Wordsworth's other productions ; with less boldness of originality, and less even of that extreme simplicity and lowliness of tone which wavered so prettily, in the Lyrical Ballads, between silliness and pathos. We have imitations of Cowper, and even of 5 Milton here ; engrafted on the natural drawl of the Lakers — and all diluted into harmony by that profuse and irrepressible wordiness which deluges all the blank verse of this school of poetry, and lubricates and weakens the whole structure of their style. 10

Though it fairly fills four hundred and twenty good quarto pages, without note, vignette, or any sort of extraneous assistance, it is stated in the title — with something of an imprudent candour — to be but "a portion" of a larger work ; and in the preface, where an 15 attempt is rather unsuccessfully made to explain the whole design, it is still more rashly disclosed, that it is . but "*a part of the second part*, of a *long* and laborious work " — which is to consist of three parts !

What Mr. Wordsworth's ideas of length are, we have 20 no means of accurately judging : But we cannot help suspecting that they are liberal, to a degree that will alarm the weakness of most modern readers. As far as we can gather from the preface, the entire poem — or one of them (for we really are not sure whether there is to 25 be one or two) is of a biographical nature ; and is to contain the history of the author's mind, and of the origin and progress of his poetical powers, up to the period when they were sufficiently matured to qualify him for the great work on which he has been so long 30 employed. Now, the quarto before us contains an account of one of his youthful rambles in the vales of Cumberland, and occupies precisely the period of three days ! So that, by the use of a very powerful *calculus*,

some estimate may be formed of the probable extent
of the entire biography.

This small specimen, however, and the statements with
which it is prefaced, have been sufficient to set our minds
at rest in one particular.   The case of Mr. Wordsworth,
we perceive, is now manifestly hopeless ; and we give
him up as altogether incurable, and beyond the power of
criticism.   We cannot indeed altogether omit taking
precautions now and then against the spreading of the
10 malady ;— but for himself, though we shall watch the
progress of his symptoms as a matter of professional
curiosity and instruction, we really think it right not to
harass him any longer with nauseous remedies, — but
rather to throw in cordials and lenitives, and wait in
15 patience for the natural termination of the disorder.   In
order to justify this desertion of our patient, however, it
is proper to state why we despair of the success of a
more active practice.

A man who has been for twenty years at work on such
20 matter as is now before us, and who comes complacently
forward with a whole quarto of it, after all the admonitions
he has received, cannot reasonably be expected to "change
his hand, or check his pride," upon the suggestion of far
weightier monitors than we can pretend to be.   Inveterate
25 habits must now have given a kind of sanctity to the
errors of early taste ; and the very powers of which we
lament the perversion, have probably become incapable
of any other application.   The very quantity, too, that
he has written, and is at this moment working up for
30 publication upon the old pattern, makes it almost hopeless
to look for any change of it.   All this is so much
capital already sunk in the concern ; which must be
sacrificed if that be abandoned ; and no man likes to give
up for lost the time and talent and labour which he has

embodied in any permanent production. We were not
previously aware of these obstacles to Mr. Wordsworth's
conversion ; and, considering the peculiarities of his
former writings merely as the result of certain wanton
and capricious experiments on public taste and indul- 5
gence, conceived it to be our duty to discourage their
repetition by all the means in our power. We now see
clearly, however, how the case stands ; — and, making
up our minds, though with the most sincere pain and
reluctance, to consider him as finally lost to the good 10
cause of poetry, shall endeavour to be thankful for the
occasional gleams of tenderness and beauty which the
natural force of his imagination and affections must still
shed over all his productions, — and to which we shall
ever turn with delight, in spite of the affectation and 15
mysticism and prolixity, with which they are so abundantly
contrasted.

Long habits of seclusion, and an excessive ambition of
originality, can alone account for the disproportion which
seems to exist between this author's taste and his genius ; 20
or for the devotion with which he has sacrificed so many
precious gifts at the shrine of those paltry idols which he
has set up for himself among his lakes and his mountains.
Solitary musings, amidst such scenes, might no doubt be
expected to nurse up the mind to the majesty of poetical 25
conception, — (though it is remarkable, that all the
greater poets lived, or had lived, in the full current of
society) : — But the collision of equal minds, — the
admonition of prevailing impressions — seems necessary
to reduce its redundancies, and repress that tendency to 30
extravagance or puerility, into which the self-indulgence
and self-admiration of genius is so apt to be betrayed,
when it is allowed to wanton, without awe or restraint, in
the triumph and delight of its own intoxication. That

its flights should be graceful and glorious in the eyes of
men, it seems almost to be necessary that they should be
made in the consciousness that men's eyes are to behold
them, — and that the inward transport and vigour by
5 which they are inspired, should be tempered by an
occasional reference to what will be thought of them by
those ultimate dispensers of glory. An habitual and
general knowledge of the few settled and permanent
maxims, which form the canon of general taste in all
10 large and polished societies — a certain tact, which
informs us at once that many things, which we still love,
and are moved by in secret, must necessarily be despised
as childish, or derided as absurd, in all such societies —
though it will not stand in the place of genius, seems
15 necessary to the success of its exertions ; and though it
will never enable any one to produce the higher beauties
of art, can alone secure the talent which does produce
them from errors that must render it useless. Those who
have most of the talent, however, commonly acquire this
20 knowledge with the greatest facility ; — and if Mr.
Wordsworth, instead of confining himself almost entirely
to the society of the dalesmen and cottagers, and little
children, who form the subjects of his book, had condescended to mingle a little more with the people that were
25 to read and judge of it, we cannot help thinking that its
texture might have been considerably improved : At
least it appears to us to be absolutely impossible, that
any one who had lived or mixed familiarly with men of
literature and ordinary judgment in poetry (of course
30 we exclude the coadjutors and disciples of his own
school) could ever have fallen into such gross faults, or
so long mistaken them for beauties. His first essays we
looked upon in a good degree as poetical paradoxes, —
maintained experimentally, in order to display talent, and

court notoriety ; — and so maintained, with no more
serious belief in their truth, than is usually generated by
an ingenious and animated defence of other paradoxes.
But when we find that he has been for twenty years
exclusively employed upon articles of this very fabric, 5
and that he has still enough of raw material on hand to
keep him so employed for twenty years to come, we cannot
refuse him the justice of believing that he is a sincere
convert to his own system, and must ascribe the peculiarities of his composition, not to any transient affectation, 10
or accidental caprice of imagination, but to a settled
perversity of taste or understanding, which has been
fostered, if not altogether created by the circumstances
to which we have alluded.

The volume before us, if we were to describe it very 15
shortly, we should characterise as a tissue of moral and
devotional ravings, in which innumerable changes are
rung upon a very few simple and familiar ideas : — But
with such an accompaniment of long words, long sen-
tences, and unwieldy phrases — and such a hubbub of 20
strained raptures and fantastical sublimities, that it is
often difficult for the most skilful and attentive student
to obtain a glimpse of the author's meaning — and altogether impossible for an ordinary reader to conjecture
what he is about. Moral and religious enthusiasm, 25
though undoubtedly poetical emotions, are at the same
time but dangerous inspirers of poetry ; nothing being so
apt to run into interminable dulness or mellifluous extravagance, without giving the unfortunate author the
slightest intimation of his danger. His laudable zeal for 30
the efficacy of his preachments, he very naturally mistakes
for the ardour of poetical inspiration ; — and, while dealing out the high words and glowing phrases which are
so readily supplied by themes of this description, can

scarcely avoid believing that he is eminently original and impressive : — All sorts of commonplace notions and expressions are sanctified in his eyes, by the sublime ends for which they are employed ; and the mystical verbiage
5 of the Methodist pulpit is repeated, till the speaker entertains no doubt that he is the chosen organ of divine truth and persuasion. But if such be the common hazards of seeking inspiration from those potent fountains, it may easily be conceived what chance Mr. Wordsworth had of
10 escaping their enchantment, — with his natural propensities to wordiness, and his unlucky habit of debasing pathos with vulgarity. The fact accordingly is, that in this production he is more obscure than a Pindaric poet of the seventeenth century ; and more verbose " than
15 even himself of yore " ; while the wilfulness with which he persists in choosing his examples of intellectual dignity and tenderness exclusively from the lowest ranks of society, will be sufficiently apparent, from the circumstance of his having thought fit to make his chief pro-
20 locutor in this poetical dialogue, and chief advocate of Providence and Virtue, *an old Scotch Pedlar* — retired indeed from business — but still rambling about in his former haunts, and gossiping among his old customers, without his pack on his shoulders. The other persons of
25 the drama are, a retired military chaplain, who has grown half an atheist and half a misanthrope — the wife of an unprosperous weaver — a servant girl with her natural child — a parish pauper, and one or two other personages of equal rank and dignity.
30 The character of the work is decidedly didactic ; and more than nine tenths of it are occupied with a species of dialogue, or rather a series of long sermons or harangues which pass between the pedlar, the author, the old chaplain, and a worthy vicar, who entertains the whole party

at dinner on the last day of their excursion. The incidents which occur in the course of it are as few and trifling
as can well be imagined ; — and those which the different
speakers narrate in the course of their discourses, are
introduced rather to illustrate their arguments or opinions, 5
than for any interest they are supposed to possess of
their own. — The doctrine which the work is intended to
enforce, we are by no means certain that we have discovered. In so far as we can collect, however, it seems
to be neither more nor less than the old familiar one, 10
that a firm belief in the providence of a wise and benefi-
cent Being must be our great stay and support under all
afflictions and perplexities upon earth — and· that there
are indications of his power and goodness in all the
aspects of the visible universe, whether living or inan- 15
imate — every part of which should therefore be regarded
with love and reverence, as exponents of those great
attributes. We can testify, at least, that these salutary
and important truths are inculcated at far greater length,
and with more repetitions, than in any ten volumes of 20
sermons that we ever perused. It is also maintained,
with equal conciseness and originality, that there is frequently much good sense, as well as much enjoyment, in
the humbler conditions of life ; and that, in spite of great
vices and abuses, there is a reasonable allowance both of 25
happiness and goodness in society at large. If there be
any deeper or more recondite doctrines in Mr. Wordsworth's book, we must confess that they have escaped
us ; — and, convinced as we are of the truth and sound-
ness of those to which we have alluded, we cannot help 30
thinking that they might have been better enforced with
less parade and prolixity. His effusions on what may be
called the physiognomy of external nature, or its moral
and theological expression, are eminently fantastic,

obscure, and affected. — It is quite time, however, that we should give the reader a more particular account of this singular performance.

* * *

5   Our abstract of the story has been so extremely concise that it is more than usually necessary for us to lay some specimens of the work itself before our readers. Its grand staple, as we have already said, consists of a kind of mystical morality: and the chief characteristics of the 10 style are, that it is prolix, and very frequently unintelligible : and though we are sensible that no great gratification is to be expected from the exhibition of those qualities, yet it is necessary to give our readers a taste of them, both to justify the sentence we have passed, 15 and to satisfy them that it was really beyond our power to present them with any abstract or intelligible account of those long conversations which we have had so much occasion to notice in our brief sketch of its contents. We need give ourselves no trouble, however, to select 20 passages for this purpose. Here is the first that presents itself to us on opening the volume ; and if our readers can form the slightest guess at its meaning, we must give them credit for a sagacity to which we have no pretension.

25   "But by the storms *of circumstance* unshaken,
          And subject neither to eclipse or wane,
          Duty exists ; — immutably survive,
          For our support, the measures and the forms,
          Which an abstract Intelligence supplies ;
30   Whose kingdom is, where Time and Space are not :
          Of other converse, which mind, soul, and heart,
          Do, with united urgency, require,
          What more, that may not perish ? "

          " 'T is, by comparison, an easy task
35   Earth to despise ; but to converse with Heav'n,

This is not easy : — to relinquish all
We have, or hope, of happiness and joy, —
And stand in freedom loosen'd from this world ;
I deem not arduous ! — but must needs confess
That 't is a thing impossible to frame   5
Conceptions equal to the Soul's desires."— pp. 144-147.

This is a fair sample of that rapturous mysticism which
eludes all comprehension, and fills the despairing reader
with painful giddiness and terror.   The following, which
we meet with on the very next page, is in the same 10
general strain : — though the first part of it affords a
good specimen of the author's talent for enveloping a
plain and trite observation in all the mock majesty of
solemn verbosity.   A reader of plain understanding, we
suspect, could hardly recognize the familiar remark, that 15
excessive grief for our departed friends is not very consistent with a firm belief in their immortal felicity, in
the first twenty lines of the following passage : — In the
succeeding lines we do not ourselves pretend to recognize
anything.   20

*   *   *

These examples, we perceive, are not very well chosen
— but we have not leisure to improve the selection; and,
such as they are, they may serve to give the reader a
notion of the sort of merit which we meant to illustrate 25
by their citation.   When we look back to them, indeed,
and to the other passages which we have now extracted,
we feel half inclined to rescind the severe sentence which
we passed on the work at the beginning : — But when we
look into the work itself, we perceive that it cannot be 30
rescinded.   Nobody can be more disposed to do justice
to the great powers of Mr. Wordsworth than we are ;
and, from the first time that he came before us, down
to the present moment, we have uniformly testified in

their favour, and assigned indeed our high sense of their value as the chief ground of the bitterness with which we resented their perversion. That perversion, however, is now far more visible than their original dignity; and
5 while we collect the fragments, it is impossible not to mourn over the ruins from which we are condemned to pick them. If any one should doubt of the existence of such a perversion, or be disposed to dispute about the instances we have hastily brought forward, we would just
10 beg leave to refer him to the general plan and character of the poem now before us. Why should Mr. Wordsworth have made his hero a superannuated pedlar? What but the most wretched affectation, or provoking perversity of taste, could induce any one to place his chosen advocate
15 of wisdom and virtue in so absurd and fantastic a condition? Did Mr. Wordsworth really imagine that his favorite doctrines were likely to gain anything in point of effect or authority by being put into the mouth of a person accustomed to higgle about tape or brass sleeve-
20 buttons? Or is it not plain that, independent of the ridicule and disgust which such a personification must excite in many of his readers, its adoption exposes his work throughout to the charge of revolting incongruity and utter disregard of probability or nature? For, after
25 he has thus wilfully debased his moral teacher by a low occupation, is there one word that he puts into his mouth, or one sentiment of which he makes him the organ, that has the most remote reference to that occupation? Is there anything in his learned, abstract and logical
30 harangues that savours of the calling that is ascribed to him? Are any of their materials such as a pedlar could possibly have dealt in? Are the manners, the diction, the sentiments in any, the very smallest degree, accommodated to a person in that condition? or are they not

eminently and conspicuously such as could not by possibility belong to it ? A man who went about selling
flannel and pocket-handkerchiefs in this lofty diction
would soon frighten away all his customers; and would
infallibly pass either for a madman or for some learned 5
and affected gentleman, who, in a frolic, had taken up
a character which he was peculiarly ill qualified for
supporting.

The absurdity in this case, we think, is palpable and
glaring : but it is exactly of the same nature with that 10
which infects the whole substance of the work — a puerile
ambition of singularity engrafted on an unlucky predilection for truisms ; and an affected passion for simplicity
and humble life, most awkwardly combined with a taste
for mystical refinements, and all the gorgeousness of 15
obscure phraseology,   His taste for simplicity is evinced
by sprinkling up and down his interminable declamations
a few descriptions of baby-houses, and of old hats with
wet brims ; and his amiable partiality for humble life,
by assuring us that a wordy rhetorician, who talks about 20
Thebes, and allegorizes all the heathen mythology, was
once a pedlar — and making him break in upon his
magnificent orations with two or three awkward notices
of something that he had seen when selling winter raiment
about the country — or of the changes in the state of 25
society, which had almost annihilated his former calling.

THE WHITE DOE OF RYLSTONE,

OR THE FATE OF THE NORTONS.

A Poem. By William Wordsworth. 4to, pp. 162. London, 1815.

THIS, we think, has the merit of being the very worst poem we ever saw imprinted in a quarto volume ; and though it was scarcely to be expected, we confess, that Mr. Wordsworth, with all his ambition, should so soon
5 have attained to that distinction, the wonder may perhaps be diminished when we state that it seems to us to consist of a happy union of all the faults, without any of the beauties, which belong to his school of poetry. It is just such a work, in short, as some wicked enemy of
10 that school might be supposed to have devised, on purpose to make it ridiculous ; and when we first took it up we could not help suspecting that some ill-natured critic had actually taken this harsh method of instructing Mr. Wordsworth, by example, in the nature of those errors, against
15 which our precepts had been so often directed in vain. We had not gone far, however, till we felt intimately that nothing in the nature of a joke could be so insupportably dull ; — and that this must be the work of one who earnestly believed it to be a pattern of pathetic simplicity,
20 and gave it out as such to the admiration of all intelligent readers. In this point of view the work may be regarded as curious at least, if not in some degree interesting ; and, at all events, it must be instructive to be made aware of the excesses into which superior understand-
25 ings may be betrayed, by long self-indulgence, and the

strange extravagances into which they may run, when
under the influence of that intoxication which is produced
by unrestrained admiration of themselves. This poetical
intoxication, indeed, to pursue the figure a little farther,
seems capable of assuming as many forms as the vulgar 5
one which arises from wine ; and it appears to require as
delicate·a management to make a man a good poet by
the help of the. one as to make him a good companion
by means of the other. In both cases, a little mistake
as to the dose or the quality of the inspiring fluid may 10
make him absolutely outrageous, or lull him over into
the most profound stupidity, instead of brightening up
the hidden stores of his genius : and truly we are concerned to say that Mr. Wordsworth seems hitherto to
have been unlucky in the choice of his liquor — or of 15
his bottle-holder. In some of his odes and ethic exhor-
tations he was exposed to the public in a state of inco-
herent rapture and glorious delirium, to which we think
we have seen a parallel among the humbler lovers of
jollity. In the Lyrical Ballads he was exhibited, on the 20
whole, in a vein of very pretty deliration; but in the
poem before us he appears in a state of low and maudlin
imbecility, which would not have misbecome Master
Silence himself, in the close of a social day. Whether
this unhappy result is to be ascribed to any adulteration 25
of his Castalian cups, or to the unlucky choice of his
company over them, we cannot presume to say. It may
be that he has dashed his Hippocrene with too large
an infusion of lake water, or assisted its operation too
exclusively by the study of the ancient historical ballads 30
of "the north countrie." That there are palpable imitations of the style and manner of those venerable compositions in the work before us is indeed undeniable;
but it unfortunately happens that while the hobbling

versification, the mean diction and flat stupidity of these models are very exactly copied, and even improved upon, in this imitation, their rude energy, manly simplicity, and occasional felicity of expression have totally disappeared; 5 and, instead of them, a large allowance of the author's own metaphysical sensibility, and mystical wordiness is forced into an unnatural combination with the borrowed beauties which have just been mentioned.

TALES OF FASHIONABLE LIFE.

By Miss Edgeworth, Author of " Practical Education," " Belinda,"
" Castle Rackrent," etc. 12mo. 3 vols. London, 1809.

IF it were possible for reviewers to *Envy* the authors
who are brought before them for judgment, we rather
think we should be tempted to envy Miss Edgeworth ; —
not, however, so much for her matchless powers of
probable invention — her never-failing good sense and 5
cheerfulness — nor her fine discrimination of characters
— as for the delightful consciousness of having done
more good than any other writer, male or female, of her
generation.   Other arts and sciences have their use, no
doubt ; and, Heaven knows, they have their reward and 10
their fame.   But the great art is the art of living ; and
the chief science the science of being happy.   Where
there is an absolute deficiency of good sense, these
cannot indeed be taught ; and, with an extraordinary
share of it, they may be acquired without an instructor : 15
but the most common case is, to be capable of learning,
and yet to require teaching ; and a far greater part of
the misery which exists in society arises from ignorance, ·
than either from vice or from incapacity.

   Miss Edgeworth is the great modern mistress in this 20
school of true philosophy ; and has eclipsed, we think,
the fame of all her predecessors.   By her many excellent
tracts on education, she has conferred a benefit on the
whole mass of the population ; and discharged, with
exemplary patience as well as extraordinary judgment, a 25
task which superficial spirits may perhaps mistake for an

humble and easy one. By her Popular Tales, she has
rendered an invaluable service to the middling and lower
orders of the people ; and by her Novels, and by the
volumes before us, has made a great and meritorious
5 effort to promote the happiness and respectability of the
higher classes. On a former occasion we believe we
hinted to her, that these would probably be the least
successful of all her labours ; and that it was doubtful
whether she could be justified for bestowing so much of
10 her time on the case of a few persons, who scarcely
deserved to be cured, and were scarcely capable of being
corrected. The foolish and unhappy part of the fashionable world, for the most part, "is not fit to hear itself
convinced." It is too vain, too busy, and too dissipated
15 to listen to, or remember any thing that is said to it.
Every thing serious it repels, by "its dear wit and gay
rhetoric"; and against every thing poignant, it seeks
shelter in the impenetrable armour of its conjunct audacity.

20   "Laugh'd at, it laughs again ; — and, stricken hard,
        Turns to the stroke its adamantine scales,
        That fear no discipline of human hands."

A book, on the other hand, and especially a witty and
popular book, is still a thing of consequence, to such of
25 the middling classes of society as are in the habit of
· reading. They dispute about it, and think of it ; and as
they occasionally make themselves ridiculous by copying
the manners it displays, so they are apt to be impressed
with the great lessons it may be calculated to teach ;
30 and, on the whole, receive it into considerable authority
among the regulators of their lives and opinions. — But a
fashionable person has scarcely any leisure to read ; and
none to think of what he has been reading. It would be
a derogation from his dignity to speak of a book in any

terms but those of frivolous derision ; and a strange desertion of his own superiority, to allow himself to receive, from its perusal, any impressions which could at all affect his conduct or opinions.

But though, for these reasons, we continue to think that Miss Edgeworth's fashionable patients will do less credit to her prescriptions than the more numerous classes to whom they might have been directed, we admit that her plan of treatment is in the highest degree judicious, and her conception of the disorder most luminous and precise.

There are two great sources of unhappiness to those whom fortune and nature seem to have placed above the reach of ordinary miseries. The one is *ennui* — that stagnation of life and feeling which results from the absence of all motives to exertion ; and by which the justice of providence has so fully compensated the partiality of fortune, that it may be fairly doubted whether, upon the whole, the race of beggars is not happier than the race of lords ; and whether those vulgar wants that are sometimes so importunate, are not, in this world, the chief ministers of enjoyment.   This is a plague that infects all indolent persons who can live on in the rank in which they were born, without the necessity of working : but, in a free country, it rarely occurs in any great degree of virulence, except among those who are already at the summit of human felicity.   Below this, there is room for ambition, and envy, and emulation, and all the feverish movements of aspiring vanity and unresting selfishness, which act as prophylactics against this more dark and deadly distemper.   It is the canker which corrodes the full-blown flower of human felicity — the pestilence which smites at the bright hour of noon.

The other curse of the happy, has a range more wide
and indiscriminate. It, too, tortures only the comparatively rich and fortunate ; but is most active among the
least distinguished ; and abates in malignity as we ascend
5 to the lofty regions of pure *ennui.* This is the desire of
being fashionable ;— the restless and insatiable passion
to pass for creatures a little more distinguished than we
really are — with the mortification of frequent failure,
and the humiliating consciousness of being perpetually
10 exposed to it. Among those who are secure of " meat,
clothes, and fire," and are thus above the chief physical
evils of existence, we do believe that this is a more
prolific source of unhappiness, than guilt, disease, or
wounded affection ; and that more positive misery is
15 created, and more true enjoyment excluded, by the
eternal fretting and straining of this pitiful ambition, than
by all the ravages of passion, the desolations of war, or
the accidents of mortality. This may appear a strong
statement ; but we make it deliberately, and are deeply
20 convinced of its truth. The wretchedness which it produces may not be so intense ; but it is of much longer
duration, and spreads over a far wider circle. It is quite
dreadful, indeed, to think what a sweep this pest has
taken among the comforts of our prosperous population.
25 To be thought fashionable — that is, to be thought
more opulent and tasteful, and on a footing of intimacy
with a greater number of distinguished persons than
they really are, is the great and laborious pursuit of
four families out of five, the members of which are
30 exempted from the necessity of daily industry. In this
pursuit, their time, spirits, and talents are wasted ; their
tempers, soured ; their affections palsied ; and their
natural manners and dispositions altogether sophisticated
and lost.

These are the giant curses of fashionable life, and Miss Edgeworth has accordingly dedicated her two best tales to the delineation of their symptoms. The history of " Lord Glenthorn " is a fine picture of *ennui* — that of " Almeria " an instructive representation of the miseries of aspirations after fashion. We do not know whether it was a part of the fair writer's *design* to represent these maladies as absolutely incurable, without a change of condition ; but *the fact* is, that in spite of the best dispositions and capacities, and the most powerful inducements to action, the hero of *ennui* makes no advances towards amendment, till he is deprived of his title and estate ! and the victim of fashion is left, at the end of the tale, pursuing her weary career, with fading hopes and wasted spirits, but with increased anxiety and perseverance. The moral use of these narratives, therefore, must consist in warning us against the first approaches of evils which can never afterwards be resisted.

WAVERLEY, OR 'TIS SIXTY YEARS SINCE.

In three volumes 12mo, pp. 1112. Third edition. Edinburgh, 1814.

IT is wonderful what genius and adherence to nature will do, in spite of all disadvantages. Here is a thing obviously very hastily, and, in many places, somewhat unskilfully written — composed, one half of it, in a
5 dialect unintelligible to four-fifths of the reading population of the country — relating to a period too recent to

---

* I have been a good deal at a loss what to do with these famous novels of Sir Walter. On the one hand, I could not bring myself to let this collection go forth, without *some* notice of works which, for many years together, had occupied and delighted me more than anything else that ever came under my critical survey : While, on the other, I could not but feel that it would be absurd, and in some sense almost dishonest, to fill these pages with long citations from books which, for the last twenty-five years, have been in the hands of at least fifty times as many readers as are ever likely to look into this publication — and are still as familiar to the generation which has last come into existence, as to those who can yet remember the sensation produced by their first appearance. In point of fact I was informed, but the other day, by Mr. Cadell, that he had actually sold not less than *sixty thousand volumes* of these extraordinary productions, in the course of the preceding year ! and that the demand for them, instead of slackening — had been for some time sensibly on the increase. In these circumstances I think I may safely assume that their contents are still so perfectly known as not to require any citations to introduce such of the remarks originally made on them as I may now wish to repeat. And I have therefore come to the determination of omitting almost all the quotations, and most of the detailed abstracts which appeared in the original

be romantic, and too far gone by to be familiar — and published, moreover, in a quarter of the island where materials and talents for novel-writing have been supposed to be equally wanting: And yet, by the mere force and truth and vivacity of its colouring, already casting 5 the whole tribe of ordinary novels into the shade, and taking its place rather with the most popular of our modern poems, than with the rubbish of provincial romances.

The secret of this success, we take it, is merely that 10 the author is a man of Genius; and that he has, notwithstanding, had virtue enough to be true to Nature throughout; and to content himself, even in the marvellous parts of his story, with copying from actual existences, rather than from the phantasms of his own imagination. The 15 charm which this communicates to all works that deal in

reviews; and to retain only the general criticism, and character, or estimate of each performance — together with such incidental observations as may have been suggested by the tenor or success of these wonderful productions. By this course, no doubt, a sad shrinking will be effected in the primitive dimensions of the articles which are here reproduced; and may probably give to what is retained something of a naked and jejune appearance. If it should be so, I can only say that I do not see how I could have helped it: and after all it may not be altogether without interest to see, from a contemporary record, what were the first impressions produced by the appearance of this new luminary on our horizon; while the secret of the authorship was yet undivulged, and before the rapid accumulation of its glories had forced on the dullest spectator a sense of its magnitude and power. I may venture perhaps also to add, that some of the general speculations of which these reviews suggested the occasion, may probably be found as well worth preserving as most of those which have been elsewhere embodied in this experimental, and somewhat hazardous, publication.

Though living in familiar intercourse with Sir Walter, I need scarcely say that I was not in the secret of his authorship; and in truth had no assurance of the fact, till the time of its promulgation.

the representation of human actions and character, is more readily felt than understood; and operates with unfailing efficacy even upon those who have no acquaintance with the originals from which the picture has been
5 borrowed. It requires no ordinary talent, indeed, to choose such realities as may outshine the bright imaginations of the inventive, and so to combine them as to produce the most advantageous effect; but when this is once accomplished, the result is sure to be something
10 more firm, impressive, and engaging, than can ever be produced by mere fiction.

The object of the work before us, was evidently to present a faithful and animated picture of the manners and state of society that prevailed in this northern part
15 of the island, in the earlier part of last century; and the author has judiciously fixed upon the era of the Rebellion in 1745, not only as enriching his pages with the interest inseparably attached to the narration of such occurrences, but as affording a fair opportunity for bringing out all the
20 contrasted principles and habits which distinguished the different classes of persons who then divided the country, and formed among them the basis of almost all that was peculiar in the national character. That unfortunate contention brought conspicuously to light, and, for the
25 last time, the fading image of feudal chivalry in the mountains, and vulgar fanaticism in the plains; and startled the more polished parts of the land with the wild but brilliant picture of the devoted valour, incorruptible fidelity, patriarchal brotherhood, and savage habits of the
30 Celtic Clans, on the one hand, — and the dark, intractable, and domineering bigotry of the Covenanters on the other. Both aspects of society had indeed been formerly prevalent in other parts of the country, — but had there been so long superseded by more peaceable habits, and

milder manners, that their vestiges were almost effaced, and their very memory nearly extinguished. The feudal principalities had been destroyed in the South, for near three hundred years, — and the dominion of the Puritans from the time of the Restoration. When the glens, and 5 banded clans, of the central Highlands, therefore, were opened up to the gaze of the English, in the course of that insurrection, it seemed as if they were carried back to the days of the Heptarchy; — and when they saw the array of the West country Whigs, they might imagine 10 themselves transported to the age of Cromwell. The effect, indeed, is almost as startling at the present moment; and one great source of the interest which the volumes before us undoubtedly possess, is to be sought in the surprise that is excited by discovering, that in our 15 own country, and almost in our own age, manners and characters existed, and were conspicuous, which we had been accustomed to consider as belonging to remote antiquity, or extravagant romance.

The way in which they are here represented must 20 satisfy every reader, we think, by an inward *tact* and conviction, that the delineation has been made from actual experience and observation ; — experience and observation employed perhaps only on a few surviving relics and specimens of what was familiar a little earlier 25 — but generalised from instances sufficiently numerous and complete, to warrant all that may have been added to the portrait : — And, indeed, the existing records and vestiges of the more extraordinary parts of the representation are still sufficiently abundant, to satisfy all who 30 have the means of consulting them, as to the perfect accuracy of the picture. The great traits of Clannish dependence, pride, and fidelity, may still be detected in many districts of the Highlands, though they do not now

adhere to the chieftains when they mingle in general
society; and the existing contentions of Burghers and
Antiburghers, and Cameronians, though shrunk into comparative insignificance, and left, indeed, without protec-
5 tion to the ridicule of the profane, may still be referred
to, as complete verifications of all that is here stated
about Gifted Gilfillan, or Ebenezer Cruickshank. The
traits of Scottish national character in the lower ranks,
can still less be regarded as antiquated or traditional;
10 nor is there any thing in the whole compass of the work
which gives us a stronger impression of the nice observation and graphical talent of the author, than the extraordinary fidelity and felicity with which all the inferior
agents in the story are represented. No one who has not
15 lived extensively among the lower orders of all descriptions, and made himself familiar with their various tempers and dialects, can perceive the full merit of those
rapid and characteristic sketches; but it requires only a
general knowledge of human nature, to feel that they
20 must be faithful copies from known originals; and to be
aware of the extraordinary facility and flexibility of hand
which has touched, for instance, with such discriminating
shades, the various gradations of the Celtic character,
from the savage imperturbability of Dugald Mahony, who
25 stalks grimly about with his battle-axe on his shoulder,
without speaking a word to any one, — to the lively un-
principled activity of Callum Beg, — the coarse unreflect-
ing hardihood and heroism of Evan Maccombich, — and
the pride, gallantry, elegance, and ambition of Fergus
30 himself. In the lower class of the Lowland characters,
again, the vulgarity of Mrs. Flockhart and of Lieutenant
Jinker is perfectly distinct and original; — as well as the
puritanism of Gilfillan and Cruickshank — the atrocity of
Mrs. Mucklewrath — and the slow solemnity of Alexander

Saunderson. The Baron of Bradwardine, and Baillie Macwheeble, are caricatures no doubt, after the fashion of the caricatures in the novels of Smollett,— or pictures, at the best, of individuals who must always have been unique and extraordinary : but almost all the other per- 5 sonages in the history are fair representatives of classes that are still existing, or may be remembered at least to have existed, by many whose recollections do not extend quite so far back as to the year 1745.

* * *   10

There has been much speculation, at least in this quarter of the island, about the authorship of this singular performance — and certainly it is not easy to conjecture why it is still anonymous. — Judging by internal evidence, to which alone we pretend to have access, we should not 15 scruple to ascribe it to the highest of those authors to whom it has been assigned by the sagacious conjectures of the public ; — and this at least we will venture to say that if it be indeed the work of an author hitherto unknown, Mr. Scott would do well to look to his laurels, 20 and to rouse himself for a sturdier competition than any he has yet had to encounter !

TALES OF MY LANDLORD.

Collected and arranged by Jedediah Cleishbotham, Schoolmaster and Parish Clerk of the Parish of Gandercleugh. 4 vols. 12mo. Edinburgh, 1816.

THIS, we think, is beyond all question a new coinage from the mint which produced Waverley, Guy Mannering, and the Antiquary : — For though it does not bear the legend and superscription of the Master on the face
5 of the pieces, there is no mistaking either the quality of the metal or the execution of the die — and even the private mark, we doubt not, may be seen plain enough, by those who know how to look for it. It is quite impossible to read ten pages of this work, in short,
10 without feeling that it belongs to the same school with those very remarkable productions ; and no one who has any knowledge of nature, or of art, will ever doubt that it is an original. The very identity of the leading characters in the whole set of stories, is a stronger proof,
15 perhaps, that those of the last series are *not* copied from the former, than even the freshness and freedom of the draperies with which they are now invested — or the ease and spirit of the new groups into which they are here combined. No imitator would have ventured so near his
20 originals, and yet come off so entirely clear of them : And we are only the more assured that the old acquaintances we continually recognise in these volumes, are really the persons they pretend to be, and no false mimics, that we recollect so perfectly to have seen them

before, — or at least to have been familiar with some of
their near relations !

We have often been astonished at the quantity of
talent — of invention, observation, and knowledge of character, as well as of spirited and graceful composition, 5
that may be found in those works of fiction in our language, which are generally regarded as among the lower
productions of our literature, — upon which no great
pains is understood to be bestowed, and which are
seldom regarded as titles to a permanent reputation. If 10
Novels, however, are not fated to last as long as Epic
poems, they are at least a great deal more popular in
their season ; and, slight as their structure, and imperfect
as their finishing may often be thought in comparison, we
have no, hesitation in saying, that the better specimens of 15
the art are incomparably more entertaining, and considerably more instructive. The great objection to them,
indeed, is, that they are too entertaining — and are so
pleasant in the reading, as to be apt to produce a disrelish
for other kinds of reading, which may be more necessary, 20
and can in no way be made so agreeable. Neither
science, nor authentic history, nor political nor professional instruction, can be rightly conveyed, we fear, in
a pleasant tale ; and therefore, all those things are in
danger of appearing dull and uninteresting to the votaries 25
of these more seductive studies. Among the most popular
of these popular productions that have appeared in our
times, we must rank the works to which we just alluded ;
and we do not hesitate to say, that they are well entitled
to that distinction. They are indeed, in many respects, 30
very extraordinary performances — though in nothing
more extraordinary than in having remained so long
unclaimed. There is no name, we think, in our literature, to which they would not add lustre — and lustre,

too, of a very enviable kind ; for they not only show great talent, but infinite good sense and good nature, — a more vigorous and wide-reaching intellect than is often displayed in novels, and a more powerful fancy, and a 5 deeper sympathy with various passion, than is often combined with such strength of understanding.

The author, whoever he is, has a truly graphic and creative power in the invention and delineation of characters — which he sketches with an ease, and colours 10 with a brilliancy, and scatters about with a profusion, which reminds us of Shakespeare himself : Yet with all this force and felicity in the representation of living agents, he has the eye of a poet for all the striking aspects external of nature ; and usually contrives, both in his 15 scenery and in the groups with which it is enlivened, to combine the picturesque with the natural, with a grace that has rarely been attained by artists so copious and rapid. His narrative, in this way, is kept constantly full of life, variety, and colour ; and is so interspersed with 20 glowing descriptions, and lively allusions, and flying traits of sagacity and pathos, as not only to keep our attention continually awake, but to afford a pleasing exercise to most of our other faculties. The prevailing tone is very gay and pleasant ; but the author's most remark- 25 able, and, perhaps, his most delightful talent, is that of representing kindness of heart in union with lightness of spirits and great simplicity of character, and of blending the expression of warm and generous and exalted affections with scenes and persons that are in themselves both 30 lowly and ludicrous. This gift he shares with his illustrious countryman Burns — as he does many of the other qualities we have mentioned with another living poet, — who is only inferior perhaps in that to which we have last alluded. It is very honorable indeed, we think, both to

the author, and to the readers among whom he is so
extremely popular, that the great interest of his pieces is
for the most part a Moral interest — that the concern we
take in his favourite characters is less on account of their
adventures than of their amiableness — and that the great 5
charm of his works is derived from the kindness of heart,
the capacity of generous emotions, and the lights of
native taste which he ascribes, so lavishly, and at the
same time with such an air of truth and familiarity, even
to the humblest of these favourites. With all his relish 10
for the ridiculous, accordingly, there is no tone of misanthropy, or even of sarcasm, in his representations ; but,
on the contrary, a great indulgence and relenting even
towards those who are to be the objects of our disappro-
bation. There is no keen or cold-blooded satire — no 15
bitterness of heart, or fierceness of resentment, in any
part of his writings. His love of ridicule is little else
than a love of mirth ; and savours throughout of the
joyous temperament in which it appears to have its
origin ; while the buoyancy of a raised and poetical 20
imagination lifts him continually above the region of
mere jollity and good humour, to which a taste, by no
means nice or fastidious, might otherwise be in danger of
sinking him. He is evidently a person of a very sociable
and liberal spirit — with great habits of observation — 25
who has ranged pretty extensively through the varieties
of human life and character, and mingled with them all,
not only with intelligent familiarity, but with a free and
natural sympathy for all the diversities of their tastes,
pleasures, and pursuits — one who has kept his heart as 30
well as his eyes open to all that has offered itself to
engage them ; and learned indulgence for human faults
and follies, not only from finding kindred faults in their
most intolerant censors, but also for the sake of the

virtues by which they are often redeemed, and the sufferings by which they have still oftener been chastised.
The temper of his writings, in short, is precisely the
reverse of those of our Laureates and Lakers, who, being
5 themselves the most whimsical of mortals, make it a conscience to loathe and abhor all with whom they happen
to disagree ; and labour to promote mutual animosity
and all manner of uncharitableness among mankind, by
referring every supposed error of taste, or peculiarity of
10 opinion, to some hateful corruption of the heart and
understanding.

With all the indulgence, however, which we so justly
ascribe to him, we are far from complaining of the writer
before us for being too neutral and undecided on the
15 great subjects which are most apt to engender excessive
zeal and intolerance — and we are almost as far from
agreeing with him as to most of those subjects. In
politics it is sufficiently manifest, that he is a decided
Tory — and, we are afraid, something of a latitudinarian
20 both in morals and religion. He is very apt at least to
make a mock of all enthusiasm for liberty or faith — and
not only gives a decided preference to the social over the
austerer virtues — but seldom expresses any warm or
hearty admiration, except for those graceful and gentle-
25 man-like principles, which can generally be acted upon
with a gay countenance — and do not imply any great
effort of self-denial, or any deep sense of the rights of
others, or the helplessness and humility of our common
nature. Unless we misconstrue very grossly the indica-
30 tions in these volumes, the author thinks no times so
happy as those in which an indulgent monarch awards a
reasonable portion of liberty to grateful subjects, who do
not call in question his right either to give or to withhold
it — in which a dignified and decent hierarchy receives

the homage of their submissive and uninquiring flocks —
and a gallant nobility redeems the venial immoralities
of their gayer hours, by brave and honourable conduct
towards each other, and spontaneous kindness to vassals,
in whom they recognise no independent rights, and not 5
many features of a common nature.

It is very remarkable, however, that, with propensities
thus decidedly aristocratical, the ingenious author has
succeeded by far the best in the representation of rustic
and homely characters ; and not in the ludicrous or con- 10
temptuous representation of them — but by making them
at once more natural and more interesting than they had
ever been made before in any work of fiction ; by showing
them, not as clowns to be laughed at — or wretches, to be
pitied and despised — but as human creatures, with as 15
many pleasures and fewer cares than their superiors —•
with affections not only as strong, but often as delicate
as those whose language is smoother — and with a vein
of humour, a force of sagacity, and very frequently an
elevation of fancy, as high and as natural as can be met 20
with among more cultivated beings. The great merit of
all these delineations, is their admirable truth and fidelity
— the whole manner and cast of the characters being
accurately moulded on their condition — and the finer
attributes that are ascribed to them so blended and 25
harmonised with the native rudeness and simplicity of
their life and occupations, that they are made interesting
and even noble beings, without the least particle of
foppery or exaggeration, and delight and amuse us,
without trespassing at all on the province of pastoral 30
or romance.

Next to these, we think, he has found his happiest
subjects, or at least displayed his greatest powers, in the
delineation of the grand and gloomy aspects of nature,

and of the dark and fierce passions of the heart. The
natural gaiety of his temper does not indeed allow him
to dwell long on such themes; — but the sketches he
occasionally introduces, are executed with admirable
5 force and spirit — and give a strong impression both
of the vigour of his imagination, and the variety of his
talent. It is only in the third rank that we would place
his pictures of chivalry and chivalrous character — his
traits of gallantry, nobleness, and honour — and that
10 bewitching combination of gay and gentle manners, with
generosity, candour, and courage, which has long been
familiar enough to readers and writers of novels, but has
never before been represented with such an air of truth,
and so much ease and happiness of execution.
15 Among his faults and failures, we must give the first
.place to his descriptions of virtuous young ladies — and
his representations of the ordinary business of courtship
and conversation in polished life. We admit that those
things, as they are commonly conducted in real life, are
20 apt to be a little insipid to a mere critical spectator ; —
and that while they consequently require more heighten-
ing than strange adventures or grotesque persons, they
admit less of exaggeration or ambitious ornament : —
Yet we cannot think it necessary that they should be
25 altogether so tame and mawkish as we generally find
them in the hands of this spirited writer, — whose powers
really seem to require some stronger stimulus to bring
them into action, than can be supplied by the flat
realities of a peaceful and ordinary existence. His love
30 of the ludicrous, it must also be observed, often betrays
him into forced and vulgar exaggerations, and into the
repetition of common and paltry stories, — though it is
but fair to add, that he does not detain us long with
them, and makes amends by the copiousness of his

assortment for the indifferent quality of some of the
specimens. It is another consequence of this extreme
abundance in which he revels and riots, and of the
fertility of the imagination from which it is supplied, that
he is at all times a little apt to overdo even those things 5
which he does best. His most striking and highly
coloured characters appear rather too often, and go on
rather too long. It is astonishing, indeed, with what
spirit they are supported, and how fresh and animated
they are to the very last; — but still there is something 10
too much of them — and they would be more waited for
and welcomed, if they were not quite so lavish of their
presence. — It was reserved for Shakespeare alone, to
leave all his characters as new and unworn as he found
them, — and to carry Falstaff through the business of 15
three several plays, and leave us as greedy of his sayings
as at the moment of his first introduction. It is no light
praise to the author before us, that he has sometimes
reminded us of this, as well as other inimitable excellences in that most gifted of all inventors. 20

To complete this hasty and unpremeditated sketch of
his general characteristics, we must add, that he is above
all things national and Scottish, — and never seems to
feel the powers of a Giant, except when he touches his
native soil. His countrymen alone, therefore, can have 25
a full sense of his merits, or a perfect relish of his
excellences ; — and those only, indeed, of them, who
have mingled, as he has done, pretty freely with the
lower orders, and made themselves familiar not only
with their language, but with the habits and traits of 30
character, of which it then only becomes expressive. It
is one thing to understand the meaning of words, as they
are explained by other words in a glossary, and another
to know their value, as expressive of certain feelings and

humours in the speakers to whom they are native, and as
signs both of temper and condition among those who are
familiar with their import.

,   We must content ourselves, we fear, with this hasty
5 and superficial sketch of the general character of this
author's performances, in the place of a more detailed
examination of those which he has given to the public
since we first announced him as the author of Waverley.
The time for noticing his two intermediate works, has
10 been permitted to go by so far, that it would probably be
difficult to recall the public attention to them with any
effect ; and, at all events, impossible to affect, by any
observations of ours, the judgment which has been passed
upon them, with very little assistance, we must say, from
15 professed critics, by the mass of their intelligent readers,
— by whom, indeed, we have no doubt that they are, by
this time, as well known, and as correctly estimated, as
if they had been indebted to us for their first impressions
on the subject.   For our own parts we must confess, that
20 *Waverley* still has to us all the fascination of a first love !
and that we cannot help thinking, that the greatness of
the public transactions in which that story was involved,
as well as the wildness and picturesque graces of its
Highland scenery and characters, have invested it with a
25 charm, to which the more familiar attractions of the other
pieces have not quite come up.   In this, perhaps, our
opinion differs from that of better judges ; — but we
cannot help suspecting, that the latter publications are
most admired by many, at least in the southern part
30 of the island, only because they are more easily and
perfectly understood, in consequence of the training
which had been gone through in the perusal of the
former.   But, however that be, we are far enough from
denying that the two succeeding works are performances

of extraordinary merit, — and are willing even to admit,
that they show quite as much power and genius in the
author — though, to our taste at least, the subjects are
less happily selected.

* * *

The scene of the story thus strikingly introduced is
laid — in Scotland of course — in those disastrous times
which immediately preceded the Revolution of 1688 ;
and exhibits a lively picture, both of the general state of
manners at that period, and of the conduct and temper
and principles of the two great parties in politics and
religion that were then engaged in unequal and rancorous
hostility. There are no times certainly, within the reach
of authentic history, on which it is more painful to
look back — which show a government more base and
tyrannical, or a people more helpless and miserable :
And though all pictures of the greater passions are full of
interest, and a lively representation of strong and
enthusiastic emotions never fails to be deeply attractive,
the piece would have been too full of distress, and
humiliation, if it had been chiefly engaged with the
course of public events, or the record of public feelings.
So sad a subject would not have suited many readers —
and the author, we suspect, less than any of them.
Accordingly, in this, as in his other works, he has made
use of the historical events which came in his way,
rather to develope the characters, and bring out the
peculiarities of the individuals whose adventures he
relates, than for any purpose of political information ;
and makes us present to the times in which he has placed
them, less by his direct notices of the great transactions
by which they were distinguished, than by his casual
intimations of their effects on private persons, and by the
very contrast which their temper and occupations often

appear to furnish to the colour of the national story.
Nothing, indeed, in this respect is more delusive, or at
least more woefully imperfect, than the suggestions of
authentic history, as it is generally — or rather universally
5 written — and nothing more exaggerated than the
impressions it conveys of the actual state and condition
of those who live in its most agitated periods. The great
public events of which alone it takes cognizance, have
but little direct influence upon the body of the people ;
10 and do not, in general, form the principal business, or
happiness or misery even of those who are in some
measure concerned in them. Even in the worst and most
disastrous times — in periods of civil war and revolution,
and public discord and oppression, a great part of the
15 time of a great part of the people is still spent in making
love and money — in social amusement or professional
industry — in schemes for worldly advancement or
personal distinction, just as in periods of general peace
and prosperity. Men court and marry very nearly as
20 much in the one season as in the other ; and are as merry
at weddings and christenings — as gallant at balls and
races — as busy in their studies and counting houses —
eat as heartily, in short, and sleep as sound — prattle
with their children as pleasantly — and thin their
25 plantations and scold their servants as zealously, as if
their contemporaries were not furnishing materials thus
abundantly for the Tragic muse of history. The quiet
undercurrent of life, in short, keeps its deep and steady
course in its eternal channels, unaffected, or but slightly
30 disturbed, by the storms that agitate its surface ; and
while long tracts of time, in the history of every country,
seem, to the distant student of its annals, to be darkened
over with one thick and oppressive cloud of unbroken
misery, the greater part of those who have lived through

the whole acts of the tragedy will be found to have enjoyed a fair average share of felicity, and to have been much less impressed by the shocking events of their day than those who know nothing else of it than that such events took place in its course. Few men, in short, are historical characters — and scarcely any man is always, or most usually, performing a public part. The actual happiness of every life depends far more on things that regard it exclusively, than on those political occurrences which are the common concern of society ; and though nothing lends such an air, both of reality and importance, to a fictitious narrative, as to connect its persons with events in real history, still it is the imaginary individual himself that excites our chief interest throughout, and we care for the national affairs only in so far as they affect him. In one sense, indeed, this is the true end and the best use of history ; for as all public events are important only as they ultimately concern individuals, if the individual selected belong to a large and comprehensive class, and the events, and their natural operation on him, be justly represented, we shall be enabled, in following out his adventures, to form no bad estimate of their true character and value for all the rest of the community.

The author before us has done all this, we think ; and with admirable talent and effect : and if he has not been quite impartial in the management of his historical persons, has contrived, at any rate, to make them contribute largely to the interest of his acknowledged inventions. His view of the effects of great political contentions on private happiness, is however, we have no doubt, substantially true ; and that chiefly because it is not exaggerated — because he does not confine himself to show how gentle natures may be roused into heroism,

or rougher tempers exasperated into rancour, by public oppression, — but turns still more willingly to show with what ludicrous absurdity genuine enthusiasm may be debased, how little the gaiety of the light-hearted and
5 thoughtless may be impaired by the spectacle of public calamity, and how, in the midst of national distraction, selfishness will pursue its little game of quiet and cunning speculation — and gentler affections find time to multiply and to meet !

10   It is this, we think, that constitutes the great and peculiar merit of the work before us. It contains an admirable picture of manners and of characters ; and exhibits, we think, with great truth and discrimination, the extent and the variety of the shades which the
15 stormy aspect of the political horizon would be likely to throw on such objects. And yet, though exhibiting beyond all doubt the greatest possible talent and originality, we cannot help fancying that we can trace the rudiments of almost all its characters in the very first
20 of the author's publications. — Morton is but another edition of Waverley ; — taking a bloody part in political contention, without caring much about the cause, and interchanging high offices of generosity with his political opponents. — Claverhouse has many of the features of
25 the gallant Fergus. — Cuddie Headrigg, of whose merits, by the way, we have given no fair specimen in our extracts, is a Dandie Dinmont of a considerably lower species ; — and even the Covenanters and their leaders were shadowed out, though afar off, in the gifted Gilfillan,
30 and mine host of the Candlestick. It is in the picture of these hapless enthusiasts, undoubtedly, that the great merit and the great interest of the work consists. That interest, indeed, is so great, that we perceive it has even given rise to a sort of controversy among the admirers

and contemners of those ancient worthies. It is a
singular honour, no doubt, to a work of fiction and
amusement, to be thus made the theme of serious attack
and defence upon points of historical and theological
discussion ; and to have grave dissertations written by 5
learned contemporaries upon the accuracy of its representations of public events and characters, or the moral
effects of the style of ridicule in which it indulges. It
is difficult for us, we confess, to view the matter in so
serious a light ; nor do we feel much disposed, even if 10
we had leisure for the task, to venture ourselves into the
array of the disputants. One word or two, however, we
shall say, before concluding, upon the two great points of
difference,   First, as to the author's profanity, in making
scriptural expressions ridiculous by the misuse of them 15
he has ascribed to the fanatics ; and, secondly, as to the
fairness of his general representation of the conduct and
character of the insurgent party and their opponents.

As to the first, we do not know very well what to
say.   Undoubtedly, all light or jocular use of Scripture 20
phraseology is in some measure indecent and profane :
Yet we do not know in what other way those hypocritical
pretences to extraordinary sanctity which generally
disguise themselves in such a garb, can be so effectually
exposed. And even where the ludicrous misapplication 25
of holy writ arises from mere ignorance, or the foolish
mimicry of more learned discoursers, as it is impossible
to avoid smiling at the folly when it actually occurs, it is
difficult for witty and humorous writers, in whose way it
lies, to resist fabricating it for the purpose of exciting 30
smiles. In so far as practice can afford any justification
of such a proceeding, we conceive that its justification
would be easy. In all our jest-books, and plays and
works of humour for two centuries back, the characters

of Quakers and Puritans and Methodists, have been
constantly introduced as fit objects of ridicule, on this
very account.   The Reverend Jonathan Swift is full of
jokes of this description ;   and the pious and correct
5 Addison himself is not a little fond of a sly and witty
application of a text from the sacred writings.   When an
author, therefore, whose aim was amusement, had to do
with a set of people, all of whom dealt in familiar
applications of Bible phrases and Old Testament adven-
10 tures, and who, undoubtedly, very often made absurd and
ridiculous applications of them, it would be rather hard,
we think, to interdict him entirely from the representation
of these absurdities ;   or to put in force, for him alone,
those statutes against profaneness which so many other
15 people have been allowed to transgress, in their hours of
gaiety, without censure or punishment.

On the other point, also, we rather lean to the side of
the author.   He is a Tory, we think, pretty plainly in
principle, and scarcely disguises his preference for a
20 Cavalier over a Puritan :   But, with these propensities, we
think he has dealt pretty fairly with both sides — especially when it is considered that, though he lays his
scene in a known crisis of his national history, his work
is professedly a work of fiction, and cannot well be
25 accused of misleading any one as to matters of fact.   He
might have made Claverhouse victorious at Drumclog, if
he had thought fit — and nobody could have found fault
with him.   The insurgent Presbyterians of 1666 and the
subsequent years, were, beyond all question, a pious,
30 brave, and conscientious race of men — to whom, and to
whose efforts and sufferings, their descendants are deeply
indebted for the liberty both civil and religious which
they still enjoy, as well as for the spirit of resistance to
tyranny, which, we trust, they have inherited along with

it. Considered generally as a party, it is impossible that they should ever be remembered, at least in Scotland, but with gratitude and veneration — that their sufferings should ever be mentioned but with deep resentment and horror — or their heroism, both active and passive, but 5 with pride and exultation. At the same time, it is impossible to deny, that there were among them many absurd and ridiculous persons — and some of a savage and ferocious character — old women, in short, like Mause Headrigg — preachers like Kettledrummle — or despera- 10 does like Balfour of Burley. That a Tory novelist should bring such characters prominently forward, in a tale of the times, appears to us not only to be quite natural, but really to be less blamable than almost any other way in which party feelings could be shown. But, 15 even he, has not represented the bulk of the party as falling under this description, or as fairly represented by such personages. He has made his hero — who, of course, possesses all possible virtues — of that persuasion ; and has allowed them, in general, the courage 20 of martyrs, the self-denial of hermits, and the zeal and sincerity of apostles. His representation is almost avowedly that of one who is not of their communion ; and yet we think it impossible to peruse it, without feeling the greatest respect and pity for those to whom it is 25 applied. A zealous Presbyterian might, no doubt, have said more in their favour, without violating, or even concealing the truth ; but, while zealous Presbyterians will not write entertaining novels themselves, they cannot expect to be treated in them with exactly the same favour 30 as if that had been the character of their authors.

With regard to the author's picture of their opponents, we must say that, with the exception of Claverhouse himself, whom he has invested gratuitously with many graces

and liberalities to which we are persuaded he has no title, and for whom, indeed, he has a foolish fondness, with which it would be absurd to deal seriously — he has shown no signs of a partiality that can be blamed, nor
5 exhibited many traits in them with which their enemies have reason to quarrel.   If any person can read his strong and lively pictures of military insolence and oppression, without feeling his blood boil within him, we must conclude the fault to be in his own apathy, and not
10 in any softenings of the partial author : — nor do we know any Whig writer who has exhibited the baseness and cruelty of that wretched government, in more naked and revolting deformity, than in his scene of the torture at the Privy Council.   The military executions of Claver-
15 house himself are admitted without palliation : and the bloodthirstiness of Dalzell, and the brutality of Lauder-dale, are represented in their true colours.   In short, if this author has been somewhat severe upon the Cove-nanters, neither has he spared their oppressors ; and the
20 truth probably is, that never dreaming of being made responsible for historical accuracy or fairness in a com-position of this description, he has exaggerated a little on both sides, for the sake of effect — and been carried, by the bent of his humour, most frequently to exaggerate on
25 that which afforded the greatest scope for ridicule.

ESSAYS ON THE NATURE AND PRINCIPLES OF TASTE.

By *Archibald Alison, LL.B., F.R.S.,* Prebendary of Sarum, etc.
2 vols. 8vo.

*   *   *   *   *

IT is unnecessary, however, to pursue these criticisms, or, indeed, this hasty review of the speculation of other writers, any farther. The few observations we have already made, will enable the intelligent reader, both to understand in a general way what has been already done 5 on the subject, and in some degree prepare him to appreciate the merits of that theory, substantially the same with Mr. Alison's, which we shall now proceed to illustrate somewhat more in detail.

The basis of it is, that the beauty which we impute to 10 outward objects, is nothing more than the reflection of our own inward emotions, and is made up entirely of certain little portions of love, pity, or other affections, which have been connected with these objects, and still adhere as it were to them, and move us anew 15 whenever they are presented to our observation. Before proceeding to bring any proof of the truth of this proposition, there are two things that it may be proper to explain a little more distinctly. First, What are the primary affections, by the suggestion of which we think 20 the sense of beauty is produced ? And, secondly, What is the nature of the connection by which we suppose that the objects we call beautiful are enabled to suggest these affections ?

With regard to the first of these points, it fortunately is not necessary either to enter into any tedious details, or to have recourse to any nice distinctions. All sensations that are not absolutely indifferent, and are, at
5 the same time, either agreeable, when experienced by ourselves, or attractive when contemplated in others, may form the foundation of the emotions of sublimity or beauty. The love of *sensation* seems to be the ruling appetite of human nature ; and many sensations, in which
10 the painful may be thought to predominate, are consequently sought for with avidity, and recollected with interest, even in our own persons. In the persons of others, emotions still more painful are contemplated with eagerness and delight : and therefore we must not be
15 surprised to find, that many of the pleasing sensations of beauty or sublimity resolve themselves ultimately into recollections of feelings that may appear to have a very opposite character. The sum of the whole is, that every feeling which it is agreeable to experience, to recal, or to
20 witness, may become the source of beauty in external objects, when it is so connected with them as that, their appearance reminds us of that feeling. Now, in real life, and from daily experience and observation, we know that it is agreeable, in the first place, to recollect our own
25 pleasurable sensations, or to be enabled to form a lively conception of the pleasures of other men, or even of sentient beings of any description. We know likewise, from the same sure authority, that there is a certain delight in the remembrance of our past, or the conception
30 of our future emotions, even though attended with great pain, provided the pain be not forced too rudely on the mind, and be softened by the accompaniment of any milder feeling. And finally, we know, in the same manner, that the spectacle or conception of the emotions

of others, even when in a high degree painful, is extremely interesting and attractive, and draws us away, not only from the consideration of indifferent objects, but even from the pursuit of light or frivolous enjoyments. All these are plain and familiar facts ; of the existence of which, however they may be explained, no one can entertain the slightest doubt — and into which, therefore, we shall have made no inconsiderable progress, if we can resolve the more mysterious fact, of the emotions we receive from the contemplation of sublimity or beauty.

Our proposition then is, that these emotions are not original emotions, nor produced directly by any material qualities in the objects which excite them ; but are reflections, or images, of the more radical and familiar emotions to which we have already alluded ; and are occasioned, not by any inherent virtue in the objects before us, but by the accidents, if we may so express ourselves, by which these may have been enabled to suggest or recal to us our past sensations or sympathies. We might almost venture, indeed, to lay it down as an axiom, that, except in the plain and palpable case of bodily pain or pleasure, we can never be *interested* in any thing but the fortunes of sentient beings ; — and that every thing partaking of the nature of mental emotion, must have for its object *the feelings*, past, present, or possible, of something capable of sensation. Independent, therefore, of all evidence, and without the help of any explanation, we should have been apt to conclude, that the emotions of beauty and sublimity must have for their objects the sufferings or enjoyments of sentient beings ; — and to reject, as intrinsically absurd and incredible, the supposition that material objects, which obviously do neither hurt nor delight the body, should yet excite, by their mere physical qualities, the very powerful emotions which are sometimes excited by the spectacle of beauty.

Of the feelings, by their connection with which external objects become beautiful, we do not think it necessary to 5 speak more minutely ; — and, therefore, it only remains, under this preliminary view of the subject, to explain the nature of that connection by which we conceive this effect to be produced. Here, also, there is but little need for minuteness, or fulness of enumeration. Almost 10 every tie, by which two objects can be bound together in the imagination, in such a manner as that the presentment of the one shall recal the memory of the other ; — or, in other words, almost every possible relation which can subsist between such objects, may serve to 15 connect the things we call sublime and beautiful, with feelings that are interesting or delightful. It may be useful, however, to class these bonds of association between mind and matter in a rude and general way.

It appears to us, then, that objects are sublime or 20 beautiful, *first*, when they are the natural signs, and perpetual concomitants of pleasurable sensations, or, at any rate, of some lively feeling of emotion in ourselves or in some other sentient beings ; or, *secondly*, when they are the arbitrary or accidental concomitants of such 25 feelings ; or, *thirdly*, when they bear some analogy or fanciful resemblance to things with which these emotions are necessarily connected. In endeavouring to illustrate the nature of these several relations, we shall be led to lay before our readers some proofs that appear to us 30 satisfactory of the truth of the general theory.

The most obvious, and the strongest association that can be established between inward feelings and external objects is, where the object is necessarily and universally connected with the feeling by the law of nature, so that it is always presented to the senses when the feeling is impressed upon the mind — as the sight or the sound of laughter, with the feeling of gaiety — of weeping, with distress — of the sound of thunder, with ideas of danger and power. Let us dwell for a moment on the last 5 instance. — Nothing, perhaps, in the whole range of nature, is more strikingly and universally sublime than the sound we have just mentioned ; yet it seems obvious, that the sense of sublimity is produced, not by any quality that is perceived by the ear, but altogether by the 10 impression of power and of danger that is necessarily made upon the mind, whenever that sound is heard. That it is not produced by any peculiarity in the sound itself, is certain, from the mistakes that are frequently made with regard to it. The noise of a cart rattling over 15 the stones, is often mistaken for thunder ; and as long as the mistake lasts, this very vulgar and insignificant noise is actually felt to be prodigiously sublime. It is so felt, however, it is perfectly plain, merely because it is then associated with ideas of prodigious power and 20 undefined danger ; — and the sublimity is accordingly destroyed, the moment the association is dissolved, though the sound itself and its effect on the organ, continue exactly the same. This, therefore, is an instance in which sublimity is distinctly proved to consist, not in any 25 physical quality of the object to which it is ascribed, but in its necessary connection with that vast and uncontrolled Power which is the natural object of awe and veneration.

* * *

The only other advantage which we shall specify as likely to result from the general adoption of the theory 30 we have been endeavouring to illustrate is, that it seems

calculated to put an end to all these perplexing and
vexatious questions about the standard of taste, which
have given occasion to so much impertinent and so
much elaborate discussion. If things are not beautiful
5 in themselves, but only as they serve to suggest interesting conceptions to the mind, then every thing which
does in point of fact suggest such a conception to any
individual, *is beautiful* to that individual; and it is not
only quite true that there is no room for disputing about
10 tastes, but that all tastes are equally just and correct,
in so far as each individual speaks only of his own
emotions. When a man calls a thing beautiful, however, he may indeed, mean to make two very different
assertions; — he may mean that it gives *him* pleasure by
15 suggesting to him some interesting emotion; and, in this
sense, there can be no doubt that, if he merely speak
truth, the thing is beautiful; and that it pleases him
precisely in the same way that all other things please
those to whom they appear beautiful. But if he mean
20 farther to say that the thing possesses some quality
which should make it appear beautiful to every other
person, and that it is owing to some prejudice or defect
in them if it appear otherwise, then he is as unreasonable
and absurd as he would think those who should attempt
25 to convince him that he felt no emotion of beauty.

All tastes, then, are equally just and true, in so far as
concerns the individual whose taste is in question; and
what a man feels distinctly to be beautiful, *is beautiful* to
him, whatever other people may think of it. All this
30 follows clearly from the theory now in question: but it
does not follow, from it, that all tastes are equally good
or desirable, or that there is any difficulty in describing
that which is really the best, and the most to be envied.
The only use of the faculty of taste is to afford an

innocent delight, and to assist in the cultivation of a
finer morality ; and that man certainly will have the most
delight from this faculty, who has the most numerous and
the most powerful perceptions of beauty.   But, if beauty
consist in the reflection of our affections and sympathies, 5
it is plain that *he* will always see the most beauty whose
affections are the warmest and most exercised — whose
imagination is the most powerful, and who has most
accustomed himself to attend to the objects by which he
is surrounded.   In so far as mere feeling and enjoyment 10
are concerned, therefore, it seems evident, that the best
taste must be that which belongs to the best affections,
the most active fancy, and the most attentive habits of
observation.   It will follow pretty exactly too, that all
men's perceptions of beauty will be nearly in proportion 15
to the degree of their sensibility and social sympathies ;
and that those who have no affections towards sentient
beings, will be as certainly insensible to beauty in external
objects, as he, who cannot hear the sound of his friend's
voice, must be deaf to its echo.   20

   In so far as the sense of beauty is regarded as a mere
source of enjoyment, this seems to be the only distinction
that deserves to be attended to ; and the only cultivation
that taste should ever receive, with a view to the gratification of the individual, should be through the indirect 25
channel of cultivating the affections and powers of observation.   If we aspire, however, to be *creators*, as well as
observers of beauty, and place any part of our happiness
in ministering to the gratification of others — as artists,
or poets, or authors of any sort — then, indeed, a new 30
distinction of tastes, and a far more laborious system of
cultivation, will be necessary.   A man who pursues only
his own delight, will be as much charmed with objects
that suggest powerful emotions in consequence of per-

sonal and accidental associations, as with those that
introduce similar emotions by means of associations that
are universal and indestructible.   To him, all objects of
the former class are really as beautiful as those of the
5 latter — and for his own gratification, the creation of
that sort of beauty is just as important an occupation :
but if he conceive the ambition of creating beauties for
the admiration of others, he must be cautious to employ
only such objects as are the *natural* signs, or the *insepara-*
10 *ble* concomitants of emotions, of which the greater part
of mankind are susceptible ; and his taste will *then* deserve
to be called bad and false, if he obtrude upon the public,
as beautiful, objects that are not likely to be associated
in common minds with any interesting impressions.

15   For a man himself, then, there is no taste that is either
bad or false ; and the only difference worthy of being
attended to, is that between a great deal and a very
little.   Some who have cold affections, sluggish imaginations, and no habits of observation, can with difficulty
20 discern beauty in any thing ; while others, who are
full of kindness and sensibility, and who have been
accustomed to attend to all the objects around them,
feel it almost in every thing.   It is no matter what other
people may think of the objects of their admiration ; nor
25 ought it to be any concern of theirs that the public would
be astonished or offended, if they were called upon to
join in that admiration.   So long as no such call is
made, this anticipated discrepancy of feeling need give
them no uneasiness ; and the suspicion of it should pro-
30 duce no contempt in any other persons.   It is a strange
aberration indeed of vanity that makes us despise persons
for being happy — for having sources of enjoyment in
which we cannot share : — and yet this is the true source
of the ridicule, which is so generally poured upon indi-

viduals who seek only to enjoy their peculiar tastes unmolested : — for, if there be any truth in the theory we have been expounding, no taste is bad for any other reason than because it is peculiar — as the objects in which it delights must actually serve to suggest to the 5 individual those common emotions and universal affec- tions upon which the sense of beauty is every where founded. The misfortune is, however, that we are apt to consider all persons who make known their peculiar relishes, and especially all who create any objects for 10 their gratification, as in some measure dictating to the public, and setting up an idol for general adoration ; and hence this intolerant interference with almost all peculiar perceptions of beauty, and the unsparing derision that pursues all deviations from acknowledged standards. 15 This intolerance, we admit, is often provoked by some- thing of a spirit of *proselytism* and arrogance, in those who mistake their own casual associations for natural or universal relations ; and the consequence is, that mortified vanity ultimately dries up, even for them, the 20 fountain of their peculiar enjoyment ; and disenchants, by a new association of general contempt or ridicule, the scenes that had been consecrated by some innocent but accidental emotion.

As all men must have some peculiar associations, all 25 men must have some peculiar notions of beauty, and, of course, to a certain extent, a taste that the public would be entitled to consider as false or vitiated. For those who make no demands on public admiration, however, it is hard to be obliged to sacrifice this source of enjoy- 30 ment ; and, even for those who labour for applause, the wisest course, perhaps, if it were only practicable, would be, to have *two* tastes — one to enjoy, and one to work by — one founded upon universal associations, according

to which they finished those performances for which they challenged univeral praise — and another guided by all casual and individual associations, through which they might still look fondly upon nature, and upon the objects
5 of their secret admiration.

WILHELM MEISTER'S APPRENTICESHIP.

A Novel. From the German of Goethe. 3 vols. 12mo, pp. 1030. Edinburgh, 1824.

THERE are few things that at first sight appear more capricious and unaccountable, than the diversities of national taste ; and yet there are not many, that, to a certain extent at least, admit of a clearer explanation. They form evidently a section in the great chapter of 5 National Character ; and, proceeding on the assumption, that human nature is everywhere fundamentally the same, it is not perhaps very difficult to indicate, in a general way, the circumstances which have distinguished it into so many local varieties. 10

These may be divided into two great classes, — the one embracing all that relates to the newness or antiquity of the society to which they belong, or, in other words, to the stage which any particular nation has attained in that great progress from rudeness to refinement, in which all 15 are engaged ; — the other comprehending what may be termed the accidental causes by which the character and condition of communities may be affected ; such as their government, their relative position as to power and civilization to neighbouring countries, their prevailing 20 occupations, determined in some degree by the capabilities of their soil and climate, and more than all perhaps, as to the question of taste, the still more accidental circumstance of the character of their first models of excellence, or the kind of merit by which their admiration and national vanity had first been excited.

It is needless to illustrate these obvious sources of peculiarity at any considerable length. It is not more
5 certain, that all primitive communities proceed to civilization by nearly the same stages, than that the progress of taste is marked by corresponding gradations, and may, in most cases, be distinguished into periods, the order and succession of which is nearly as uniform and determined.
10 If tribes of savage men always proceed, under ordinary circumstances, from the occupation of hunting to that of pasturage, from that to agriculture, and from that to commerce and manufactures, the sequence is scarcely less invariable in the history of letters and art. In
15 the former, verse is uniformly antecedent to prose — marvellous legends to correct history — exaggerated sentiments to just representations of nature. Invention, in short, regularly comes before judgment, warmth of feeling before correct reasoning — and splendid declamation and
20 broad humour before delicate simplicity or refined wit. In the arts again, the progress is strictly analogous — from mere monstrosity to ostentatious displays of labour and design, first in massive formality, and next in fantastical minuteness, variety, and flutter of parts ; — and then,
25 through the gradations of startling contrasts and overwrought expression, to the repose and simplicity of graceful nature.

These considerations alone explain much of that contrariety of taste by which different nations are dis-
30 tinguished. They not only start in the great career of improvement at different times, but they advance in it with different velocities — some lingering longer in one stage than another — some obstructed and some helped forward, by circumstances operating on them from within

or from without. It is the unavoidable consequence, however, of their being in any one particular position, that they will judge of their own productions and those of their neighbours, according to that standard of taste which belongs to the place they then hold in this great 5 circle ; — and that a whole people will look on their neighbours with wonder and scorn, for admiring what their own grandfathers looked on with equal admiration, — while they themselves are scorned and vilified in return, for tastes which will infallibly be adopted by the 10 grandchildren of those who despise them.

What we have termed the accidental causes of great differences in beings of the same nature, do not of course admit of quite so simple an exposition. But it is not in reality more difficult to prove their existence and explain 15 their operation. Where great and degrading despotisms have been early established, either by the aid of super-stition or of mere force, as in most of the states in Asia, or where small tribes of mixed descent have been engaged in perpetual contention for freedom and superiority, as in 20 ancient Greece — where the ambition and faculties of individuals have been chained up by the institution of castes and indelible separations, as in India and Egypt, or where all men practise all occupations and aspire to all honours, as in Germany or Britain — where the sole 25 occupation of the people has been war, as in infant Rome, or where a vast pacific population has been for ages inured to mechanical drudgery, as in China — it is needless to say, that very opposite notions of what conduces to delight and amusement must necessarily 30 prevail; and that the Taste of the nation must be affected both by the sentiments which it has been taught to cultivate, and the capacities it has been led to unfold.

The influence of early models, however, is perhaps the most considerable of any ; and may be easily enough understood. When men have been accustomed to any particular kind of excellence, they naturally become good 5 judges of it, and account certain considerable degrees of it indispensable, — while they are comparatively blind to the merit of other good qualities to which they had been less habituated, and are neither offended by their absence, nor at all skilful in their estimation. Thus those nations 10 who, like the English and the Dutch, have been long accustomed to great cleanliness and order in their persons and dwellings, naturally look with admiration on the higher displays of those qualities, and are proportionately disgusted by their neglect ; while they are apt to under-15 value mere pomp and stateliness, when destitute of these recommendations : and thus also the Italians and Sicilians, bred in the midst of dirt and magnificence, are curiously alive to the beauties of architecture and sculpture, and make but little account of the more homely 20 comforts which are so highly prized by the others. In the same way, if a few of the first successful adventurers in art should have excelled in any particular qualities, the taste of their nation will naturally be moulded on that standard — will regard those qualities almost exclusively 25 as entitled to admiration, and will not only consider the want of them as fatal to all pretentions to excellence, but will unduly despise and undervalue other qualities, in themselves not less valuable, but with which their national models had not happened to make them timeously 30 familiar. If, for example, the first great writers in any country should have distinguished themselves by a pompous and severe regularity, and a certain elaborate simplicity of design and execution, it will naturally follow, that the national taste will not only become critical and

rigorous as to those particulars, but will be proportionally
deadened to the merit of vivacity, nature, and invention,
when combined with irregularity, homeliness, or confusion.
While, if the great patriarchs of letters had excelled in
variety and rapidity of invention, and boldness and truth 5
of sentiment, though poured out with considerable
disorder and incongruity of manner, those qualities would
come to be the national criterion of merit, and the
correctness and decorum of the other school be despised,
as mere recipes for monotony and tameness.   10

These, we think, are the plain and certain effects of
the peculiar character of the first great popular writers of
all countries. But still we do not conceive that they
depend altogether on any thing so purely accidental as
the temperament or early history of a few individuals. 15
No doubt the national taste of France and of England
would at this moment have been different, had *Shakespeare*
been a Frenchman, and Boileau and Racine written in
English. But then, we do not think that Shakespeare
could have been a Frenchman ; and we conceive that his 20
character, and that of other original writers, though no
doubt to be considered on the whole as casual, must yet
have been modified to a great extent by the circumstances
of the countries in which they were bred. It is plain
that no original force of genius could have enabled 25
Shakespeare to write as he had done, if he had been
born and bred among the Chinese or the Peruvians.
Neither do we think that he could have done so, in any
other country but England — free, sociable, discursive,
reformed, familiar England — whose motley and mingling 30
population not only presented "every change of many-
coloured life" to his eye, but taught and permitted every
class, from the highest to the lowest, to know and to
estimate the feelings and the habits of all the others — and

thus enabled the gifted observer not only to deduce the
true character of human nature from this infinite variety
of experiments and examples, but to speak to the sense
and the hearts of each, with that truly universal tongue,
5 which every one feels to be peculiar, and all enjoy as
common.

We have said enough, however, or rather too much, on
these general views of the subject — which in truth is
sufficiently clear in those extreme cases, where the
10 contrariety is great and universal, and is only perplexing
when there is a pretty general conformity both in the
causes which influence taste and in the results. Thus,
we are not at all surprised to find the taste of the
Japanese or the Iroquois very different from our own —
15 and have no difficulty in both admitting that our human
nature and human capacities are substantially the same,
and in referring this discrepancy to the contrast that
exists in the whole state of society, and the knowledge,
and the opposite qualities of the objects to which we
20 have been respectively accustomed to give our admiration.
That nations living in times or places altogether remote,
should disagree in taste, as in every thing else, seems to
us quite natural. They are only the nearer cases that
puzzle. And, that great European countries, peopled by
25 the same mixed races, educated in the admiration of the
same classical models — venerating the same remains of
antiquity — engaged substantially in the same occupations
— communicating every day, on business, letters, and
society — bound up in short in one great commonwealth,
30 as against the inferior and barbarous parts of the
world, should yet differ so widely — not only as to the
comparative excellence of their respective productions,
but as to the constituents of excellence in all works of
genius or skill, does indeed sound like a paradox, the

solution of which every one may not be able to deduce
from the preceding observations.

The great practical equation on which we in this
country have been hitherto most frequently employed,
has been between our own standard of taste and that 5
which is recognized among our neighbours of France : —
And certainly, though feelings of rivalry have somewhat
aggravated its *apparent*, beyond its real amount, *there is*
a great and substantial difference to be accounted for, —
in the way we have suggested — or in some other way. 10
Stating that difference as generally as possible, we would
say, that the French, compared with ourselves, are more
sensitive to faults, and less transported with beauties —
more enamoured of art, and less indulgent to nature —
more charmed with overcoming difficulties, than with that 15
power which makes us unconscious of their existence —
more averse to strong emotions, or at least less covetous
of them in their intensity — more students of taste, in
short, than adorers of genius — and far more disposed
than any other people, except perhaps the Chinese, to 20
circumscribe the rules of taste to such as they themselves
have been able to practise, and to limit the legitimate
empire of genius to the provinces they have explored.
There has been a good deal of discussion of late
years, in the face of literary Europe, on these debatable 25
grounds ; and we cannot but think that the result has
been favourable, on the whole, to the English, and that
the French have been compelled to recede considerably
from many of their exclusive pretensions — a result which
we are inclined to ascribe, less to the arguments of our 30
native champions, than to those circumstances in the
recent history of Europe, which have compelled our
ingenious neighbours to mingle more than they had ever
done before with the surrounding nations — and thus to

become better acquainted with the diversified forms which genius and talent may assume.

But while we are thus fairly in the way of settling our differences with France, we are little more than beginning them, we fear, with Germany ; and the perusal of the extraordinary volumes before us, which has suggested all the preceding reflections, has given us, at the same time, an impression of such radical, and apparently irreconcilable disagreement as to principles, as we can scarcely hope either to remove by our reasonings, or even very satisfactorily to account for by our suggestions.

This is allowed, by the general consent of all Germany, to be the very greatest work of their very greatest writer. The most original, the most varied and inventive, — the most characteristic, in short, of the author, and of his country. We receive it as such accordingly, with implicit faith and suitable respect ; and have perused it in consequence with very great attention and no common curiosity. We have perused it, indeed, only in the translation of which we have prefixed the title : But it is a translation by a professed admirer ; and by one who is proved by his Preface to be a person of talents, and by every part of the work to be no ordinary master, at least of one of the languages with which he has to deal. We need scarcely say, that we profess to judge of the work only according to our own principles of judgment and habits of feeling ; and, meaning nothing less than to dictate to the readers or the critics of Germany what they should think of their favourite authors, propose only to let them know, in all plainness and modesty, what we, and we really believe most of our countrymen, actually think of this *chef-d'œuvre* of Teutonic genius.

We must say, then, at once, that we cannot enter into

the spirit of this German idolatry ; nor at all comprehend
upon what grounds the work before us could ever be
considered as an admirable, or even a commendable
performance.   To us it certainly appears, after the
most deliberate consideration, to be eminently absurd, 5
puerile, incongruous, vulgar, and affected ; — and, though
redeemed by considerable powers of invention, and some
traits of vivacity, to be so far·from perfection, as to be,
almost from beginning to end, one flagrant offence
against every principle of taste, and every just rule of 10
composition.   Though indicating, in many places, a mind
capable both of acute and profound reflection, it is full
of mere silliness and childish affectation ; — and though
evidently the work of one who had seen and observed
much, it is throughout altogether unnatural, and not so 15
properly improbable, as affectedly fantastic and absurd —
kept, as it were, studiously aloof from general or ordinary
nature — never once bringing us into contact with real
life or genuine character — and, where not occupied with
the professional squabbles, paltry jargon, and scenical 20
profligacy of strolling players, tumblers, and mummers
(which may be said to form its staple), is conversant only
with incomprehensible mystics and vulgar men of whim,
with whom, if it were at all possible to understand them,
it would be a baseness to be acquainted.   Every thing, 25
and every body we meet with, is a riddle and an oddity;
and though the tissue of the story is sufficiently coarse,
and the manners and sentiments infected with a strong
tinge of vulgarity, it is all kept in the air, like a piece of
machinery at the minor theatres, and never allowed to 30
touch the solid ground, or to give an impression of
reality, by the disclosure of known or living features.   In
the midst of all this, however, there are, every now and
then, outbreakings of a fine speculation, and gleams of a

warm and sprightly imagination — an occasional wild and exotic glow of fancy and poetry — a vigorous heaping up of incidents, and touches of bright and powerful description.

5   It is not very easy certainly to account for these incongruities, or to suggest an intelligible theory for so strange a practice.   But in so far as we can guess, these peculiarities of German taste are to be referred, in part, to the comparative newness of original composition 10 among that ingenious people, and to the state of European literature when they first ventured on the experiment — and in part to the state of society in that great country itself, and the comparatively humble condition of the greater part of those who write, or to whom writing is 15 there addressed.

The Germans, though undoubtedly an imaginative and even enthusiastic race, had neglected their native literature for two hundred years — and were chiefly known for their learning and industry.   They wrote huge 20 Latin treatises on Law and Theology — and put forth bulky editions and great tomes of annotations on the classics.   At last, however, they grew tired of being respected as the learned drudges of Europe, and reproached with their consonants and commentators ;   and 25 determined, about fifty years ago, to show what metal they were made of, and to give the world a taste of their quality, as men of genius and invention.   In this attempt the first thing to be effected was at all events to avoid the imputation of being scholastic imitators of the classics. 30 *That* would have smelt too much, they thought, of the old shop ;   and in order to prove their claims to originality, it was necessary to go a little into the opposite extreme, — to venture on something decidedly modern, and to show at once their independence on their old masters, and

their superiority to the pedantic rules of antiquity. With
this view some of them betook themselves to the French
models — set seriously to study how to be gay — *apprendre
à être vif*—and composed a variety of petites pieces and
novels of polite gallantry, in a style — of which we shall 5
at present say nothing. This manner, however, ran too
much counter to the general character of the nation to
be very much followed — and undoubtedly the greater
and better part of their writers turned rather to us, for
hints and lessons to guide them in their ambitious career. 10
There was a greater original affinity in the temper and
genius of the two nations — and, in addition to that
consideration, our great authors were indisputably at once
more original and less classical than those of France.
England, however, we are sorry to say, could furnish 15
abundance of bad as well as of good models — and even
the best were perilous enough for rash imitators. As
it happened, however, the worst were most generally
selected — and the worst parts of the good. Shakespeare
was admired — but more for his flights of fancy, his daring 20
improprieties, his trespasses on the borders of absurdity,
than for the infinite sagacity and rectifying good sense
by which he redeemed those extravagancies, or even the
profound tenderness and simple pathos which alternated
with the lofty soaring or dazzling imagery of his style. 25
Altogether, however, Shakespeare was beyond their
rivalry; and although Schiller has dared, and not inglori-
ously, to emulate his miracles, it was plainly to other
merits and other rivalries that the body of his ingenious
countrymen aspired. The ostentatious absurdity — the 30
affected oddity — the pert familiarity — the broken style,
and exaggerated sentiment of Tristram Shandy — the
mawkish morality, dawdling details, and interminable
agonies of Richardson — the vulgar adventures, and

homely, though, at the same time, fantastical speculations
of John Buncle and others of his forgotten class, found
far more favour in their eyes. They were original,
startling, unclassical, and puzzling. They excited curiosity
5 by not being altogether intelligible — effectually excluded
monotony by the rapidity and violence of their transitions,
and promised to rouse the most torpid sensibility, by the
violence and perseverance with which they thundered at
the heart. They were the very things, in short, which
10 the German originals were in search of ; — and they were
not slow, therefore, in adopting and improving on them.
In order to make them thoroughly their own, they had
only to exaggerate their peculiarities — to mix up with
them a certain allowance of their old visionary philosophy,
15 misty metaphysics, and superstitious visions — and to
introduce a few crazy sententious theorists, to sprinkle
over the whole a seasoning of rash speculation on morality
and the fine arts.

The style was also to be relieved by a variety of odd
20 comparisons and unaccountable similes — borrowed, for
the most part, from low and revolting objects, and all the
better if they did not exactly fit the subject, or even
introduced new perplexity into that which they professed
to illustrate.

25   This goes far, we think, to explain the absurdity,
incongruity, and affectation of the works of which we are
speaking.   But there is yet another distinguishing quality
for which we have not accounted — and that is a peculiar
kind of vulgarity which pervades all their varieties, and
30 constitutes, perhaps, their most repulsive characteristic.
We do not know very well how to describe this unfortunate peculiarity, except by saying that it is the vulgarity
of pacific, comfortable burghers, occupied with stuffing,
cooking, and providing for their coarse personal accommo-

dations. There certainly never were any men of genius
who condescended to attend so minutely to the *non-
naturals* of their heroes and heroines as the novelists of
modern Germany. Their works smell, as it were, of
groceries — of brown papers filled with greasy cakes and 5
slices of bacon, — and fryings in frowsy back parlours.
All the interesting recollections of childhood turn on
remembered tidbits and plunderings of savoury store-
rooms. In the midst of their most passionate scenes
there is always a serious and affectionate notice of 10
the substantial pleasures of eating and drinking. The
raptures of a tête-à-tête are not complete without a bottle
of nice wine and a "trim collation." Their very sages
deliver their oracles over a glass of punch ; and the
enchanted lover finds new apologies for his idolatry in 15
taking a survey of his mistress's "combs, soap, and
towels, with the traces of their use." These baser
necessities of our nature, in short, which all other writers
who have aimed at raising the imagination or touching
the heart have kept studiously out of view, are osten- 20
tatiously brought forward, and fondly dwelt on by the
pathetic authors of Germany.

We really cannot well account for this extraordinary
taste. But we suspect it is owing to the importance that
is really attached to those solid comforts and supplies of 25
necessaries, by the greater part of the readers and writers
of that country. Though there is a great deal of freedom
in Germany, it operates less by raising the mass of the
people to a potential equality with the nobles, than by
securing to them their inferior and plebeian privileges ; 30
and consists rather in the immunities of their incor-
porated tradesmen, which may enable them to become
rich as such, than in any general participation of national
rights, by which they may aspire to dignity and elegance,

as well as opulence and comfort.   Now, the writers, as
well as the readers in that country, belong almost entirely
to the plebeian and vulgar class.   Their learned men are
almost all wofully poor and dependent ; and the com-
5 fortable burghers who buy entertaining books by the
thousand at the Frankfort fair, probably agree with
their authors in nothing so much as the value they
set on those homely comforts to which their ambition
is mutually limited by their condition ; and enter into no
10 part of them so heartily as those which set forth their
paramount and continual importance.

It is time, however, that we should proceed to give
some more particular account of the work which has
given occasion to all these observations.

MEMOIRS OF ZEHIR-ED-DIN MUHAMMED BABER, EMPEROR OF HINDUSTAN.

Written by himself, in the Jaghatai Turki, and translated, partly by the late John Leyden, Esq., M.D., partly by William Erskine, Esq.

THIS is a very curious, and admirably edited work. But the strongest impression which the perusal of it has left on our minds is the boundlessness of authentic history ; and, if we might venture to say it, the useless- ness of all history which does not relate to our own 5 fraternity of nations, or even bear, in some way or other, on our own present or future condition.

We have here a distinct and faithful account of some hundreds of battles, sieges and great military expeditions, and a character of a prodigious number of eminent indi- 10 viduals, — men famous in their day, over wide regions, for genius or fortune — poets, conquerers, martyrs — founders of cities and dynasties — authors of immortal works — ravagers of vast districts abounding in wealth and population. Of all these great personages and 15 events, nobody in Europe, if we except a score or two of studious Orientalists, has ever heard before ; and it would not, we imagine, be very easy to show that we are any better for hearing of them now. A few curious traits, that happened to be strikingly in contrast with our 20 own manners and habits, may remain on the memory of a reflecting reader — with a general confused recollection of the dark and gorgeous phantasmagoria. But no one,

we may fairly say, will think it worth while to digest or
develope the details of the history ; or be at the pains to
become acquainted with the leading individuals, and fix
in his memory the series and connection of events.   Yet
5 the effusion of human blood was as copious — the display
of talent and courage as imposing — the perversion of
high moral qualities, and the waste of the means of
enjoyment as unsparing, as in other long-past battles
and intrigues and revolutions, over the details of which
10 we still pore with the most unwearied attention ; and to
verify the dates or minute circumstances of which, is still
regarded as a great exploit in historical research, and
among the noblest employments of human learning and
sagacity.

15   It is not perhaps very easy to account for the eagerness with which we still follow the fortunes of Miltiades,
Alexander, or Cæsar — of the Bruce and the Black Prince,
and the interest which yet belongs to the fields of Mara-
thon and Pharsalia, of Crecy and Bannockburn, compared
20 with the indifference, or rather reluctance, with which we
listen to the details of Asiatic warfare — the conquests
that transferred to the Moguls the vast sovereignties of
India, or raised a dynasty of Manchew Tartars to the
Celestial Empire of China.   It will not do to say, that
25 we want something nobler in character, and more exalted
in intellect, than is to be met with among those murderous
Orientals — that there is nothing to interest in the contentions of mere force and violence ; and that it requires
no very fine-drawn reasoning to explain why we should
ɔ turn with disgust from the story, if it had been preserved,
of the savage affrays which have drenched the sands of
Africa or the rocks of New Zealand — through long
generations of murder — with the blood of their brutish
population.   This may be true enough of Madagascar

or Dahomy ; but it does not apply to the case before us.
The nations of Asia generally—at least those composing
its great states — were undoubtedly more polished than
those of Europe, during all the period that preceded their
recent connexion. Their warriors were as brave in the 5
field, their statesmen more subtle and politic in the
cabinet : In the arts of luxury, and all the elegancies of
civil life, they were immeasurably superior ; in ingenuity
of speculation — in literature — in social politeness — the
comparison is still in their favour. 10

It has often occurred to us, indeed, to consider what
the effect would have been on the fate and fortunes of
the world, if, in the fourteenth, or fifteenth century,
when the germs of their present civilisation were first
disclosed, the nations of Europe had been introduced 15
to an intimate and friendly acquaintance with the great
polished communities of the East, and had been thus led
to take *them* for their masters in intellectual cultivation,
and their models in all the higher pursuits of genius,
polity, and art. The difference in our social and moral 20
condition, it would not perhaps be easy to estimate :
But one result, we conceive, would unquestionably have
been, to make us take the same deep interest in their
ancient story, which we now feel, for similar reasons, in
that of the sterner barbarians of early Rome, or the more 25
imaginative clans and colonies of immortal Greece. The
experiment, however, though there seemed oftener than
once to be some openings for it, was not made. Our
crusading ancestors were too rude themselves to estimate
or to feel the value of the oriental refinement which 30
presented itself to their passing gaze, and too entirely
occupied with war and bigotry, to reflect on its causes or
effects ; and the first naval adventurers who opened up
India to our commerce, were both too few and too far off

to communicate to their brethren at home any taste
for the splendours which might have excited their own
admiration.   By the time that our intercourse with those
regions was enlarged, our own career of improvement had
5 been prosperously begun ; and our superiority in the art,
or at least the discipline of war, having given us a signal
advantage in the conflicts to which that extending intercourse immediately led, naturally increased the aversion
and disdain with which almost all races of men are apt
10 to regard strangers to their blood and dissenters from
their creed.   Since that time the genius of Europe has
been steadily progressive, whilst that of Asia has been at
least stationary, and most probably retrograde ; and the
descendants of the feudal and predatory warriors of the
15 West have at last attained a decided predominancy over
those of their elder brothers in the East; to whom, at
that period, they were unquestionably inferior in elegance
and ingenuity, and whose hostilities were then conducted
on the same system with our own.   *They*, in short, have
20 remained nearly where they were ; while *we*, beginning
with the improvement of our governments and military
discipline, have gradually outstripped them in all the
lesser and more ornamental attainments in which they
originally excelled.

25   This extraordinary fact of the stationary or degenerate
condition of the two oldest and greatest families of mankind — those of Asia and Africa, has always appeared
to us a sad obstacle in the way of those who believe
in the general progress of the race, and its constant
30 advancement towards a state of perfection.   Two or
three thousand years ago, those vast communities were
certainly in a happier and more prosperous state than
they are now ; and in many of them we know that their
most powerful and flourishing societies have been cor-

rupted and dissolved, not by any accidental or intrinsic
disaster, like foreign conquest, pestilence, or elemental
devastation, but by what appeared to be the natural
consequences of that very greatness and refinement
which had marked and rewarded their earlier exertions. 5
In Europe, hitherto, the case has certainly been different :
For though darkness did fall upon its nations also, after
the lights of Roman civilisation were extinguished, it is
to be remembered that they did not burn out of themselves, but were trampled down by hosts of invading 10
barbarians, and that they blazed out anew, with increased
splendour and power, when the dulness of that superin-
cumbent mass was at length vivified by their contact, and
animated by the fermentation of that leaven which had
all along been secretly working in its recesses.   In 15
Europe certainly there has been a progress : And the
more polished of its present inhabitants have not only
regained the place which was held of old by their illustrious masters of Greece and Rome, but have plainly
outgone them in the most substantial and exalted of 20
their improvements.   Far more humane and refined
than the Romans — far less giddy and turbulent and
treacherous than the Greeks, they have given a security
to life and property that was unknown to the earlier ages
of the world — exalted the arts of peace to a dignity 25
with which they were never before invested ; and, by the
abolition of domestic servitude, for the first time extended
to the bulk of the population those higher capacities and
enjoyments which were formerly engrossed by a few.   By
the invention of printing, they have made all knowledge, 30
not only accessible, but imperishable ; and by their improvements in the art of war, have effectually secured
themselves against the overwhelming calamity of barbarous invasion — the risk of subjugation by mere numerical

or animal force : Whilst the alternations of conquest and defeat amongst civilised communities, who alone can now be formidable to each other, though productive of great local and temporary evils, may be regarded on the whole 5 as one of the means of promoting and equalising the general civilisation. Rome polished and enlightened all the barbarous nations she subdued — and was herself polished and enlightened by her conquest of elegant Greece. If the European parts of Russia had been 10 subjected to the dominion of France, there can be no doubt that the loss of national independence would have been compensated by rapid advances both in liberality and refinement; and if, by a still more disastrous, though less improbable contingency, the Moscovite hordes were 15 ever to overrun the fair countries to the south-west of them, it is equally certain that the invaders would speedily be softened and informed by the union ; and be infected more certainly than by any other sort of contact, with the arts and knowledge of the vanquished.

20 All these great advantages, however — this apparently irrepressible impulse to improvement — this security against backsliding and decay, seems peculiar to Europe,[1] and not capable of being communicated, even by her, to the most docile races of the other quarters of the world : 25 and it is really extremely difficult to explain, upon what are called philosophical principles, the causes of this superiority. We should be very glad to ascribe it to our

---

[1] When we speak of Europe, it will be understood that we speak, not of the land, but of the people — and include, therefore, all the settlements and colonies of that favoured race, in whatever quarter of the globe they may now be established. Some situations seem more, and some less, favourable to the preservation of the original character. The Spaniards certainly degenerated in Peru — and the Dutch perhaps in Batavia ; — but the English remain, we trust unimpaired in America.

greater political Freedom : — and no doubt, as a secondary
cause, this is among the most powerful ; as it is to the
maintenance of that freedom that we are indebted for the
self-estimation, the feeling of honour, the general equity
of the laws, and the substantial security both from sudden 5
revolution and from capricious oppression, which distinguish our portion of the globe. But we cannot bring
ourselves to regard this freedom as a mere accident in
our history, that is not itself to be accounted for, as well
as its consequences : And when it is said that our 10
greater stability and prosperity is owing to our greater
freedom, we are immediately tempted to ask, by what
that freedom has itself been produced ? In the same
way we might ascribe the superior mildness and humanity
of our manners, the abated ferocity of our wars, and 15
generally our respect for human life, to the influence of
a Religion which teaches that all men are equal in the
sight of God, and inculcates peace and charity as the
first of our duties. But, besides the startling contrast
between the profligacy, treachery, and cruelty of the 20
Eastern Empire after its conversion to the true faith, and
the simple and heroic virtues of the heathen republic, it
would still occur to inquire, how it has happened that the
nations of European descent have alone embraced the
sublime truths, and adopted into their practice the mild 25
precepts, of Christianity, while the people of the East
have uniformly rejected and disclaimed them, as alien to
their character and habits — in spite of all the efforts of
the apostles, fathers, and martyrs, in the primitive and
most effective periods of their preaching ? How, in 30
short, it has happened that the sensual and sanguinary
creed of Mahomet has superseded the pure and pacific
doctrines of Christianity in most of those very regions
where it was first revealed to mankind, and first

established by the greatest of existing governments?
The Christian revelation is no doubt the most precious
of all Heaven's gifts to the benighted world. But it is
plain, that there was a greater aptitude to embrace and
5 to profit by it in the European than in the Asiatic race.
A free government, in like manner, is unquestionably the
most valuable of all human inventions — the great
safeguard of all other temporal blessings, and the main-
spring of all intellectual and moral improvement : — But
10 such a government is not the result of a lucky thought
or happy casualty ; and could only be established among
men who had previously learned both to relish the benefits
it secures, and to understand the connexion between the
means it employs and the ends at which it aims.
15   We come then, though a little reluctantly, to the
conclusion, that there is a natural and inherent difference
in the character and temperament of the European and
the Asiatic races — consisting, perhaps, chiefly in a
superior capacity of patient and persevering thought in
20 the former — and displaying itself, for the most part, in
a more sober and robust understanding, and a more
reasonable, principled, and inflexible morality. It is
this which has led us, at once to temper our political
institutions with prospective checks and suspicious provi-
25 sions against abuses, and, in our different orders and
degrees, to submit without impatience to those checks
and restrictions ; — to extend our reasonings by repeated
observation and experiment, to larger and larger conclusions — and thus gradually to discover the paramount
30 importance of discipline and unity of purpose in war,
and of absolute security to person and property in all
peaceful pursuits — the folly of all passionate and vindictive assertion of supposed rights and pretensions, and
the certain recoil of long-continued injustice on the heads

of its authors — the substantial advantages of honesty
and fair dealing over the most ingenious systems of
trickery and fraud ; — and even — though this is the last
and hardest, as well as the most precious, of all the
lessons of reason and experience — that the toleration 5
even of religious errors is not only prudent and merciful
in itself, and most becoming a fallible and erring being,
but is the surest and speediest way to compose religious
differences, and to extinguish that most formidable
bigotry, and those most pernicious errors, which are 10
fed and nourished by persecution. It is the want of this
knowledge, or rather of the capacity for attaining it, that
constitutes the palpable inferiority of the Eastern races ;
and, in spite of their fancy, ingenuity, and restless
activity, condemns them, it would appear irretrievably, to 15
vices and sufferings, from which nations in a far ruder
condition are comparatively free. But we are wandering
too far from the magnificent Baber and his commentators,
— and must now leave these vague and general speculations for the facts and details that lie before us. 20

CHRONOLOGICAL LIST

OF

ESSAYS.

———◦◦———

DATES IN JEFFREY'S LIFE.

1773, Oct. 23, Jeffrey born in Edinburgh.

1781–91, studies in Edinburgh and Glasgow.

1791–92, studies at Queen's College, Oxford.

1792–93, attends law lectures in Edinburgh.

1794, is admitted to the bar.

1798, visits London; returns to Edinburgh.

1801, marries Miss Catherine Wilson.

1802, publishes articles in the *Monthly Review*.

1802, Oct. 10, first number of the *Edinburgh Review*.

1803, becomes editor of the *Edinburgh Review* at a salary of £300.

1804, is making £240 at the bar.

1805, his wife dies.

1806, visits London; duel with Moore.

1813–14, visits America and marries Miss Wilkes.

1815, settles at Craigcrook, three miles north-west of Edinburgh.

1829, elected dean of the Faculty of Advocates, Edinburgh.

1829, resigns the editorship of the *Edinburgh Review*.

1830, is made Lord Advocate.

1831, is elected to Parliament.

1834, accepts a judgeship in the Court of Sessions; becomes Lord Jeffrey.

1850, Jan. 26, death of Jeffrey.

Dictionary of National Biography.

ENGLISH REVIEWS.

1749, the *Monthly Review;* Ralph Griffiths.

1755, the first *Edinburgh Review;* Adam Smith, Blair, Robertson.

1756, the *Critical Review;* Archibald Hamilton and Smollett.

1756, the *Literary Magazine or Universal Review;* Dr. Johnson a
    contributor.

1793, the *British Critic or Theological Review;* Archdeacon Nares.

1802, the *Edinburgh Review;* Jeffrey.

1809, the *Quarterly Review;* Gifford.

1824, the *Westminster Review;* Bowring.

———•◦•———

l 19. *Mr. Weber.* Henry Weber was a learned and eccentric German who served Scott as amanuensis from 1804 to 1813. Besides his
edition of Ford he published an edition of Beaumont and Fletcher, a
collection of early Metrical Romances, and a collection of Popular
Romances of oriental origin. In 1813 he went mad and tried to
force Scott to fight a duel with pistols. He died in an asylum in
1818. Cf. Lockhart's *Life of Scott,* Aug. 1804, and Jan. 1814. His
edition of Ford is now worth remembering only as an early attempt
to make the Elizabethan dramatists better known. Interest in these
dramatists had begun to revive about 1800. In 1798 appeared
Joanna Baillie's *Plays on the Passions.* In 1802 Charles Lamb
published his *John Woodvil,* a play that unmistakably drew its inspiration from the Elizabethans. In 1805 Gifford brought out his
edition of Massinger. In 1808 Lamb published his *Specimens of
English Dramatic Poets.* In 1811 appeared Weber's *Ford* and from
that date on editions followed rapidly. The tone of the *Edinburgh
Review* toward this revival was ultimately very favorable. Lamb's
John Woodvil had been contemptuously treated and his *Specimens*
was passed over in silence. But on the appearance of Weber's *Ford,*
Jeffrey hastened to use it as the text for a warmly eulogistic discourse
on the Elizabethans. In his essay of 1820 on Keats he takes credit
to himself for having swayed the popular taste toward these older
models. Doubtless his essays were influential; but it is equally
certain that the Romantic current had been setting with all its force
in the same direction. Coleridge and Hazlitt had lectured and written in honor of the age of Elizabeth, and the vogue of the Elizabethans was owing to far more important causes than even the *ipse
dixit* of "King Jamfray." Bulwer-Lytton explains the return to the
older writers as an attempt to justify innovation by an appeal to pre-
cedent. See his *England and the English,* bk. iv, chap. 2.

2 30. *The Reformation . . . but one symptom.* The essay on *Ford*
is specially interesting because of Jeffrey's frequent use of the historical method.   This mention of the Reformation is a case in point;
later, he explains historically the prevalence of French fashions in
English literature ; and still further on, he accounts for the English
love of Shakspere as owing to the accommodation of Shakspere's
"forms of excellence" to "the peculiar character, temperament,
and situation," of the English nation.   The other essays of Jeffrey
that best show his grasp of the historical method are those on
Madame de Staël's *De la Littérature, etc.*, and on Goethe's *Wilhelm
Meister.* Madame de Staël's book was itself a plea for the use of
the historical method in the study of literature ; she wished "to
show that all the peculiarities in the literature of different ages and
countries may be explained by a reference to the condition of
society, and the political and religious institutions of each."   The
book appeared in 1812, but it is plain from this essay on *Ford* that
Jeffrey was by no means indebted to it for an introduction to the
historical method.

5 17. *Jeremy Taylor.* Jeffrey shared his admiration for Taylor
with the Romanticists.   Coleridge's fondness for Taylor was pro-
verbial.   Peacock makes Mr. Flosky, who in *Nightmare Abbey*
stands for Coleridge, appear on one occasion, "jeremitaylorically
pathetic."

8 20. *This new Continental style.* The pseudo-classicism of modern German criticism.   Cf. Körting, *Grundriss der Geschichte der
englischen Litteratur*, p. 272.

12 16. *Akenside and Gray.* Jeffrey's sneering mention of Gray
seems hard to explain.   The decorative beauty of Gray's *Odes*, their
combination of imaginative splendor with sanity of mood and freedom from transcendental affectations, are the very qualities that
might be expected to catch Jeffrey's applause.

13 20. *The mawkish tone of pastoral innocence.* Cf. the attacks on
Wordsworth in the essay on Crabbe's *Poems*, p. 58. and in the essays
on the *Excursion* and the *White Doe*, pp. 105 and 118.   Of these,
the essay on Crabbe (1808) is the earliest.

15 26. *Forms of excellence . . . accommodated to their . . . character.* This view of the relativity of artistic excellence will be found
more adequately expounded in the essay on Madame de Staël's *De
la Littérature, etc.* (1812) " With regard to the author again, or artist
of any other description, who pretends to *bestow* the pleasure, his
object of course should be, to give as much, and to as many persons

as possible ; and especially to those who, from their rank and education, are likely to regulate the judgment of the remainder. It is
his business, therefore, to ascertain what does please the greater part
of such persons ; and to fashion his productions according to the
rules of taste, which may be deduced from that discovery. Now, we
humbly conceive it to be a complete and final justification for the
whole body of the English nation, who understand French as well
as English and yet prefer Shakespeare to Racine, just to state mod-
estly and firmly, the fact of that preference ; and to declare, that
their habits and tempers and studies and occupations, have been
such as to make them receive far greater pleasure from the more
varied imagery — the more flexible tone — the closer imitation of
nature — the more rapid succession of incident, and vehement bursts
of passion of the English author, than from the unvarying majesty
— the elaborate argument — and epigrammatic poetry of the French
dramatist. For the taste of the nation at large, we really cannot
conceive that any other apology can be necessary."

19 14. *Shakespeare.* Cf. Matthew Arnold : " Shakespeare himself, divine as are his gifts, has not, of the marks of the Master,
this one : perfect sureness of hand in his style. Alone of English
poets, alone in English art, Milton has it." *Mixed Essays*, ed. 1883,
p. 200.

21 4. *An encomium on Shakespeare.* The book was published
in 1817; 2d edition, 1818. It was dedicated to Charles Lamb.
" Hazlitt received £100 for it. The first edition went off in six
weeks; the sale of the second was spoilt, as he thought, by an attack
in the ' Quarterly Review.' For this and a later assault Hazlitt
revenged himself by a vigorous letter to William Gifford." *Dict. of
Nat. Biog.* § Hazlitt.

21 14. *Our own admiration.* Jeffrey takes too much credit for
his admiration of Shakspere ; even the eighteenth century was
alive to Shakspere's merits. For a list of dates marking the
course of the Shakspere revival in the eighteenth century, see
Körting, *Grundriss der Geschichte der englischen Litteratur*, p. 313.
Cf. Hettner, *Geschichte der englischen Litteratur*, p. 529.

22 6. *A fine sense of the beauties of the author.* In this work of
Hazlitt's, Jeffrey has chanced on a genuine piece of impressionistic
criticism and he treats it on the whole very sympathetically. He
himself never loiters over a poem, yields luxuriously to the mood it
induces, and fashions a new bit of imaginative literature out of the
dreams it suggests. He is much too responsible a person to practice

such intellectual vagrancy, but he looks on it in others tolerantly and even sympathetically.

24 3. *Relative to mental emotion.* Cf. *Selections,* p. 91, l. 27, p. 150, l. 18, and p. 152.

26 2. *Stephen Duck* (b. 1705, d. 1756). He was for many years a farm-laborer, but became interested in reading, got together a few books, and gained some familiarity with literature. About 1729 he began to be known as a writer of verse. In 1730 he was brought to the notice of Queen Caroline, who made him keeper of one of her libraries and gave him a pension of £30 a year. Later he took orders, preached for a time in Kew Chapel, and in 1751 received a living in Surrey. In 1756, in a fit of despondency, he drowned himself in the Thames. He had the honor of having his poems edited, in 1736, by Joseph Spence, "late Professor of Poetry in the University of Oxford"; and "an account of the author" was prefixed, written in 1730, in which Spence gives many curious details about Duck's study and reading, his ideas on poetry, his methods of composition. A few lines from one of his earliest poems will illustrate the character of his effusions. The poem is addressed "to a gentleman who requested a copy of verses from the author":

> " I have before the Time prescrib'd by you,
> Expos'd my weak Production to your view;
> Which may, I hope, have pardon at your hand,
> Because produc'd to light by your Command.
> Perhaps you might expect some finish'd Ode,
> Or sacred Song, to sound the Praise of God;
> A glorious thought and laudable !" etc., etc.

26 2. *Thomas Dermody.* He rivalled Chatterton in precocity and misfortunes, and surpassed him in learning, but had little poetic genius. He was born in County Clare, Ireland in 1775; at the age of nine he was assistant in Greek and Latin in his father's school, and before fourteen was thoroughly at home in Greek, Latin, French and Italian, and knew some Spanish. He was taken up by Henry Grattan, Bishop Percy and other influential men, but ruined all his chances by persistent dissipation. He lived in London for a time, where he finally died in destitution in 1802. A two-volume life of Dermody was published in 1806 and his complete poems appeared in 1807. His best work was done about 1791 in imitation of Burns. Such lines as the following, in memory of an old crony, might almost be mistaken for the Scotch poet's:

> " No curate now can work thy throat,
> And alter clean thy jocund note;
> Charon has plump'd thee in his boat,
> And run ahead :
> My curse on death, the meddling sot !
> Gay Johnny 's dead."

A couple of stanzas from *My Own Elegy* are also worth quoting :

> " Gude faith ! with all thy roguish trick,
> Thy Pegasus has got a kick ;
> Flat as a tomb-stone, dumb as stick,
> Thou liest at last :
> God send, thou gang'st not to old Nick
> For frolics past !"

> " I do remember thee right well ;
> Thou didst in witty pranks excel ;
> Can all thy deeds of sly note tell,
> Thou great verse-fighter ;
> But, ah ! auld Death has borne the bell,
> And bit the biter."

32 10. *German plays.* Between 1796 and 1815 the English stage was overrun with translations and adaptations of the plays of the German dramatist Kotzebue ; during these twenty years there were published no less than eighty-nine editions of one or another of his plays. *Die Spanier in Peru* was perhaps the greatest favorite. Monk Lewis's translation, called *Rolla*, was published in 1797 and reached a second edition in 1799. Sheridan's adaption, *Pizarro*, was made in 1799 and reached its twenty-sixth edition in 1800. Meanwhile there were also other fairly popular translations. Perhaps Kotzebue's next most popular play was *Menschenhass und Reue*, which, as the *Stranger*, remained for many years a favorite ; the part of Mrs. Haller was one of Mrs. Siddons's most famous impersonations. All these dramas indulged in much weak sentimentality, condemned, at least implicitly, conventional morals, and represented passion as its own justification. For the various translations of Kotzebue's works see the *British Museum Catalogue*. Probably these were the plays that Jeffrey had chiefly in mind, though he may even here be glancing at Schiller's *Die Räuber*, which he mentions a moment later. The earliest English account of *Die Räuber* (1781) was that given by Henry Mackenzie in a lecture before the Royal Society of Edinburgh in 1788. The first translation of *Die Räuber* was made by A. F. Tytler, Lord Woodhouselee, in 1792 ; 4th edition, 1800. Two

other translations appeared in 1799, and still a third in 1800.   See the *British Museum Catalogue.*

33 31.   *The heroics only of the hulks.*   Within a year the first two cantos of *Childe Harold* were published, and within five years the heroics of the hulks had become the favorite cant of all Europe.

37.   *Second edition.*   The first edition of the *Lady of the Lake* was published in May, 1810, and consisted of 2,050 copies; four more editions, comprising 18,250 copies, followed in the same year. Lockhart's *Life of Scott,* 1st ed. II, 290.

37 3.   *The race of popularity.*   The tone of faint praise in this article may have been in part prompted by Jeffrey's knowledge of the leading part Scott had taken in the establishment of the Tory *Quarterly Review* (Feb., 1809).   At the same time, it should be remembered that Jeffrey's article on *Marmion* (1808) was fully as severe.   "We must remind our readers," he says, in that article, "that we never entertained much partiality for this sort of composition, and ventured on a former occasion to express our regret that an author endowed with such talents should consume them in imitations of obsolete extravagance, and in the representation of manners and sentiments in which none of his readers can be supposed to take much interest, except the few who can judge of their exactness. To write a modern romance of chivalry seems to be much such a phantasy as to build a modern abbey or an English pagoda."   A day or two after the appearance of the *Marmion* article Jeffrey dined at Scott's house.   He was treated by his host with precisely the old-time frankness and friendship.   But as he was bowing himself out Mrs. Scott took her woman's revenge by saying in her broken English, "Well, good night, Mr. Jeffrey — dey tell me you have abused Scott in de Review, and I hope Mr. Constable has paid *you* very well for writing it."   Lockhart's *Scott,* 1st ed., II, 149.   The little sneer is interesting historically as illustrating the feeling prevalent for many years that paid reviewing was a disgraceful trade, and that the reviewer was a bookseller's hack.   It was his fear of this prejudice that had made Jeffrey hesitate about becoming editor of the *Review ;* soon after accepting the editorship he writes tartly to Horner, "Do not fancy that I am to take your orders as if I were a shopman of Constable's."   In point of fact, it was owing to the business policy of the *Edinburgh Review,* and to the high character of the contributors it secured, that this prejudice against writing review-articles for pay was finally broken down.

Ostensibly the publication of the *Marmion* essay made no difference in the personal relations between Jeffrey and Scott. Nevertheless, after this date Scott sent no more articles to the *Edinburgh;*
and in about six months he was in active correspondence with
Canning and Gifford about the establishment of a new Tory Review.
The first number of the *Quarterly Review* was dated February, 1809.

44 8. *Song by a person of quality.*

> " I said to my heart between sleeping and waking,
> Thou wild thing, that always art leaping or aching,
> What black, brown, or fair, in what clime, in what nation,
> By turns has not taught thee a pit-a-pat-ation?
>
> Thus accused, the wild thing gave this sober reply:
> See the heart without motion, though Celia pass by!
> Not the beauty she has, or the wit that she borrows,
> Gives the eye any joys, or the heart any sorrows.
>
> When our Sappho appears, she whose wit's so refined,
> I am forced to applaud with the rest of mankind;
> Whatever she says, is with spirit and fire;
> Ev'ry word I attend; but I only admire.
>
> Prudentia as vainly would put in her claim,
> Ever gazing on heaven, though man is her aim:
> 'T is love, not devotion, that turns up her eyes;
> Those stars of this world are too good for the skies.
>
> But Cloe, so lively, so easy, so fair,
> Her wit so genteel, without art, without care;
> When she comes in my way, the motion, the pain,
> The leapings, the achings, return all again.
>
> O wonderful creature! a woman of reason!
> Never grave out of pride, never gay out of season!
> When so easy to guess who this angel should be,
> Would one think Mrs. Howard ne'er dreamt it was she?"
>   — Swift's *Works,* Scott's 2d ed., XIII, 331.

By the "person of quality" is said to have been meant the Earl
of Peterborough.

44 31. *Those who first sought to excite it.* It is in such passages
as this that Jeffrey's imperfect grasp of the historical method is most
apparent. Of course, he utterly fails to realize here the conditions
under which the earliest poetry was produced. He conceives of the
first makers of verse as men of the world, polished and educated
and reflective, consciously choosing their subjects and their methods
with a view to producing the best possible effects. For a suggestive

account of the conditions under which the earliest poetry of a race
or tribe is produced, see Wilhelm Scherer's *Poetik*, pp. 73-117.
Cf. the *Introduction* to Professor Gummere's selection of *English
and Scottish Ballads* (Athenæum Press Series), pp. xxxv ff.

45 16. *Some of them . . . set themselves.* The chances seem to
be that in this rather superficial contrast between modern and ancient
poetry, Jeffrey had three or four very recent poets in mind as representing his classes of "after-poets." By those who "set themselves
to observe and delineate both characters and external objects with
greater minuteness and fidelity" he probably meant Cowper and
Crabbe; by those who "analyze more carefully the mingling passions
of the heart, etc.," he probably meant Campbell; and the poets of
the third sort, who distort nature or dissect it, were doubtless the
Lake poets. "Fantastical" is his favorite sneer for Wordsworth.
Cf. the essay on *Mrs. Hemans*, where he speaks of "the fantastical
emphasis of Wordsworth," and the essay on *Crabbe's Poems*, p. 57,
where he asserts that Wordsworth and his associates are trying to
bring back "the fantastical oddity and puling childishness of
Withers, Quarles, or Marvel."

46 7. *Modern sculpture.* The superficiality of Jeffrey's art criticism is most glaring when we contrast such passages as this with
the best work of German or French critics or with later English
criticism. Jeffrey's characterization of ancient and of modern poetry
should be compared with Hegel's treatment of the same subject in
the *Introduction* to his *Philosophy of Fine Art* (Bosanquet's translation); and the apologetic suggestion of a likeness between modern
poetry and modern sculpture should be contrasted with Hegel's
analysis of the two arts and of their relative fitness to give imaginative
expression to modern life. Jeffrey seems never to have attempted
any thorough comparative study of the fine arts with a view to
determining their relative limitations and scope.

52 3. *The sudden light and colour of some moral affection.* Doubtless Scott's descriptions are, as Jeffrey says, atmospheric and
suggestive of moods. But the suggestion usually depends on the
time of day, or the season, or historical associations, or the incidents
of the actual story. A morning landscape breathes hope and
cheerful confidence; an autumn landscape is wan and dispiriting;
a famous battle-field kindles a glow of patriotism. These moods
are very simple and the associations very obvious. As for any
more complex moods or subtler associations, we must look elsewhere for them than in Scott,

53 5. *We rejoice in his resurrection.* The same reasons that led Jeffrey to republish so many of his essays on Crabbe seem to justify rather generous selections from those essays. The reasons are given in Jeffrey's note, p. 53. Crabbe's unpopularity has been more than made up to him by the devotion of his chosen admirers. "Women and young people never will like him, I think; but I believe every thinking man will like him more as he grows older." *Letters and Literary Remains of Edward FitzGerald*, ed. Wright, I, p. 398. This was the verdict of one of Crabbe's most patient and insinuating advocates, Edward FitzGerald, the translator of Omar Khayyám. Jeffrey's admiration for Crabbe was probably somewhat stimulated by detestation of what seemed to him unendurable affectation in Wordsworth's treatment of every-day life and by the desire to make Wordsworth's mysticism more grotesque by contrasting it sharply with Crabbe's common sense.

54 1. *Upwards of twenty years.* Cf. the *Preface* to the third edition of Crabbe's *Poems*, London, 1808: "About twenty-five years since was published a Poem called *The Library;* which, in no long time, was followed by two others, *The Village* and *The Newspaper*. These with a few alterations and additions are here reprinted; and are accompanied by a Poem of greater length, and several shorter attempts, now, for the first time, before the public." The "Poem of greater length" was *The Parish Register*.

57 28. *Whimsical and unheard-of beings.* Cf. Coleridge, *Biographia Literaria*, chap. 14: "The thought suggested itself . . . that a series of poems might be composed of two sorts. In the one, the incidents and agents were to be, in part at least, supernatural; and the excellence aimed at was to consist in the interesting of the affections by the dramatic truth of such emotions, as would naturally accompany such situations, supposing them real. . . . For the second class, subjects were to be chosen from ordinary life; the characters and incidents were to be such as will be found in every village and its vicinity where there is a meditative and feeling mind to seek after them, or to notice them when they present themselves." Jeffrey's words in the text are almost a parody, unconscious, of course, on this passage. Jeffrey's "unheard-of beings" and "incredible situations" are Coleridge's "incidents and agents . . . in part at least supernatural": and Jeffrey's "strained and exaggerated moralization" is what Coleridge and Wordsworth regard as the natural commentary of "a meditative and feeling mind" on "subjects . . . chosen from ordinary life." Coleridge's *Ancient Mariner* seemed

to Jeffrey an "unheard-of being," and Wordsworth's *Resolution and Independence*, with its interpretation of the leech-gatherer's life, seemed full of "strained and exaggerated moralization."

58 11. *Their own capricious feelings.* It is to the subjectivity of Wordsworth's poetry that Jeffrey takes exception. Wordsworth, he insists, gives us never the actual fact but always his somewhat grotesque reaction on the fact. He puts before us, not the actual leech-gatherer of real life, but a fantastical creature into which the leech-gatherer is transformed when seen through the poet's mists of emotion.

60 13. *A lover trots away.* This is, of course, an utterly unfair account of the famous little poem, "Strange fits of passion have I known." The poem illustrates the way in which an over-mastering mood colors all nature with its own hue and wrests all natural sights and sounds into symbols. The moon setting over his mistress's cottage seems to the lover in the poem to portend disaster. A similar interpretation of nature in terms of an over-mastering mood may be found in Tennyson's *Maud*, xiv, 4 : "I heard no sound where I stood."

61 6. *An old nurse, . . . or a monk, or parish clerk is always at hand.* These are the *conventional* spokesmen for tales of misery. Jeffrey pleads for conventions and condemns Wordsworth's realism. He regards poetry as something *artificial*, to be consciously wrought out in harmony with laws and precedents and conventions. Jeffrey never wholly escaped from this shallow view of the poet's art. Cf. Wordsworth's *Preface* to the *Lyrical Ballads*, where he takes to task the "men who talk of Poetry as of a matter of amusement and idle pleasure; who will converse with us as gravely about a *taste* for Poetry, as they express it, as if it were a thing as indifferent as a taste for rope-dancing, or Frontiniac or Sherry." Wordsworth's *Poems*, Macmillan, 1890, p. 855.

68 15. *Little fragments of sympathy.* Cf. Jeffrey's essay on the *Nature and Principles of Taste*, pp. 151-2.

88. *John Keats.* This article was published in August, 1820. The notorious attacks on Keats had appeared about two years earlier in *Blackwood's Magazine* and in the *Quarterly Review*. That in *Blackwood's* is supposed to have been by Lockhart; at any rate the article made use of information about Keats's early life that Bailey, an intimate friend of Keats, had supplied in confidence to Lockhart in the hope of securing for Keats fair treatment in *Blackwood's.* The article in the *Quarterly* has been usually attributed to

the editor, William Gifford. The *Blackwood* article is much the more savage and abusive, but the *Quarterly* article has been longer and more widely remembered because of Shelley's allusions to it in *Adonais*, and because of Byron's well-known epigram:

> " Who kill'd John Keats?
> 'I,' says the *Quarterly*,
> So savage and Tartarly,
> ' 'T was one of my feats.'"

The story that Keats's suffering under these attacks sent him into a decline is no longer credited. See Colvin's *Life of Keats*, chap. 6, and cf. the very careful review of all the evidence in the case in Rossetti's *Life of Keats*, chap. 5. Mr. Rossetti thinks that Jeffrey's article in the *Edinburgh* had an important influence in righting Keats with the public.

SS 4. *That imitation of our old writers.* Cf. 1–19.

SS 19. *The flowers of poetry.* Cf. note, 96-8, and *Introduction*, p. xxii. Keats's poetry lends itself more readily than the poetry of Wordsworth, Shelley, or Byron to interpretation as merely decorative work. It is in this way that Jeffrey conceives of it, and hence he can reconcile himself to its richness and gorgeousness and patronize it with a safe conscience. He finds it no more revolutionary than the poetry of Campbell or Moore. In point of fact, Keats's Romanticism was a vital principle, as has been shown by his influence in developing modern æstheticism.

S9 17. *Imagination . . . subordinate to reason.* Cf. Brandl's account of the process of poetic composition: " A deeply felt situation is the starting point. Kindred representations join, often by means of external associations, and add new features, and thus the image grows. The combining power consists in an excitation of feeling, supported by a richly endowed memory. The understanding has only to watch that no inconsistency creeps in. To which side of these two qualities the balance shall incline depends chiefly on the taste of the day. In the pseudo-classical era feeling was too much controlled by reflection. The original mental picture did not spontaneously grow, but had to be helped on by conscious, capricious aids, according to mechanical rules; so that the work, despite the careful arrangement of the parts, gives rather the impression of an artificial than of an organic product. The writers themselves felt this, and selected by preference subjects addressed to the understanding — such as moral poems and satires. The Romantic school, on the other hand, failed from not being critical enough." Brandl's *Life of Coleridge* (Lady Eastlake's translation), chap. 4. Cf. Dilthey's *Das Schaffen des Dichters,* in *Philosophische Aufsätze, Eduard Zeller . . . gewidmet,* Leipzig, 1887.

90 15. *Any one who would . . . represent the whole poem as despicable.* Of course, it is to the author of the *Quarterly* article on Keats that Jeffrey is here paying his compliments.

90 29. *The true genius of English poetry.* Cf. the passage on Pope, p. 10, and that on Shakspere, p. 15. These passages mark unmistakably Jeffrey's advance beyond the point of view of the pseudo-classicists. Poetry must be something more than rhymed rhetoric; it must be the work of the imagination. So far Jeffrey was willing to go with the Romanticists in their criticisms on the pseudo-classicists. He also admitted that poetry might well enough take us into a land of enchantment, as it often does in the works of the Elizabethans. But when a poet tried to find this land of enchantment in the very midst of every-day life by looking on common things merely as symbols of an infinitely beautiful spiritual world, Jeffrey at once refused to follow; his common sense rebelled; he was too much of a man of the world to tolerate transcendentalism.

91 27. *Those mysterious relations, etc.* Cf. *Selections,* pp. 150 and 152.

94. *Childe Harold's Pilgrimage.* The first and second cantos had been published in 1812.

95 15. *The Lake poets.* Jeffrey has an inkling here of an important truth that he never thoroughly grasped. Byron's madly egoistic revolt and Wordsworth's high spiritual conservatism were alike attempts to give life greater richness of coloring and wealth of emotion than it had had in the eighteenth century. The full significance of this similarity of aim Jeffrey never realized; but he noted the greater imaginativeness of style, intensity of temper, and fervor of utterance that are characteristic of both poets and that distinguish their portrayal of life from that of the pseudo-classicists.

96 8. *Lofty flights.* This is another of those tricks of speech that betray Jeffrey's theory of poetry. Certain subjects, he implies, furnish the poet with more or less favorable "occasions" for making verse; and on these "occasions" the poet "takes his flights." If he has "good taste," these occasions will never be "mean," particularly in case his "flight" is to be "lofty." Poetry is, in other words, merely the pretty pastime of clever men. Cf. 100-27 and 103-4.

99 33. *A moral teacher.* This essay is a good illustration of Jeffrey's criticism of literature from the ethical point of view.

Jeffrey boasted of having first made this kind of criticism current in England. Cf. the *Introduction*, p. xxv, and note p. 155–16. The ethical critic of to-day pushes his analysis far beyond the point where Jeffrey stopped. Compare with this essay of Jeffrey's Mr. John Morley's essay on *Byron* in his *Critical Miscellanies*, vol. I. Jeffrey is content with an analysis of Byron's typical hero and a warning against the type. Mr. Morley shows why the type originated, and why it was so popular. Jeffrey regards Byron's ethics as merely the expression of the poet's own self-will; Mr. Morley points out the connection between Byron's ethics and the social conditions in the midst of which the poet wrote, and brings the spirit of Byron's work into intelligible relation with the spirit of the times.

100 27. · *Necessary agents.* This passage is a perfect illustration of the view of poetry, described in note 96–8. A poet "deals in heroes," he has certain "extraordinary adventures to detail," and he must " bring about the catastrophe of his story " properly. In other words, a poet merely invents more or less mechanically an ingenious fable for the delectation of his readers, and clothes this story in richly imaginative language.

101 17. *We had the good fortune.* Jeffrey discreetly omits all mention of the first encounter between the *Edinburgh Review* and Lord Byron. Brougham's contemptuous article on Byron's *Hours of Idleness* had appeared in the *Edinburgh* in 1808, and had provoked from Byron in 1809 the fiercest and most effective satire in English since Churchill, *English Bards and Scotch Reviewers.* " As to the Edinburgh Reviewers " Byron says in his Preface to the second edition (Oct. 1809), " it would indeed require a Hercules to crush the Hydra; but if the author succeeds in merely 'bruising one of the heads of the serpent,' though his own hand should suffer in the encounter, he will be amply satisfied." It should be noted, however, that Jeffrey himself did not fare badly in the Satire : he is termed, and justly termed, "self-constituted judge of poesy," is charged with a reckless eagerness for clever articles, true or false, and, as arch-critic of his time, has to suffer indirectly when Byron sneers at the typical reviewer. Otherwise, he comes off with little damage. Byron's account of the qualities of the successful reviewer should be noted :

> " A man must serve his term to every trade
> Save censure — critics all are ready made.
> Take hackneyed jokes from Miller, got by rote,
> With just enough of learning to misquote ;

A mind well skill'd to find or forge a fault ;
A turn for punning, call it Attic salt ;
To Jeffrey go, be silent and discreet
His pay is just ten sterling pounds per sheet :
Fear not to lie, 'twill seem a sharper hit ;
Shrink not from blasphemy, 'twill pass for wit ;
Care not for feeling — pass your proper jest,
And stand a critic, hated, yet caress'd."

101 26. *Official observer.* Jeffrey's various descriptions of his
duties as critic are worth careful comparison. Here he speaks of
himself as merely an official observer, bound to watch lest the public
overlook some good thing. In the essay on Scott's *Lady of the
Lake,* p. 37, he pretends "to be privileged, in ordinary cases, to
foretell the ultimate reception of all claims on public admiration."
In his essay on Scott's novels in 1817, he professes to believe it
impossible ' to affect by any observations of his, the judgment which
had been passed upon' those works of fiction. Similarly, in the
present instance he deems it hardly worth while to comment on
Byron's poems, inasmuch as the world has already pronounced so
decisively in their favor. From all these passages it is plain that
Jeffrey regarded himself as having authority chiefly as the representative of the best taste of the most cultivated people ; he was the
spokesman of the intelligent public. Whenever, then, he felt this
intelligent public behind him he played the austere and pitiless judge
to perfection. It was in this high mood that he dealt with Wordsworth ; "This will never do," he declares of the *Excursion ;* later,
he laments Wordsworth's disregard of "all the admonitions he has
received "; and he finally refuses to "rescind the severe sentence "
he has passed on Wordsworth's work. In these attacks Jeffrey
feels that he has "the world " behind him, and it is as the highest
exponent of the most cultivated taste that he claims authority. In
this spirit he later takes Goethe to task. His confidence in his
public leads him to substitute abuse for argument. He accuses
Goethe of "affectation," "vulgarity," "childishness," "mere folly,"
"sheer nonsense," etc., etc. These terms are merely violent ways
of expressing dislike ; they have no scientific value ; they are not
open to discussion. In such essays, Jeffrey is the dogmatic critic,
pure and simple ; he dogmatizes boldly because he is sure of his
public ; he dogmatizes picturesquely because he has humor, infinite ·
readiness in illustration, and a sparkling style ; and he dogmatizes
serviceably because of his acuteness, his tact, and his close sympathy

with the public he serves. It was a great relief and a great advantage to the public of Jeffrey's day to know just *how* they felt about the books that they read ; and it was part of Jeffrey's mission to tell them this picturesquely and amusingly.

103 4. *Great force of writing.* In such passages as this Jeffrey fails to appreciate the organic relation between literature and life. He regards Byron as catching the popular taste by clever devices of style ; he does not see that Byron was the product of his time and that he received so eager a welcome because he was giving utterance to ideas and feelings that had long been fermenting in the minds and hearts of many people. If Jeffrey had thoroughly grasped this relation between author and public, his theory of art and his practice of criticism would both have been modified. He would have got beyond the view of poetry that makes it a mere pastime ; and in criticising contemporary poetry he would have considered it in its relation to social conditions and as the expression of a spirit whose presence must be historically accounted for.

105 1. *This will never do.* These words have done Jeffrey's reputation an infinite deal of damage. Wordsworth finally conquered the public, and Jeffrey's epigrammatic contempt became for Wordsworth's admirers a mark of the critic's irredeemable shallowness. Of late years, however, opinion has been shifting away from Wordsworth ; the estimate of Wordsworth's poetry that Mr. Courthope has included in chap. 16 of his *Life of Pope*, tallies in many respects with Jeffrey's estimate. Mr. Courthope takes exception to Wordsworth's constant interpretation of life in terms of his own quaint emotion and to his persistent neglect of the point of view and the moods of the vast majority of cultivated people. These are, of course, precisely the objections Jeffrey urges on pages 109–10. On the whole, then, a fair-minded reader of Jeffrey's essay, particularly if he be no devotee of transcendentalism, will find it sound in many of its strictures, and irresistibly droll in its play upon the poet's solemn egotism. The article certainly fails to do Wordsworth justice; but that it is totally wrong in its cavilling, as the poet's admirers used to urge, no critic now will assert.

108 21. *The admonitions he has received.* This is the very tone and manner of pedagogic criticism. The author is a schoolboy with an ill-written exercise and the critic is the master or " monitor " who rates him for his blunders. In the essays he selected for preservation Jeffrey is rarely so magisterial. Cf. 101–26.

109 29. *Prevailing impressions.* Cf. Courthope's *Life of Pope*, chap. 16 : "The two main points of difference between the classical and the modern romantic schools are here brought into vivid relief. Pope, the antagonist of the metaphysical school, had taught that the essence of poetry was the presentation, in a perfect form, of imaginative materials common to the poet and the reader — ' What oft was thought, but ne'er so well expressed.' Wordsworth maintained, on the contrary, that matter, not in itself stimulating to the general imagination, might become a proper subject for poetry if glorified by the imagination of the poet."

110 6. "*An occasional reference to what will be thought of them.*" Cf. Keats's assertion: "When I am writing for myself for the mere sake of the moment's enjoyment, perhaps nature has its course with me — but a Preface is written to the Public. . . . I never wrote one single line of Poetry with the least shadow of public thought." *Letters of John Keats*, April 9, 1818. Cf. also Sydney Dobell's *Thoughts on Art*, p. 48 : "Poetry . . . is the expression of a mind according to its own laws; Rhetoric is the expression of a mind according to the laws of its Hearer." Wordsworth rejected emphatically the conventional taste of the world as a standard of poetic excellence. Cf. his letter to Lady Beaumont, May 21, 1807 : "It is impossible that any expectations can be lower than mine concerning the immediate effect of this little work upon what is called the public. I do not here take into consideration the envy and malevolence, and all the bad passions which always stand in the way of a work of any merit from a living poet; but merely think of the pure, absolute, honest ignorance in which all worldlings of every rank and situation must be enveloped, with respect to the thoughts, feelings, and images, on which the life of my poems depends. The things which I have taken, whether from within or without, what have they to do with routs, dinners, morning calls, hurry from door to door, from street to street, on foot or in carriage; with Mr. Pitt or Mr. Fox, Mr. Paul or Sir Francis Burdett, the Westminster election or the borough of Honiton ? In a word — for I cannot stop to make my way through the hurry of images that present themselves to me — what have they to do with endless talking about things nobody cares anything for except as far as their own vanity is concerned, and this with persons they care nothing for but as their vanity or *selfishness* is concerned ? — What have they to do (to say all at once) with a life without love ? . . . It is an awful truth, that there neither is, nor can be, any genuine enjoyment of poetry among

nineteen out of twenty of those persons who live, or wish to live, in the broad light of the world — among those who either are, or are striving to make themselves, people of consideration in society." Christopher Wordsworth's *Memoirs of Wordsworth*, Boston, 1851, I, 333.

111 11. *A settled perversity of taste.* What is unpardonable in Jeffrey is not his rejection of Wordsworth's transcendentalism but his failure to comprehend it. He insists on regarding it either as a mere affectation of singularity for the sake of effect, or as an inexplicable mental aberration. Apparently he never made a serious effort to understand Wordsworth's theory of poetry or theory of life. He never examined Wordsworth's work in a scientific spirit and with the simple purpose of mastering Wordsworth's ideas. In such essays as this the injurious effects of the dogmatic spirit in criticism are most unmistakable.

113 10. *The old familiar one.* In this passage Jeffrey disregards all that is genuinely distinctive in Wordsworth's new poetical Pantheism, and makes of him merely a somewhat quaint exponent of the old-time view of the mechanical relation of the universe to a great First Cause. Neglecting entirely Wordsworth's doctrine of the immanence of God in nature, Jeffrey, of course, failed to understand his mystical interpretation of nature and found it merely a mass of "moral and devotional ravings."

118 *The White Doe.* Wordsworth's explanation of his aim in this poem should be read in connection with Jeffrey's criticism. "The subject being taken from feudal times has led to its being·compared to some of Walter Scott's poems that belong to the same age and state of society. The comparison is inconsiderate. Sir Walter pursued the customary and very natural course of conducting an action, presenting various turns of fortune, to some outstanding point on which the mind might rest as a termination or catastrophe. The course I attempted to pursue is entirely different. Everything that is attempted by the principal personages in 'The White Doe' fails, so far as its object is external and substantial. So far as it is moral and spiritual it succeeds. . . . The anticipated beatification, if I may say so, of [the heroine's] mind, and the apotheosis of the companion of her solitude, are the points at which the Poem aims, and constitute its legitimate catastrophe, far too spiritual a one for instant or widely-spread sympathy, but not therefore the less-fitted to make a deep and permanent impression upon that class of minds who think and feel more independently, than the many do, of the

surfaces of things and interests transitory because belonging more to the outward and social forms of life than to its internal spirit." Christopher Wordsworth's *Memoirs of Wordsworth*, chap. 36.

122 18. *The impenetrable armour of its conjunct audacity.* The phrase is unusually epigrammatic for Jeffrey, who, despite his reputation among his contemporaries for brilliancy and sparkle of style, rarely gives his readers a phrase they can quote.

127 12. *True to Nature.* To-day Scott's sins against truth are a favorite topic with the realists; in Jeffrey's day Scott seemed "true to nature throughout," and was praised for "copying from actual existences." This well illustrates how relative a matter is realism in fiction; one man's truth is another man's lie.

131 20. *Mr. Scott.* This good guess must duly be noted as an illustration of Jeffrey's acuteness.

133 6. *Works of fiction.* Jeffrey's apologies for treating novels as serious literature are historically interesting. He has himself alluded to these apologies and explained them in his preface to those of his essays that deal with novels and tales.

"As I perceive I have, in some of the following papers, made a sort of apology for seeking to direct the attention of my readers to things so insignificant as *Novels*, it may be worth while to inform the present generation that, *in my youth*, writings of this sort were rated very low with us — scarcely allowed indeed to pass as part of a nation's permanent literature — and generally deemed altogether unworthy of any grave critical notice. Nor, in truth — in spite of Cervantes and Le Sage — and Marivaux, Rousseau, and Voltaire abroad — and even our own Richardson and Fielding at home — would it have been easy to controvert that opinion, in our England, at the time: For certainly a greater mass of trash and rubbish never disgraced the press of any country, than the ordinary Novels that filled and supported our circulating libraries, down nearly to the time of Miss Edgeworth's first appearance. There had been, the Vicar of Wakefield, to be sure, before; and Miss Burney's Evelina and Cecilia — and Mackenzie's Man of Feeling, and some bolder and more varied fictions of the Misses Lee. But the staple of our Novel market was, beyond imagination, despicable: and had consequently sunk and degraded the whole department of literature, of which it had usurped the name.

"All this, however, has since been signally, and happily, changed; and that rabble rout of abominations driven from our confines for ever. The *Novels* of Sir Walter Scott are, beyond all question, the most remarkable productions of the present age; and have made a sensation, and produced an effect, all over Europe, to which nothing parallel can be mentioned since the days of Rousseau and Voltaire; while, in our own country, they have attained a place, inferior only to that which must be filled for ever by the unapproachable glory of Shakespeare. With the help, no doubt, of their political revolutions, they have produced, in France, Victor Hugo, Balzac, Paul de Kock, etc., the *Promessi Sposi* in Italy — and Cooper, at least, in America. — In England, also, they have had imitators enough; in the persons of Mr. James, Mr. Lover, and others. But the works most akin to them in excellence have rather, I think, been related as collaterals than as descendants. Miss Edgeworth, indeed, stands more in the line of their ancestry; and I take Miss Austen and Sir E. L. Bulwer to be as intrinsically original; — as well as the great German writers, Goethe, Tieck, Jean Paul Richter, etc. Among them, however, the honour of this branch of literature has at any rate been splendidly redeemed; — and now bids fair to maintain its place, at the head of all that is graceful and instructive in the productions of modern genius."

136 21. *Graceful and gentleman-like principles.* In such passages as this Jeffrey's powers of analysis and of quick and sure generalization come out very strikingly. This account of the ethics of the author of the five new anonymous novels tallies perfectly with the conclusions that careful study of Scott's complete works and life has established as regards his ideas of conduct. These essays on Scott are examples of Jeffrey's best manner. He is confident without being supercilious, severe without being captious or harsh; his alertness and sureness of touch are conspicuous, as are also the swiftness and eager variety of his style; the insight into the sources of the author's power, the analysis of methods, and the ready appreciation of general effects are all characteristic of Jeffrey's best critical work; and finally his interpretation of the ethical spirit of Scott's novels is just and suggestive, and illustrates the kind of literary discussion in which Jeffrey felt himself most original and effective.

138 25. *So tame and mawkish.* Jeffrey here recognizes the limitation in Scott's genius that Scott himself confessed to in his well-known eulogy on Jane Austen : " The big bow-wow strain I can do myself, like any now going ; but the exquisite touch which renders ordinary commonplace things and characters interesting from the truth of the description and the sentiment is denied to me." Scott's Diary in Lockhart's *Life of Scott*, March 14, 1826.

149 1. *These criticisms.* In the opening pages of this essay Jeffrey has considered two possible views of Beauty : first, that Beauty is a special quality inherent in all beautiful objects, and that this quality is recognized by a special sense or faculty called the power of taste ; secondly, that the Beautiful is merely the agreeable. The first theory he finds untenable because of men's conflicting judgments about beauty. If beauty were, like color, a simple quality, perceived directly by a peculiar sense, all men ought to agree in their

perceptions of beauty as they agree in their perceptions of color ; a beautiful object ought to force its beauty on a man's sense of beauty as unmistakably and individually as a colored object forces its color on his sense of sight.   In point of fact, men differ irreconcilably, not simply as to the degree or kind of beauty in a given object, but as to whether it has beauty at all. Hence, Jeffrey contends, Beauty cannot be a simple quality perceived by a single sense.   Nor, in the second place, can the Beautiful be merely the agreeable. For it is plain on a moment's thought, that there are countless objects, such as sugar, an easy chair, an old friend, which are agreeable without being beautiful. After disposing briefly of these two impossible theories of Beauty, Jeffrey propounds his own theory in a single sentence ; that sentence is not worth repeating, inasmuch as Jeffrey at once expounds his theory in the second paragraph of the extract in the text. Finally, Jeffrey takes up historically the most important theories of Beauty from the times of the Greeks to his own day, summarizes each, and suggests its shortcomings. It is at this point that the extract in the text begins.

149 8. *Mr. Alison's.* Rev. Archibald Alison (1757–1839) was the father of the well-known historian, Sir Archibald Alison.   Though Scotch by birth, he was educated at Balliol College, Oxford, took orders in the English Church, and held various livings in different parts of England.   In 1800 he was made minister of the Episcopal Chapel, Cowgate, Edinburgh, and the rest of his life was spent in the Scottish capital.   He published various sermons, of which those on the seasons were specially admired. Brougham is said to have called the sermon on autumn "one of the finest pieces of composition in the language." Alison's *Essay on the Nature and Principles of Taste* appeared in 1790; the second edition (1811) gave occasion for Jeffrey's review, which was published in the *Edinburgh* for May, 1811. Jeffrey's article was afterwards enlarged and included in the *Encyclopædia Britannica*, where it formed the discussion on *Beauty*.   It was omitted in the ninth edition.   To examine adequately the theory that Jeffrey expounds would require a complete essay and a consideration of many difficult questions. The reader who may be interested in determining the precise grounds on which Lord Jeffrey's theory is discredited may find them convincingly set forth in the *Westminster Review*, LIII, 1–58, April, 1850. He may also consult Prof. Knight's *Philosophy of the Beautiful*, London, 1893, Part ii, 39–45.   No one contends to-day that a man's individual experience has manufactured his sense of beauty;

or that the associations that are drawn from his past life, as an independent, conscious being, can account for his delight in the contemplation of a beautiful object. Cf. Spencer's *Principles of Psychology*, New York, 1873, II, p. 636 ff. The extracts in the text, then, are given, not because of any permanent worth in the theory they express, but because of their historical significance and because of the light they throw on Jeffrey's principles of criticism and ways of conceiving of literature. Cf. *Introduction*, p. xxiv.

149 11. *The reflection of our own inward emotions.* Cf. the comment of Burns in a letter to Alison acknowledging the receipt of his *Essay*. "I own, sir, that at first glance several of your propositions startled me as paradoxical. That the martial clangor of a trumpet had something in it vastly more grand, heroic, and sublime, than the twingle-twangle of a jews-harp; that the delicate flexure of a rose-twig, when the half-blown flower is heavy with the tears of the dawn, was infinitely more beautiful and elegant than the upright stub of a burdock, and that from something innate and independent of all associations of ideas; — these I had set down as irrefragable, orthodox truths, until perusing your book shook my faith." *Poems, Songs, and Letters of Robert Burns*, Globe edition, p. 489.

151 33. *Material objects.* Cf. the review of Knight's *Principles of Taste*, in the *Edinburgh* for Jan., 1806: "It is hard to say what others feel; but we have often experienced that the sublime of natural objects, after the first effect of *unexpectedness* is over, leaves a kind of disappointment, a vacuity and want of satisfaction in the mind. It is not until our imaginations have infused life, and therefore power, into the still mass of nature, that we feel real emotions of sublimity. This we do, sometimes by impersonating the inanimate objects themselves; sometimes by associating real or fancied beings with the scenes which we behold. This is that which distinguishes the delight of a rich and refined imagination, amidst the grandest scenery of Wales or Scotland, from the rude stare of a London cockney. The one sees mere rocks and wildernesses, and sighs in secret for Whitechapel; the other acknowledges in every mountain a tutelary genius of the land, and peoples every glen with the heroes of former times; — defends the passage of Killicranky with Dundee; or rushes with Caractacus from the heights of Snowdon."

154 28. *What a man feels to be distinctly beautiful, is beautiful to him.* Jeffrey's conclusion, then, seems to be as follows: Any object is beautiful to that individual out of whose past it has the subtle

power of evoking strangely-blent chords of pleasure and pain. Any object may therefore be beautiful to some special individual. But there are objects that have this subtle evocative power over the past of "the greater part of mankind," by means of "associations that are universal and indestructible." These objects are beautiful *par excellence;* the ability to create or portray this kind of beauty is the characteristic of the great artist, and the ability to recognize it the characteristic of the good critic. Jeffrey, however, suggests no means of determining abstractly what associations are universal and indestructible, and hence no means of discriminating in thought between a man's own peculiar objects of beauty and those objects which may be regarded as universally or absolutely beautiful. Jeffrey's standard of beauty therefore becomes purely arbitrary. He has to appeal for a decision as regards the relative worth of associations and emotions to the taste of a capriciously chosen minority. Cf. his essay on the *Lady of the Lake,* p. 39, lines 13–29. His judges are "persons eminently qualified, by natural sensibility, and long experience and reflection, to perceive all beauties that really exist, as well as to settle the relative value and importance of all the different sorts of beauty." How these judges are to be recognized or chosen, — whether, for example, Gifford of the *Quarterly Review* is one of these judges, and how they are to settle their disputes among themselves, — these are questions that Jeffrey leaves unanswered. In other words, Jeffrey can discover no objective standard of beauty, and the only escape from absolute lawlessness, that he suggests, consists in his offer of himself as "self-constituted judge of poesy."

155 11. *The best taste . . . belongs to the best affections.* It seems singular that Jeffrey could have maintained this belief after a glance at his most intimate friends. Sydney Smith, for example, was a man of overflowing social sympathies, of quick and lively fancy, of great readiness of observation; yet he had only the slightest interest in art; he boasted of having spent but fifteen minutes in the Louvre; and in all his book-reviews there is no trace of appreciation of beauties of style, or of the purely artistic qualities of prose or of verse.

155 16. *Sensibility and social sympathies.* It is interesting to note how this theory of the nature of beauty falls in with Jeffrey's principles and practice in literary criticism, — particularly with his ethical interpretation of literature. The recognition of beauty depends, in Jeffrey's view of the matter, wholly on a man's uncon-

scious revival of past emotions of sympathy with his fellows. Accordingly, a man who has been immersed in himself, and has felt no love or pity for his kind, will have a very narrow range of æsthetic emotion ; and a man who has loved, or pitied, or feared, or hated on wrong occasions, *i. e.*, immorally, will have a debased and ignoble taste in art. On this theory of the origin of taste, it is plain that the ethical value of literature, the moral spirit of an author, must assume for the critic a great importance; and that the discussion of an author's moral tone will be in the highest degree necessary, not simply because of the moral influence his writings will be likely to exert, but because the key to the writer's feeling for the beautiful is likely to be found in his moral feelings. From this point of view, then, Jeffrey's development of the ethical criticism of literature, — a kind of criticism for which in the introduction to his collected essays he takes special credit, — is seen to follow necessarily from his general theory of art. Cf. *Introduction*, p. xxv.

159. *Wilhelm Meister's Apprenticeship.* This was, of course, Carlyle's translation of *Wilhelm Meisters Lehrjahre.* Jeffrey's specific judgments on the book are worthless, but his speculations on the relation between National Character and National Taste are worth preserving, and should be compared with his ideas on the same subject as expressed in the essay on Madame de Staël's *De la Littérature* (1812), and in the essay on the *Memoirs of Baber* (1827). An increase in Jeffrey's firmness of grasp on at least the theory of the historical method is certainly noticeable.

159 7. *Human nature . . . fundamentally the same.* Cf. Jeffrey's conclusion, two years later, touching "inherent" differences of character between Asiatic and European races. See the essay on the *Memoirs of Baber*, p. 180 ff.

159 11. *Two great classes.* This passage recalls Taine's classification of the forces that shape and determine a nation's literature. Such forces may be grouped, according to Taine, under the three categories, — *race, milieu, moment,* race, surroundings, and epoch. "What we call the race," Taine explains, "are the innate and hereditary dispositions which man brings with him into the world, and which, as a rule, are united with the marked differences in the temperament and structure of the body." This element in the problem Jeffrey neglects in the present essay ; two years later, however, in the essay on the *Memoirs of Baber*, Jeffrey admits explicitly that races differ inherently in character, and after such an admission he could hardly have denied the influence of such differences on

national literatures. Taine's account of his second class of forces is as follows : " Man is not alone in the world ; nature surrounds him, and his fellow-men surround him ; accidental and secondary tendencies overlay his primitive tendencies, and physical or social circumstances disturb or confirm the character committed to their charge. Sometimes the climate has had its effect. . . . Sometimes the state policy has been at work. . . . Sometimes the social conditions have impressed their mark, as eighteen centuries ago by Christianity, and twenty-five centuries ago by Buddhism." The parallelism is unmistakable between this class of causes and Jeffrey's " accidental causes . . . such as . . . government . . . relative position as to power and civilization to neighbouring countries . . . prevailing occupations . . . soil and climate." Finally, of the influence of the epoch, Taine says : " There is yet a third rank of causes ; for, with the forces within and without, there is the work which they have already produced together, and this work itself contributes to produce that which follows. . . . It is with a people as with a plant ; the same sap, under the same temperature, and in the same soil, produces, at different steps of its progressive development, different formations, buds, flowers, fruits, seed-vessels, in such a manner that the one which follows must always be preceded by the former, and must spring up from its death." All these influences, which Taine includes under the general name of epoch, correspond precisely to those that Jeffrey has in mind when he speaks of "the newness or antiquity" of a society, and of the various stages, through which nations inevitably pass, in their " progress from rudeness to refinement." In this essay, then, Jeffrey anticipates very strikingly the points of view, the analysis, and the classification of facts, that Taine did so much to make popular forty years later, in the *Introduction* to his *Histoire de la littérature anglaise.* For Taine's theory see his *History of English Literature*, Van Laun's translation, New York, 1891, *Introduction.* For suggestive criticisms on Taine's position see Sainte-Beuve, *Causeries du lundi*, Paris, 3d ed., XIII, p. 249 ff. ; Paul Bourget, *Essais de psychologie contemporaine*, Paris, 1887, I, p. 180 ff; Émile Hennequin, *La critique scientifique*, Paris, 1888, pp. 93–127.

161 31. *The Taste of the Nation.* The reader should bear in mind Jeffrey's theory of Beauty, as expounded in the article on the *Nature and Principles of Taste*, p. 149 ff. Objects are beautiful according as they wake in the mind echoes of past passions, — love, hate, pity, fear, — which have been associated with these objects in actual experi-

ence. Now it is at once plain that such widely differing civilizations as those Jeffrey describes in the text would lead to wide and radical differences in the associations of pleasure and pain that would cling about the same object in two different nations. Hence, the same object would have wholly different æsthetic values for two different nations. In some such way as this Jeffrey would apply his theory of Beauty to explain the variations in national standards of Taste.

163 14. *On anything so purely accidental.* Jeffrey is here not far from the view of the modern scientific critic, — from that of Taine, for example. To be sure, Jeffrey regards the character of Shakspere and the characters of other writers as "on the whole casual"; but by this phrase he merely denotes that residuum of inexplicableness in every individuality that defies the keenest scientific analysis. Such a residuum remains to-day in spite of all the advances in physiology and biology, and psychology and sociology, and in spite of all the talk about heredity and environment. For Taine, as for Jeffrey, individual character was still inexplicable, though Taine perhaps brought the "casual" element within narrower limits than Jeffrey would have believed possible. ·The important point to note is that Jeffrey pleads in this essay for a view of literature that makes it a growth in accordance with law. Shakspere's poetry, he contends, could not have been produced in France; could have been produced only in England. Shakspere's poetry was therefore determined in character by the *milieu* in the midst of which it was written. Of the nature and degree of the influence of the epoch Jeffrey is not so sure; and of the influence of race he has only the vaguest notions. But at least for the time being, and in theory, he is convinced that literature is something more than the artificial product of ingenious men, who, in writing verse and prose, follow idly their own whims and caprices. Cf. 168–22.

168 8. *Peculiarities of German taste.* In trying to account for German taste, Jeffrey considers first those influences that Taine would group under the term *moment*, and secondly, those that Taine would class as *milieu*. Of course the discussion that follows is grotesquely inadequate; it could not fail to be inadequate, inasmuch as Jeffrey had only the merest smattering of a second-hand knowledge of German literature, and was familiar with German history only as an intelligent English reader might be familiar with it who had kept close watch on current European politics. Of German metaphysics and of German literary criticism Jeffrey was consciously

and proudly ignorant. Under these circumstances, his explanation of German taste was bound to be merely a botch of random guesses, more or less happy intuitions, and superficially clever generalities. A few years later Carlyle undertook the same problem with an altogether different equipment and with altogether different results.

168 22. *They grew tired of being respected.* It seems strange to find Jeffrey relapsing here into the superficial view of literature as merely the work of clever artificers trying to show skill and win fame. His whole preceding argument has tended to prove that the literature of any epoch is made what it is because of its spontaneous adaptation to the social needs of the times. At least, this is the interpretation that a modern reader, familiar with the views of Taine and his school, would put on the opening pages of this essay. The present passage, however, seems to show that Jeffrey only partly realized the conclusions to which his arguments lead. His problem is to explain the characteristics of various periods in German literature. In trying to solve this problem he does not consider how the literature of each period corresponded to the social needs of the time, and gave imaginative expression to the ideals of life that were current in the period in question. He considers literature apart from the life of the times and regards it merely as the work of "authors" writing for their own delectation or for public applause. He sees that in their choice of subjects and in their methods of treatment these authors must have been influenced somewhat by surroundings and epoch. But his analysis of the nature of this influence is very unconvincing; and he does not conceive either of the life of the German nation or of its expression in the literature of its authors as an evolution in accordance with law. This essay is almost the only one where Jeffrey ever attempts to use the historical method in the study of contemporary literature. His failure here shows just how far he comprehended and had control of the method in question. He understood in its main principles the theory on which the use of the method depends for its justification. He even applied the method with some success to explain the characteristics of certain earlier periods of English literature. But in the study of contemporary literature he never used the method successfully; partly because he was more interested in judging than in explaining; partly because he was not broad enough in his sympathies to enter into all the conflicting ideals of life and of art that surrounded him; partly because he had no adequate conception of society as an organism complex in structure and manifold in functions, and no clear insight into the subtle interplay of social forces.

169 32. *Tristram Shandy . . . Richardson.* For a somewhat similar account of the influence of English models on German authors of the baser sort, see Coleridge's *Biographia Literaria*, Bohn's edition, chap. 23.

170 1. *The fantastical speculations of John Buncle.* Thomas Amory, the author of *The Life of John Buncle, Esq.*, was born about 1691 and died in 1788. He is believed to have known Swift, was at one time intimate with Toland and other Deists, but later lived almost a hermit's life, and is thought to have been not quite sane. The first volume of his *John Buncle* appeared in 1756, the second in 1766. The work is a strange compound of romantic adventures, rhapsodies over natural scenery, and theological speculations. Buncle marries and buries seven wives in the course of his tale, all of them beautiful creatures whom he chances upon in his peregrinations through the English lake region. One noteworthy point in the book is the author's genuine appreciation of picturesque scenery. Hazlitt devotes Number 18 of his *Round Table* to a eulogy of Amory, whom he calls the English Rabelais. Lamb was also a reader of *Buncle.* Cf. his essay on the *Two Races of Men.*

173 1. *A very curious . . . work.* As the extracts in the text deal hardly at all with Baber it is not worth while to go into the details of his life. The extracts have been given because they express Jeffrey's latest ideas touching the influence of race on civilization, and because they supplement suggestively the speculations at the beginning of the essay on *Wilhelm Meister.*

180 16. *A natural and inherent difference.* Cf. 159-7 and 159-11.

ADVERTISEMENTS

ATHENÆUM PRESS SERIES.

ISSUED UNDER THE GENERAL EDITORSHIP OF

PROFESSOR GEORGE LYMAN KITTREDGE, *of Harvard University*,

AND

PROFESSOR C. T. WINCHESTER, *of Wesleyan University*.

IT is proposed to issue a series of carefully edited works in English Literature, under the above title. This series is intended primarily for use in colleges and higher schools; but it will furnish also to the general reader a library of the best things in English letters in editions at once popular and scholarly. The works selected will represent, with some degree of completeness, the course of English Literature from Chaucer to our own times.

The volumes will be moderate in price, yet attractive in appearance, and as nearly as possible uniform in size and style. Each volume will contain, in addition to an unabridged and critically accurate text, an Introduction and a body of Notes. The amount and nature of the annotation will, of course, vary with the age and character of the work edited. The notes will be full enough to explain every difficulty of language, allusion, or interpretation. Full glossaries will be furnished when necessary.

The introductions are meant to be a distinctive feature of the series. Each introduction will give a brief biographical sketch of the author edited, and a somewhat extended study of his genius, his relation to his age, and his position in English literary history. The introductory matter will usually include a bibliography of the author or the work in hand, as well as a select list of critical and biographical books and articles. *See also Announcements.*

Sidney's Defense of Poesy.

Edited with an Introduction and Notes by ALBERT S. Cook, Professor of English iu Yale University. 12mo. Cloth. xlv + 103 pages. By mail, 90 cents; for introduction, 80 cents.

William Minto, *Late Prof. of Literature, University of Aberdeen:* It seems to me to be a very thorough and instructive piece of work. The interests of the student are consulted in every sentence of the Introduction and Notes, aud the paper of questions is admirable as a guide to the thorough study of the substance of the essay.

Ben Jonson's Timber: or Discoveries

Made upon Men and Matter, as they have Flowed out of his Daily Readings, or had their Reflux to his Peculiar Notions of the Times.

Edited, with Introduction and Notes, by FELIX E. SCHELLING, Professor in the University of Pennsylvania. 12mo. Cloth. xxxviii + 166 pages. Mailing price, 90 cents; for introduction, 80 cents.

THIS is the first attempt to edit a long-neglected English classic, which needs only to be better known to take its place among the best examples of the height of Elizabethan prose. The introduction and a copious body of notes have been framed with a view to the intelligent understanding of an author whose wide learning and wealth of allusion make him the fittest exponent of the scholarship as well as the literary style and feeling of his age.

Edward Dowden, *Prof. of English, Trinity College, Dublin, Ireland :* It is a matter for rejoicing that so valuable and interesting a piece of literature as this prose work of Jonson should be made easily accessible, and should have all the advantages of scholarly editing.

Selections from the Essays of Francis Jeffrey.

Edited, with Introduction and Notes, by LEWIS E. GATES, Instructor in English in Harvard University. 12mo. Cloth. xlv + 213 pages. By mail, $1.00; for introduction, 90 cents.

THE selections are chosen to illustrate the qualities of Jeffrey's style and his range and methods as a literary critic. The introduction gives a brief sketch of the history of Reviews in England down to 1802 and suggests some of the more important changes in critical methods and in the relations between critic and public which were brought about by the establishment of the *Edinburgh Review*. This volume is especially valuable for classes that are beginning the independent study of literary topics and methods of criticism.

H. Humphrey Neill, *Prof. of English, Amherst College:* It will surprise many lay readers in English literature to find that the writings of one now counted a back number in literature are so full of interest, and even of modern spirit. The introduction is well done. The third section is especially valuable and interesting to the readers of modern periodicals; and the whole book stands well beside the other contributions to the study of literature now issuing from your press.

Old English Ballads.

Selected and edited, with Notes and Introduction, by Professor F. B. GUMMERE of Haverford College. 12mo. Cloth.   pages. By mail,   cents; for introduction,   cents.

THE aim has been to present the best of the traditional English and Scottish ballads and also to make the collection representative. The texts are printed with no "improvements" whatsoever, and but few changes in arrangement. The *Gest* of Robin Hood is given entire, not only for its intrinsic merits, but to assist in the study of epic development. The pieces have been arranged by subject, but not divided into groups or classes. The glossary will be found full, but simple. Philological details have been given only when the explanation of the passage rendered them necessary. The notes have been prepared according to the same principle, — the elucidation of the text and the thought. The introduction presents a detailed study of popular poetry and the views of its chief critics, with notes on metre, style, etc.

Selections from the Poetry and Prose of Thomas Gray.

Edited, with Introduction and Notes, by WM. LYON PHELPS, Instructor in English Literature at Yale College. 12mo. Cloth.   pages. By mail,   cents; for introduction,   cents.

THIS volume contains all of the poems of Gray that are of any real interest and value, and the prose selections include the *Journal in the Lakes* entire, and extracts from his Letters of autobiographical and literary interest. The Introduction, besides containing a Life of Gray, a Bibliography, etc., gives a summary of his historical significance, with a critical review of his work. A special feature will be an article on *Gray's Knowledge of Norse*, by Professor Kittredge of Harvard. The text is taken directly from the original editions, and is printed entire with scrupulous accuracy. The Notes on the Poems explain every doubtful or obscure passage, all allusions to historical or literary matters, and give the most important parallel passages with exact references. The Notes on the Prose are very brief, and simply explanatory. This volume of Gray, besides being adapted for the general reader, will be especially useful in schools and colleges.

Minto's Manual of English Prose Literature.

Designed mainly to show characteristics of style. By WILLIAM MINTO, M.A., Professor of Logic and English Literature in the University of Aberdeen, Scotland. 12mo. Cloth. 566 pages. Mailing price, $1.65; for introduction, $1.50.

THE main design is to assist in directing students in English composition to the merits and defects of the principal writers of prose, enabling them, in some degree at least, to acquire the one and avoid the other. The Introduction analyzes style: elements of style, qualities of style, kinds of composition. Part First gives exhaustive analyses of De Quincey, Macaulay, and Carlyle. These serve as a key to all the other authors treated. Part Second takes up the prose authors in historical order, from the fourteenth century up to the early part of the nineteenth.

Hiram Corson, *Prof. English Literature, Cornell University :* Without going outside of this book, an earnest student could get a knowledge of English prose styles, based on the soundest principles of criticism, such as he could not get in any twenty volumes which I know of.

Katherine Lee Bates, *Prof. of English, Wellesley College:* It is of sterling value.

John M. Ellis, *Prof. of English Literature, Oberlin College:* I am using it for reference with great interest. The criticisms and comments on authors are admirable — the best, on the whole, that I have met with in any text-book.

J. Scott Clark, *Prof. of Rhetoric, Syracuse University :* We have now given Minto's English Prose a good trial, and I am so much pleased that I want some more of the same.

A. W. Long, *Wofford College, Spartanburg, S.C.:* I have used Minto's English Poets and English Prose the past year, and am greatly pleased with the results.

Minto's Characteristics of the English Poets,

from Chaucer to Shirley.

By WILLIAM MINTO, M.A., Professor of Logic and English Literature in the University of Aberdeen, Scotland. 12mo. Cloth. xi + 382 pages. Mailing price, $1.65; for introduction, $1.50.

College Requirements in English.

Entrance Examinations.

By Rev. ARTHUR WENTWORTH EATON, B.A., Instructor in English in the Cutler School, New York. 12mo. Cloth. 74 pages. Mailing price, 90 cents; to teachers, 80 cents.

Selections in English Prose from Elizabeth to
Victoria. 1580-1880.

By JAMES M. GARNETT, Professor of the English Language and Literature in the University of Virginia. 12mo. Cloth. ix + 701 pages. By mail, $1.65: for introduction, $1.50.

THE selections are accompanied by such explanatory notes as have been deemed necessary, and will average some twenty pages each. The object is to provide students with the texts themselves of the most prominent writers of English prose for the past three hundred years, in selections of sufficient length to be characteristic of the author, and, when possible, they are complete works or sections of works.

H. N. Ogden, *West Virginia University:* The book fulfills my expectations in every respect, and will become an indispensable help in the work of our senior English class.

F. B. Gummere, *Prof. of English, Haverford College:* I like the plan, the selections, and the making of the book.

Macaulay's Essay on Milton.

Edited, with Introduction and Notes, by HERBERT A. SMITH, Instructor in English in Yale University. 12mo. Paper. pages. Mailing price, cents; for introduction, cents.

A CONVENIENT and well-edited edition of Macaulay's masterly essay on Milton. The introduction and notes are especially valuable to students.

Defoe's History of the Plague in London.
Journal of the Plague Year.

Edited by BYRON S. HURLBUT, Instructor in English in Harvard University. 12mo. Cloth. pages. Mailing price, cents; for introduction, cents.

THE book is intended to meet the requirements of students preparing to take the college entrance examinations, and to supply a convenient edition for general use.

Biography. Phillips Exeter Lectures.

By Rev. PHILLIPS BROOKS, D.D. 12mo. Paper. 30 pages. Mailing price, 12 cents; for introduction, 10 cents.

The Art of Poetry:

The Poetical Treatises of Horace, Vida, and Boileau, with the translations by Howes, Pitt, and Soame.

Edited by ALBERT S. COOK, Professor of the English Language and Literature in Yale University. 12mo. Cloth. lviii + 303 pages. Mailing price, $1.25; for introduction, $1.12.

Bliss Perry, *Prof. of English, Princeton College:* The fullness and accuracy of the references in the notes is a testimony to his patience as well as his scholarship. . . . I wish to express my admiration of such faithful and competent editing.

Shelley's Defense of Poetry.

Edited, with Introduction and Notes, by ALBERT S. COOK, Professor of English in Yale University. 12mo. Cloth. xxvi + 86 pages. Price by mail, 60 cents; for introduction, 50 cents.

John F. Genung, *Prof. of Rhetoric, Amherst College:* By his excellent editions of these three works, Professor Cook is doing invaluable service for the study of poetry. The works themselves, written by men who were masters alike of poetry and prose, are standard as literature; and in the introduction and notes, which evince in every part the thorough and sympathetic scholar, as also in the beautiful form given to the books by the printer and binder, the student has all the help to the reading of them that he can desire.

Cardinal Newman's Essay on Poetry.

With reference to Aristotle's Poetics. Edited, with Introduction and Notes, by ALBERT S. COOK, Professor of English in Yale University. 8vo. Limp cloth. x + 36 pages. Mailing price, 35 cents; for introduction, 30 cents.

Addison's Criticisms on Paradise Lost.

Edited by ALBERT S. COOK, Professor of the English Language and Literature in Yale University. 12mo. Cloth. xxvi + 200 pages. Mailing price, $1.10; for introduction, $1.00.

V. D. Scudder, *Instructor in English Literature, Wellesley College:* It seems to me admirably edited and to be welcome as an addition to our store of text-books.

"What is Poetry?" Leigh Hunt's Answer to

the Question, including Remarks on Versification.

Edited by ALBERT S. COOK, Professor of the English Language and Literature in Yale University. 12mo. Cloth. 104 pages. Mailing price, 60 cents; for introduction, 50 cents.

Bliss Perry, *College of New Jersey, Princeton, N.J.:* Professor Cook's beautiful little book will prove to the teacher one of the most useful volumes in the series it represents.

The Beginnings of the English Romantic Movement.

A Study in Eighteenth Cen ury Literature. By WILLIAM LYON
PHELPS, Ph.D., Instructor iɩ ʼɩnglish Literature, Yale University.
12mo. Cloth. viii + 192 page ɩ Mailing price, $1.10; for introduc-
tion, $1.00.

THIS book is a study of tɩ ᐧ germs of English Romanticism
between 1725 and 1765. No other work in this field has
ever been published, hence the rɩsʼɩʼts given here are all the fruit
of first-hand investigation. The ᐟɔɔk discusses, with abundant
references and illustrations, the variots causes that brought about
the transition of taste from Classicism to Romanticism — such as
the Spenserian revival, the influence of Milton's minor poetry, the
love of mediæval life, the revival of ballad literature, the study of
Northern mythology, etc. It is believed that this book is a con-
tribution to our knowledge of English literary history; and it
will be especially valuable to advanced classes of students who
are interested in the development of literature.

Archibald MacMechan, *Professor
of English, Dalhousie College, Hal-
ifax, N.S.:* It is a valuable contri-
bution to the history of English
literature in the eighteenth century.

    Barrett Wendell, *Professor of*

English, Harvard University: All
along I have thought it among the
most scholarly and suggestive books
of literary history. . . . It is certainly based on an amount of original study by no means usual.

Studies in the Evolution of English Criticism.

By LAURA JOHNSON WYLIE, Graduate Student of English in Yale
University. 12mo. Cloth.   pages. Mailing price, $
for introduction, $

THE critical principles of Dryden and Coleridge, and the conditions on which the evolution of their opposite theories
depended, are the subjects chiefly discussed in this book. The
classical spirit is first traced from its beginnings in the sixteenth
century to its adequate expression by Dryden; the preparation
for a more philosophic criticism is then sought in the widening
sympathy and knowledge of the eighteenth century; and, finally,
Coleridge's criticism is considered as representing the reaction
against the philosophy of the preceding school.

A Primer of English Verse.

By HIRAM CORSON, Professor of English Literature in Cornell University. 12mo. Cloth. iv + 232 pages. By mail, $1.10; for introduction, $1.00.

THE leading purpose of this volume is to introduce the student to the æsthetic and organic character of English Verse — to cultivate his susceptibility to verse as an inseparable part of poetic expression. To this end, the various effects provided for by the poet, either consciously or unconsciously on his part, are given for the student to practice upon, until those effects come out distinctly to his feelings.

J. H. Gilmore, *Prof. of English, University of Rochester:* It gives a thoroughly adequate discussion of the principal forms of English verse.

The University Magazine, *New York:* Professor Corson has given us a most interesting and thorough treatise on the characteristics and uses of English metres. He discusses the force and effects of various metres, giving examples of usage from various poets. The book will be of great use to both the critical student and to those who recognize that poetry, like music, is constructed on scientific and precise principles.

Analytics of Literature.

A Manual for the Objective Study of English Prose and Poetry. By L. A. SHERMAN, Professor of English Literature in the University of Nebraska. 12mo. Cloth. xx + 468 pages. Mailing price, $1.40; for introduction, $1.25.

THIS book was written to embody a new system of teaching literature that has been tried with great success. The chief features of the system are the *recognition of elements,* and *insuring an experience of each,* on the part of the learner, according to the laboratory plan. The principal stages in the evolution of form in literature are made especial subjects of study.

Edwin M. Hopkins, *Instructor of English, University of Kansas:* I am delighted with the fruitful and suggestive way in which he has treated the subject.

Bliss Perry, *College of New Jersey, Princeton, N.J.:* I have found it an extremely suggestive book. . . It has a great deal of originality and earnestness.

Daniel J. Dorchester, Jr., *Prof. of Rhetoric and English Literature, Boston University:* It is a very useful book. I shall recommend it.

www.ingramcontent.com/pod-product-compliance
Lightning Source LLC
Chambersburg PA
CBHW020346030726
47496CB00007B/2022